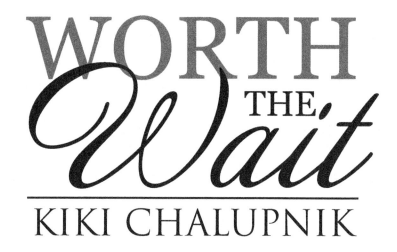

WORTH THE Wait

KIKI CHALUPNIK

WESTBOW
PRESS®
A DIVISION OF THOMAS NELSON
& ZONDERVAN

This is a work of fiction. All of the characters, names, incidents, organizations, and dialogue in this novel are either the products of the author's imagination or are used fictitiously.

WestBow Press books may be ordered through booksellers or by contacting:

WestBow Press
A Division of Thomas Nelson & Zondervan
1663 Liberty Drive
Bloomington, IN 47403
www.westbowpress.com
1 (866) 928-1240

ISBN: 978-1-5127-3536-9 (sc)
ISBN: 978-1-5127-3538-3 (hc)
ISBN: 978-1-5127-3537-6 (e)

Library of Congress Control Number: 2016904602

Print information available on the last page.

WestBow Press rev. date: 04/11/2016

Acknowledgements

Thank you to my daughter, Janet, and daughter-in-law, Sue, who encouraged me one Christmas to write this book. After I told them I had an idea for a book rolling around in my head and in my heart, their response was, "Mom, go for it." This was all I needed to hear, and my journey as an unknown author began.

Thank you to the many friends that I have been so blessed with. Their encouragement and support have meant so much to me; too many to mention by name. Thank you to Malinda Bastedo and Linda VanNoy who willingly offered to read and critique my first manuscript.

Thank you to Jon and Babs Woolston, who made publishing possible.

Thank you to my daughter-in-law, Sue, who agreed to do the final editing of my book. Agreeing to do this for me was a tremendous blessing. You may be our daughter-in-law but we prefer to leave the "in-law" part off. You truly are a daughter to us. We love you so much.

Thank you to my life-long friends that have always given me unconditional love and support: Joann Swaback Brooke, Dorothy Carlson, Dorothy McLean, and Elaine Sola. We have shared fifty years plus of fantastic memories.

Thank you to my husband, Rick, who patiently sat alone many days and nights as I wrote. He has always been my rock and encourager, not only in writing but in 54 plus years of marriage. I love you with all my heart.

God has graciously blessed us with two amazing children and their spouse: Rick and Sue, Mike and Janet; I love you. You have given us much joy.

And to my four awesome grandchildren: Kali Joy, Tyler, Trevor, and Travis, I love you MORE!!

I pray this book is not simply a fictional love story but that the message is caught and speaks to hearts young and old. Our culture is changing and we have lost the importance of what I believe God would shout: It is, "Worth the Wait."

Chapter 1

"Trust in the Lord with all your heart, and lean
not on your own understanding; in all your ways
acknowledge Him, and he shall direct your paths."
Proverbs 3:5 – 6 NKJ

Abby awoke gazing at this verse every morning for the past five and a half months. This was one of many verses that had been beautifully cross-stitched by her mom, and it hung lovingly on one of the walls in her bedroom. The verse had become Abby's very strength. This had been her bedroom growing up until her second year in college when her mom decided to redecorate and make it a lovely guest bedroom—that once again became Abby's. Each morning for the past five and a half months, Abby did all she could do to pull her weary and aching body out of bed as she tried to accomplish simple tasks. Some days the sadness and depression were too overwhelming for her; she could barely cope. She wondered if the hole in her heart would ever heal. The first couple of months, no one pushed her; they knew she needed the time to heal both physically and emotionally. Abby's parents and Thomas's parents had been encouraging her now to "get on with her life" and her career—but it was easier said than done. However, she knew today had to be different.

It was difficult for Abby to believe that just six months ago, on a beautiful December afternoon, she became Mrs. Thomas Sinclair—and then two hours later, the widow of Thomas Sinclair.

Abby met her handsome husband Thomas their third year in college. Thomas went on to seminary after graduation, and Abby got her master's in finance and then her PhD. Thomas always dreamed of being a pastor one day, and Abby could not have been more supportive of his decision. Their wedding was perfect. Her wedding gown, one she had dreamed about as a little girl, flowed with lots and lots of raw silk and, had a scoop neckline with seed pearls covering the bodice and cap sleeves. Of course Thomas was even more than handsome in his tux, and she could still see his amazing smile as he watched her with anticipation walking down the aisle—with only him in her eyes and her in his. Thinking of their wedding day always brought a flow of tears to her eyes, and she promised herself she would have no more of it...but she couldn't help it. Maybe it would get easier one day, but not today, as the memories of that day flooded her soul.

They had left the church excited, looking forward to the reception with friends and family—but even more excited for the night to come. Thomas and Abby made a promise that they would keep themselves pure until their wedding night, a promise Abby had made to herself while in high school. Now she wasn't so sure if that was the right thing to do. Thomas never knew what it would be to have Abby give herself completely to him, nor would she. And it hurt so much to think of that. It didn't seem worth the wait as far as Abby was concerned. *All things work together for good—really?*

After their picture perfect wedding, Tim, Thomas's best man, drove his Dad's vintage Chrysler to take them from the church to the reception venue. The rest of the bridal party followed in the limo. With horns honking and so much excitement, Tim never saw or heard the pickup truck barreling through the red light. Four teens had never slowed down for the red light since they were running from the cops after holding up a 7-Eleven. They were also high on drugs and drunk. They slammed into the Chrysler with such force that it instantly killed Thomas and Tim. It left Abby with a broken leg, broken ribs, and a severe concussion. Abby was in an induced coma for two weeks until the swelling in her brain subsided. Waking to the news that her Thomas was killed left her not only devastated but with no desire to live herself. A combined memorial service had been held for Thomas and Tim. The doctors did not believe Abby would have any memory of life as she knew it. Fortunately—or unfortunately—Abby remembered everything about her life and her wedding day with Thomas. Coming back to live with her parents instead of her new home with her husband was more than she could bear. They had so much to live for: Thomas getting his first church two towns over, and her looking for a job after they were settled. It was a fairytale romance and a life they desired. Every day Abby asked God why, and every day that verse kept staring at her: "And lean not on your own understanding." So many verses would flood her soul, but each day no answer came. Abby promised herself that today would be different. It just had to be.

Chapter 2

Abby applied and was offered the position of CFO for a very high-end resort chain in Forestville, Texas. She accepted the position and was excited about the fresh start for her life. She would miss being close to family and friends in Arkansas who had become such an important part in her healing. She also knew that God would give her the strength and courage she would need to face the challenges she was bound to have.

Two weeks prior to Abby moving to Forestville, she and her dad, William Sullivan, drove to Forestville with the furniture she had—furniture she and Thomas received as wedding gifts, with most being used pieces given to them from both their parents. Abby and Thomas had planned that one day they would be able to afford a few new pieces, but they were thankful for all they were given to set up a home.

Abby met with the executive manager of the resort at the time she and her dad arrived with her furniture. He assured her that when she came out in two weeks she would meet the CEO and owner of the resort chain. Stevenson Enterprises owned three such luxury resorts: one in Florida, another in Southern California, and the Texas resort where the corporate office was located. Abby was pleased to have found the cutest little house to rent just seven miles from the resort in the small town of Forestville.

Her car, a silver Chevy Malibu, was filled to the brim with clothes, kitchen gadgets, and small appliances that were mostly wedding gifts. Abby wanted to return all her shower and wedding gifts, but no one would hear of it. Thankful for all her loving friends and family, Abby knew she would miss them terribly. With the help of her mom and dad, Abby finished packing her car. She was excited to be starting her new job as CFO at the Lone Star Resort and Spa in Forestville, Texas. Not far from Galveston, it was a very upscale resort boasting of Texas charm and elegance. It was also known for providing the rich and famous some peace and quiet away from the paparazzi and clamor of LA or New York City. Shedding a few tears, she was off for the 488 mile trip from the little town outside of Little Rock to Texas. She promised her mom, Lois, that she would call every day. Lois knew how difficult it had been for Abigail to even get in a car after the accident, much less drive one, but with all the encouragement they could muster they knew Abby had to do this on her own. She left with a heavy heart leaving behind so many memories. All she would have of Thomas were memories, and she vowed that she would always cherish the good ones. Only the heartache and sadness would she leave behind... hopefully.

Abby was good about calling her mom and dad the two nights she was on the road and she called the minute she arrived at her new home in Forestville. Her parents were grateful for the phone call and that she had arrived safely. Abby was thankful that she and her dad were able to get all the furniture set up two weeks earlier, which was a job in itself; because of this, unloading her car did not take her long. Exhausted and weary from the drive and unloading her car, she could not wait to soak in the tub before getting into bed. The next day was Saturday and she could put away and organize what she could the next two days. As much as she wanted to find a church on Sunday, she knew she had better stay home, unpack all her boxes, and get ready for her first day of work on Monday.

As she collapsed on the couch Sunday night, Abby couldn't believe how much she had accomplished in the past two days.

Thinking about what to wear her first day at the resort, she realized she could barely put two sentences together let alone think of what she should wear tomorrow. She would get up early and handle that task in the morning.

Rising early Monday morning, Abby put the coffee pot on while she headed for the shower. After going through her closet, she thought she would wear her pale green suit, matching it with a floral silk blouse and hot pink mules, as the same pink was in the blouse. Thomas always said the pale green made her green eyes pop. She put her long auburn hair up in a loose twist, keeping a few tendrils on the side. Thomas told her she was the most beautiful woman he had ever seen, but then again, he had been the love of her life. Come to think of it, there was one other man that always told her that—Jack. Abby was not about to think about him, not ever. She always felt somewhat attractive, but with her freckles and dimples she was not thoroughly convinced. Light makeup covered her freckles, but she couldn't do anything about her dimples—well, maybe just not smile too much. Trying not to think about it; today would be six months since her wedding day, six months since her life was turned upside down.

Abby wanted to be at the resort in plenty of time so she could get an early start. Feeling fairly confident in how she looked, she slipped on her mules and grabbed her Coach bag. Appearance was everything her first day on the job.

Chapter 3

Abby entered the resort at half-past seven in the morning, knowing it would give her time to meet Wade Jenson, the Executive Manager of the resort. She had interviewed with him, and he seemed to be a pleasant man. Abby was anxious to see her new office and familiarize herself with the resort. As far as Abby was concerned, the Texas resort lobby was breathtaking and elegant beyond belief. One would expect a rustic western theme, but this lobby had beautiful crystal chandeliers, marble floors, mahogany counter and desk, damask couches and chairs that were perfectly placed for the guests to enjoy each other's company—it was magnificent. Abby could not believe this is where she would actually be working. The concierge was seated at the desk, a very attractive woman in her early forties, Abby would guess. Abby introduced herself and told her she was meeting Mr. Jenson. The concierge introduced herself and said Mr. Jenson was expecting her and she would call him. Abby waited patiently for Mr. Jenson to arrive. She didn't wait long before he entered the lobby with arm extended, giving Abby a very strong handshake. He was meticulously dressed in a dark blue suit, white shirt, and red tie. Abby wondered if she was appropriately dressed for this new position. Of course he insisted she call him Wade and not Mr. Jenson, and she in turn told him to call her Abby or Abigail instead of Mrs. Sinclair. A few weeks prior, Abby had interviewed in his private office, which was behind the registration counter. She had not yet seen where her office was located. Wade said the main offices, salon, and spa, were located on the seventh floor. He escorted Abby to the private employee elevator which was located down the hall towards the rear entrance. This was no ordinary employee elevator. It was beautifully appointed with walnut paneling, plush forest green carpeting, and beautiful bronze light fixtures. Abby just knew this was not going to be a typical place to work. After arriving on the seventh floor, they entered another beautiful lobby where the receptionist welcomed guests and directed them to the spa, salon, and indoor pool. The offices were located down another hall and Wade opened the door to Abby's office. It was beautifully furnished with a new mahogany desk, cushiony leather chair, matching file cabinets, and computer. Abby went directly to the floor to ceiling windows to see the view she had, and it was breathtaking. It overlooked the back of the resort property that backed up to a woodsy area boasting of tall poplar and oak trees, and beyond a beautiful crystal blue lake. "Wade this is absolutely beautiful. I never expected such an elegant office, and the view is breathtaking."

Abby felt somewhat uncomfortable when she noticed he never took his eyes off of her, but when her eyes met his, he looked away.

"I'm pleased you like it, Abby, and welcome to the Lone Star Resort and Spa. Mr. Stevenson will probably be in to personally welcome you as well. He's returning from a business meeting in Florida and should be arriving shortly. Make yourself at home and see if there is anything you may need. You will find our staff very accommodating and pleasant to work with."

Abby held out her hand to thank Wade for everything and told him how much she looked forward to working there.

Abby spent the afternoon reviewing spreadsheets and familiarizing herself with company data. Her attention was then drawn to a three drawer mahogany cabinet matching her desk. She had no problem with the first two drawers, but the third drawer was completely stuck. Abby could tell something was jammed, but no matter what she tried, it would not open. She finally gave up and gave maintenance a call. They said they would have someone up immediately. Determined to get this drawer open, Abby got down on her knees and was bent over in a very precarious position when maintenance showed up. At least she thought he was from maintenance. Clearing his throat when he entered, Abby looked up into the most beautiful ocean-blue eyes she had ever seen. He was quite tall, and he had very neatly combed sandy colored hair, and he had somewhat of a stubble beard…and looked extremely handsome in his khaki pants and black polo shirt. It was obvious he spent a lot of time working out, as his broad chest and shoulders barely fit his shirt. Abby chided herself for taking notice of this handsome man standing over her; after all she lost her husband just six months ago. Abby thanked him for coming to her aid so quickly. "You must be from maintenance. Thank you for coming to my rescue. As you can see, I am having a terrible time trying to open the bottom drawer of this cabinet. By the way, my name is Abby, and what is your name?" Rob was slow to reply to such a simple question.

A little flustered, but after noticing a gold plaque positioned on the front of Abby's desk which read, York Brothers Furniture, Rob replied, "Bob, Bob York." He could not take his eyes off of her as she tried getting up from the floor. Bob quickly reached out his hand and helped her to her feet. Thanking him, Abby asked if he thought he could fix her cabinet.

"Yes, yes of course I can fix it. That's why I'm in maintenance." Bob was completely taken aback when he first laid eyes on Abby. He expected a forty or fifty year old widow, not a gorgeous brunette with amazing green eyes…maybe her hair was auburn colored. It really didn't matter, she was beautiful. He said he would be right back after he picked up the tools needed to fix the cabinet. He knew what he really had to do was head off the real maintenance guy. He also wanted to tell everyone to call him Bob York, and that he worked in maintenance. Bob or really, Rob, got a lot of strange looks, but since he was the boss, no one would dare argue with him. He told Wade to pass this along to all the staff. He did not want Abby to know he was not only her boss but CEO and President of Stevenson Enterprises. She certainly did not recognize him, and he liked this just fine. It would be great to have someone like him for himself. Not for his fame and fortune. It was obvious that Abby never read any tabloid magazines to know who he was, and as long as he could be Bob from maintenance that would be fine with him. He wanted to be liked for who he was, not what the magazines made him out to be.

Rob Stevenson was a self-made billionaire. A millionaire at twenty-eight and now a billionaire at thirty-two, he enjoyed a lifestyle that kept him in the limelight, and of course, plenty of women; especially models and movie stars that wanted to be seen with him. After all, he was dubbed most handsome and eligible bachelor for 2014. His picture was constantly showing up on the cover of every tabloid magazine with some beauty. Dodging the paparazzi was always a problem that he wished he did not have to put up with. He was not a movie star or some TV personality, but simply a guy with a lot of money—and he had to admit, fairly good looking. He did however enjoy the life of the rich and famous. *Man, it would be nice once in a while to just be normal and not have a camera pushed in my face so much.* Making his way back to Abby's office, Rob thought he would give the cabinet another try.

Abby was sitting at her desk going over the spreadsheets that she brought up. It was going to take her a little time to get a handle on everything. She had her reading glasses on when Rob walked in and he thought it made her look even cuter. Her hair was up in a loose twist, but after her struggle with the cabinet some of her locks had fallen out and were cascading down around her shoulders. Rob wanted to walk over to her and push some of the beautiful locks behind her ear, but he refrained. It sure looked like it had some natural curl to it—and it looked like it must be really long. Thinking how soft her hair must be, Rob wanted to pull the clip out and see just how long her hair actually was. Snapping out of his fantasy, Rob gave the cabinet another try.

"No, sorry I can't seem to get it. This drawer is really stubborn. I think I'll have to come back in the morning and try." Rob only said this so he would have an excuse to return in the morning.

"Okay", said Abby, somewhat ignoring him as she continued working.

"How long will you be working?" asked Rob.

"I'm sure at least until five o'clock. I have no idea what time it is."

"It's almost five," said Rob. "Actually it will be in about five minutes. I know you are new here and all. Would you like to get a bite to eat?" Rob raised his eyebrows, questioning if it was the right move or not. "Hey it's just for a burger or something. We can eat right here in the Texas Grill. They have great burgers."

Abby hesitated, but also knew she was starving as she worked through her lunch. "Well, I guess it would be okay. I haven't eaten since breakfast and I really have no idea what the restaurants are like in town. I was going to grab something on my way home but your offer sounds good. Thanks. Give me a few minutes to close everything and I'll be ready to go." Abby wondered what in the world she was doing. She just met this guy a few hours ago. *Oh well, it's simply a burger at the grill… and I have no one else to eat with.*

Rob was relieved that word spread quickly as to his new identity. He got a lot of second glances as he walked into the Texas Grill with Abby. They were seated at a booth towards the back of the grill. Abby was in awe how this restaurant was decorated, it had a western classiness that was indescribable: beautiful dark oak wood tables, along with red and gold fabric covered chairs and booths. The pictures, that looked to be original oils, were all western scenes of beautiful horses and landscapes that had to be from Arizona or Texas. They each ordered a burger, Rob with fries and Abby with sweet potato fries, one of her favorites. Rob ordered a beer and Abby ordered a Diet Coke. Rob changed his drink to a Diet Coke as well. They were given a lot of attention by their waiter and other restaurant staff. Abby commented on all the attention and Rob simply said it was because she was new and they wanted to make a good impression on her.

"How long have you lived in Texas, or are you new to the area?" asked Rob. He already knew but did not want her to know this.

"I just moved here on Friday from Arkansas. I really do not know anyone yet and thought I would start looking for a church this Sunday. I was too exhausted yesterday and needed to finish unpacking and putting things away, so I did not go anywhere. I think it's important to find a good church home, and it's a great place to connect with other like-minded people. What about you, Bob, do you attend a church?"

Rob felt a little uneasy but managed to let Abby know that his life was pretty busy right now. "There was a time growing up that I attended church a lot. My mom and aunt made sure I went to church with them, but once I got into college, my plans and my priorities became success and money."

"So this is why you're in maintenance? How's that working for you?" Abby did not mean to sound sarcastic or condescending but was sure that's how it came across.

Rob, being caught off guard, knew once the words were out of his mouth, it was not the response he should have given. *What was I thinking? My priorities were success and money?* He only hoped he could dig himself out of this one. "Well, you know how it is when you're in college and you think you have the world by the tail, and that's what most guys think about, success and money. Hasn't happened for me though; maybe one day."

Abby simply nodded and seemed to accept his reasoning. "I guess working here can keep you pretty busy." Their conversation flowed easily, and Abby was totally impressed with Bob's quick wit and humor. They laughed and bantered easily, and Rob could not help but notice how Abby's beautiful green eyes sparkled as she laughed. She seemed to smile with her eyes and Rob couldn't help but notice the dimples that showed when she smiled. Rob was enraptured by her. Abby felt guilt flood over her for all her laughter, and feeling so totally comfortable with Bob—she had not laughed like this in the past six months. *Was it wrong to enjoy being with Bob, someone I just met a few hours ago?*

"Oh my goodness," Abby squealed looking at her watch and noticing the time. "It's already past eight! Where has the time gone? I really need to get going. We better get our checks. I can't believe we sat here for over three hours."

Bob motioned for the waiter to come over with the check, and he simply signed for it. Abby sat with money in her hand ready to pay her part of the bill, but when Bob simply signed for it he could see the confusion in her eyes. "Oh, employees get all their meals covered in any of the restaurants or coffee shops here. Didn't Wade tell you this when you were hired?"

"Yes, he did, but I believe he only said that lunch was covered when you were on company time."

"No, every meal is covered no matter what time...company time or not. He will have to go over this with you. It must have slipped his mind."

"Well, that's an exceptional policy and benefit that I have never heard of, but I won't complain. I better be on my way. Thanks so much for dinner and the company."

As Abby slid out of the booth, Bob stood and began walking her to the door. "I'll be in to work on your cabinet in the morning then."

"I'd appreciate that. Thank you." Abby felt a little flushed and couldn't understand why her stomach seemed to flip as she said goodbye to him. She knew that getting to sleep tonight was not going to be easy.

Chapter 4

Abby stopped in the coffee shop at the resort and picked up a vanilla latte coffee and a biscotti, another favorite. Expecting to pay for it, the young girl at the counter simply waved her off. She was surprised that Wade had already got the word out regarding her comp meals. She was certainly going to enjoy this extra perk. This coffee shop was on the seventh floor in the wing that housed the indoor pool and spa. Close enough to her office; Abby knew she would be visiting this little spot often. It was an adorable little shop, painted in pale pastels with several small round tables and chairs—it was very French looking, although she had never been to France. They had quite an assortment of pastries and gourmet coffees.

Abby walked into her office to see Bob already at work on her cabinet. Looking up from the floor, he had a big smile on his face. "I think I got it fixed this time. You shouldn't have any more problems with it."

"Thank you so much," said Abby, as she wondered if she would be seeing much more of Bob, now that his job was finished.

Rob couldn't help staring at her, thinking how beautiful she looked this morning. She was wearing a form fitting pencil skirt, mint green silk blouse, and three inch heels. Her hair was up once again but this time twisted with a simple clip. Rob smiled and winked at her saying he would see her around; then walked out.

Abby felt certain sadness in his leaving, and immediately wondered what she could break to get him back up to her office. Guilt flooded her spirit again and all she could think of was how comfortable Bob was making her feel, *friendship, that's all it is.*

Abby found a friend, and it felt good to have someone she could talk to. Once she met other employees and found a church home, she was certain she would make friends; that had never been a problem for her.

Abby spent the next few days absorbed in reviewing resort accounts. She was finally getting a handle on the finances for not only the Texas resort but also the resort in California, and the most recent Florida resort. She totally enjoyed her job and the challenges she encountered every day. She was talking to the finance directors at the other two resorts, and building quite a rapport with each of them. She was also getting acquainted with the crew to the corporation's personal jet. They called often to discuss flight times, fuel, and other services needed. By Thursday afternoon Abby was exhausted, but in a good way. Sometimes she thought her head was going to explode with all she was trying to keep in order, and each new task. It was getting close to quitting, when to Abby's surprise Bob poked his head inside the door. "How has your week been?" Bob asked out of genuine concern, but also hoping for an opportunity to see her.

Abby's stomach fluttered and she thought it was due to hunger, but her heart definitely skipped a beat when she saw Bob in the doorway. She didn't realize until then how much she missed not seeing him the past several days. "My week has been quite busy, but I think I'm getting a handle on everything. I'm sure it will take me a while before I can say I really know what I'm doing, but all in all it's going quite well."

"So are you enjoying working here…any problems with your cabinet?" Of course Bob asked this in jest and couldn't help but give her his slightly crooked smile and a wink.

Abby giggled and was quick to tell him that she really was enjoying her new job quite a bit. It was a lot of work but she always loved a challenge. She found that her job as CFO was not simply about keeping her nose in the books and glued to a computer screen all day, but also afforded her the opportunity to communicate with so many other employees; not only in Texas but the California and Florida resorts as well.

"Hey, want to grab a bite to eat with me?" Bob asked with a hopeful expression in his eyes. How could Abby refuse, especially with her stomach growling? She nodded and said she would be ready to leave in about an hour. Bob looked at his watch and said that wouldn't be until well after five. "Are you sure you can't leave at five?"

Abby thought about it but also knew what she had to do. "No, I really have too much to do, and with a weekend coming up, I don't want to leave any loose ends."

"Okay, I'll be back at five-thirty. Is that okay with you?"

"Sure, I should be ready by then." *Is this a date?* No, Abby would not think of it as such. Bob was a friend and someone she enjoyed being with, even if it had been only one other time. Then why did she feel a little giddy and excited to be going out for dinner with him tonight? *He is a friend—that's all.*

Bob was knocking on her door promptly at five-thirty. As Rob watched Abby clearing her desk, he felt a warm feeling rush over him. Man, she was beautiful. Even after working all day, she looked fresh and radiant. There was definitely something about her that set her apart from all the other women Rob had known. He couldn't put his finger on it but she was definitely different.

Abby heard his knock and acknowledged him; she said she would be ready in a minute. Fortunately, she had touched up her blush and lipstick before Bob came. She was pleased she wore a fitted pant suit today. Her suit jacket was over her desk chair and she started to slip it on when she got up. Bob came over to help, and she couldn't help but think what a gentleman he was. Walking to the door, Rob put his hand on the small of her back gently guiding her out the door. A little tingle went up her spine and Abby dismissed it as simply a feeling she was unfamiliar with since Thomas. He always had his hand on the small of her back when he was guiding her through a crowd, or simply directing her to a seat.

"Are we going to the grill tonight?" asked Abby with some excitement in her voice that she could not stifle. She certainly did not want to sound anxious…because she wasn't.

"I think we'll try one of the other restaurants tonight, seeing it's a little later than the other night. Have you eaten in the main dining room?"

"No, I have not." Abby answered with some hesitation. What did this mean to be eating in the main dining room? She knew the Black Stallion was outrageously expensive and wondered if they would be taking advantage of the company by eating there. "I really don't think we should take advantage of the company's policy, and I am perfectly content to pay for my own meal this evening, wherever we go."

Giving her a questioning look, Rob agreed to her misgivings. "Hey, I'm inviting you and I have full intentions of it being my treat. No strings, believe me. You really should eat at all the resort's restaurants so you know what they're like. Believe me when I tell you, you will love the food."

"No doubt I will, but I have heard the prices may be way out of our league."

Upon entering the restaurant, Rob immediately went over to the desk. The maître d' reached behind the desk and helped him on with a dinner jacket. Rob put out his arm for Abby to take and they followed the maître d' to a table in the back of the restaurant that overlooked the outdoor pools and waterfalls. The pools were quite a distance below giving the bathers privacy. And with the floor-to-ceiling windows it made the view breathtaking. Abby asked if the ocean was very far from there and Rob pointed to a patch of crystal blue way in the distance. He said it was actually about twelve miles from where they were.

Pulling out the chair for her, Abby sat comfortably in the very cushioned leather chair. "What a beautiful room and amazing views. You're absolutely right; I would hate to have missed dining here."

Rob was pleased to see the sparkle in her eyes and asked if she wanted him to order for her. She agreed to let him do this, and was pleased he first asked if she wanted steak, which they were famous for, or fish. "I love steak, and would be delighted to have you choose for me."

After a relaxing dinner and great conversation, Rob walked Abby to her car that was parked out back. "Thank you so much for a lovely dinner tonight, Bob. Have a great weekend."

Chapter 5

Several weeks went by with Abby not seeing much of Bob at all. She was sure he had to be quite busy in a huge resort like this. She was busy, and found herself doing some serious investigating in the finances for the California resort. Abby discovered a charge for a new Oriental rug which would be for the foyer in the resort. She knew the cost was probably ridiculous to begin with, but when she saw it was $250,000 she lost it. *What was this rug made of... gold,* thought Abby. This was really a puzzle and she would not stop until she knew it was the actual cost. As she researched, and contacted several other companies, she was able to find the same rug, and same size, for half the cost. To Abby this was still absurd, and an amount she could barely get her head around. She knew she had to talk to the CEO, Robert Stevenson, but he had been very elusive, and she had not yet met him. Abby wanted to fly out to California and check this carpet out before it was actually delivered. She needed to compare it to what she found at Hotel Furnishings here in Texas. If it was indeed the same carpet, something was amiss, and we may have an employee stealing money from the company. Just the thought of this gave her shivers. *Could someone really be that dishonest and steal from a company—especially ours that is more than fair and generous with their employees?* The thought sickened her. Abby knew she would have to call Mr. Stevenson, explain what she had discovered, and suggest she make a trip out to California.

Abby picked up her phone and dialed Mr. Stevenson, not knowing if he was in this building or at one of the other resorts. As far as she knew, he could be up in the air on his private jet. One of the flight crew would have been in contact with her... or maybe not. Abby was sure Mr. Stevenson could make his own arrangements if need be. "Hello Mr. Stevenson. This is Abigail Sinclair, your CFO; although I have not had the pleasure of meeting you," she so wanted to say she had been working for him for the past four weeks, and had not yet met him, but she did not. "There seems to be quite a discrepancy in a very large purchase being made for the California resort. I would like permission to take a trip out there and investigate the matter for myself. If my inclination is correct, I believe someone may be stealing money from the company."

There was a very long pause before he spoke. "Well, Miss Sinclair do you think this is something you are capable of handling?" Abby really sensed an arrogance and sarcasm to his voice, which did not bode well with her. *The jerk, he hasn't even had the courtesy to introduce himself to me, and now he is questioning my ability? She had explained everything quite clearly and still he did not see the importance of this?*

"Go ahead Miss Sinclair. Are you able to make the arrangements for the company jet?"

"It's Mrs. Sinclair by the way, and yes, I'm sure I can manage. I have spoken to the crew several times in the past... four weeks." She really emphasized how long she had been with the company, and felt pretty confident that she actually found such a serious discrepancy to the California purchase. In fact she was quite proud of herself. "I will make arrangements to fly out Monday morning and I should return Tuesday or Wednesday at the latest. If all goes well, I may be able to return the same day. Is this acceptable to you?"

"Fine, Mrs. Sinclair. I expect a full report when you return."

"Yes sir. Would you like me to call from California and let you know my findings?"

"That would work, and I would appreciate a call when you arrive in San Diego." He wanted the assurance that she was safe and a phone call from her would definitely confirm this.

Abby slammed the receiver down and was seeing red. *What kind of a boss do I have anyway?* She was still fuming when Bob walked into her office. He could not help but notice how upset she was, and knew it had to be over him.

"What happened? You seem really upset, feel like talking about it?"

"Who is Mr. Stevenson anyway? I can't believe he is such a jerk. I've been here four weeks and haven't even met the man. Can you believe he thinks I'm incapable of handling a situation that came up in California?" Abby was not about to tell Bob what she had discovered, and knew this was a very confidential matter.

"Want to tell me about it? I can't believe Mr. Stevenson could be that nasty to you. He must have his reasons. He's usually a pretty decent guy, so tell me about it." She really was kind of cute when she was angry; her green eyes looked even greener, and he knew he shouldn't be enjoying this. Rob didn't realize he was putting her in an awkward situation and felt bad after the words came out. On the other hand, he would see if she could keep something this serious to herself.

"No I don't think it's something I can talk about, and it is confidential. But thanks for caring. I just needed to blow off some steam. It's really not like me to get this upset. I'm really sorry."

Changing the subject so she wouldn't have to be pressured into talking about the situation, or Mr. Stevenson, Abby wanted to tell Bob about an idea she had been thinking about the past few days. But now she wondered if it was something she would ever be able to ask Mr. Stevenson about, "How much property does the resort own to the south?"

"Have you eaten lunch?" asked Bob rather casually. "We can talk about your question over lunch."

"I've been bringing my lunch the past few weeks so I can keep working. It's great having a little fridge in my office, and I enjoy simply having a yogurt for lunch."

Rob realized that was why he never saw her at any of the restaurants or coffee shops around lunchtime. He was sure the staff must be having a good laugh after asking them to keep a

21

look out for her, and to let him know where she was eating. "We can go to one of the coffee shops if you like, or how about the grill?'

"That sounds good, I am starving and this will give me a chance to cool off." Abby was surprised at how upset Mr. Stevenson's comments had made her; she never lost her cool. After shutting down her computer and grabbing her purse, she was ready and anxious to go.

"Shall we go to the grill then?" Bob tried not to show any expression as to how pleased he was to have lunch with her.

"Sure, that works for me." Bob came up behind her putting his hand on her back as he led her out the door. Once again she tingled and wondered if it was from his touch, or just the reminder of the way Thomas would walk with her.

They were seated in a booth to the back of the restaurant and they noticed a little bit of a crowd. After being seated Bob reminded her of the question she had for him back in the office, and asked why the question.

"It looks from what you pointed out earlier that there is plenty of property to have an additional resort. I think it would be awesome to have a dude ranch with horseback riding, chuck wagon dinners, and even water activities, such as boat rentals. You did say that the lake out back belongs to the resort, did you not?"

"Yes, I believe it does. You are quite the visionary, and I'm sure when you have a chance, Mr. Stevenson would love hearing your ideas." Abby rolled her eyes but Rob was totally impressed with this woman and how she could be this beautiful and this smart all in one package. "Do you know how to ride horses?" *This will really be the icing on the cake.*

Abby's eyes lit up. "Why yes, I love riding."

"Did you know that we have horses on the property already? We use them for getting to the unreachable part of the property. Maybe you would like to go riding sometime. I'll check if there's a way we can get a couple of horses one day."

Abby couldn't hold her excitement in just thinking about getting back on a horse. "When I was younger I had my own horse and rode just about every day. We had horse property so riding every day was no problem."

"Well then. It should be a lot of fun riding together sometime."

"That would be great, Bob. I would love it."

Bob, really Rob, blurted out, "Great! Hey Abby, how would you like to go boating this weekend? I have a friend with a boat, and it would be fun to get away. It's supposed to be a really hot weekend." Rob had no idea where this idea even came from.

"I don't know. Is the boat on the lake here?" Abby was giving it some thought as she only knew Bob for all of four weeks. From what other people had said, he was a really nice man. He gave her no reason not to be able to trust him...and there would be someone else along.

"The boat is docked in the Galveston marina about twelve miles from here. We could take off Friday afternoon. It's a cabin cruiser and plenty big, and since you have church on Sunday, we can be back sometime Saturday night if need be." He waited to see her reaction wondering if he crossed the line inviting her to a weekend on the boat. "If you feel at all uncomfortable, we'll leave. I promise."

Bob had never given her any reason to not trust him, and especially working together she could not imagine he would take advantage in any way. "I think it would be fun, but I don't know about leaving work early tomorrow. I guess I could miss church if we don't make it back in time."

Man, she was a dedicated employee. Rob wished they were all like her. "Shouldn't be a problem, but you can check with Wade if it would be okay. I know I'll be done with my work early afternoon. How about I pick you up around three o'clock? You can pack a bag and we'll leave from here."

"Okay." She wondered why she did not have any reservations about her decision. If she did later tonight or early tomorrow, she would back out. Abby learned early on to listen to her gut.

Rob needed to call Jeff, his captain, and tell him they would have to reverse roles. Jeff was a good friend and piloted his yacht for the past five years. The purchase of his boat was one of the things he did when he made his first million. He absolutely loved boating and hoped Abby would as well.

Rob filled Jeff in on what was going on with Abby and how he couldn't believe she knew absolutely nothing about him—not even that he was her boss. Jeff agreed to play along; after all he had no choice in the matter.

"What about your car, boss? Won't it give it away if you show up with your Lamborghini?" Jeff was more than willing to trade vehicles as well.

"Man, I never thought of that. But that's not a problem. You can come by tomorrow and we'll switch vehicles." Rob knew Jeff was more than pleased having the chance to drive his Lamborghini. He knew he could take his Land Rover, but that too would be a little over the top for a maintenance guy. He felt a little devious, and how long he could keep this up would be another question. Hopefully, Abby would understand his motive. The last thing he wanted was for her to be so angry with him that she would quit her job and leave.

Chapter 6

Abby packed her bag taking extra clothes as she knew being on the water always meant getting wet, and wishing you had something to change into. She also packed two swimsuits. Packing her bag made her sad because they were the clothes she bought for her honeymoon and never had a chance to wear them. She was a little apprehensive over the suits as they were both bikinis. She would simply leave a shirt on as much as possible. And she couldn't forget her big floppy hat. Abby hated to admit it, but she was excited. For over four weeks now she felt as if she had no life.

Rob stopped by right at three o'clock. He certainly was punctual, thought Abby. He asked if she had talked to Wade about getting off early. He already knew she had but did not want to let on. In fact, Rob had called Wade first thing in the morning to let him know. "Yes, I did talk to Wade this morning and he said he saw no problem in me leaving early. Of course I did not tell him my reason for wanting out early, and it was good he never asked."

"Are you all set to go?" asked Rob.

"Yes I am. I did pack a bag and I hope I didn't take too much. I absolutely hate getting all wet and not have anything to change into. Will there be room on the boat for me to change?" Abby wore a white gauze skirt, a turquoise cotton shirt that tied in the front, and matching sandals—casual for work but a little dressy for a boat. She would put her shorts on when she got on the boat.

"Oh, that won't be a problem. There should be plenty of room." *Evidently Abby was not listening when I told her it was a cabin cruiser.*

Switching cars with Jeff worked out well, and although Jeff had a decent vehicle, it was no Lamborghini. It took Rob a while to get used to how slow Jeff's truck traveled; maybe it wasn't the truck but him. He liked traveling in the fast lane. The ride to the marina was quiet, but not awkward. Rob asked Abby about church, "Have you had any luck in finding a church home?"

"Yes, I think I have. I love the music, and the pastor and my small group are really good. The only problem when you're single is that many of the married women think you're after their husband. The older women are great though, and they have made me feel very welcome."

Time flew by as conversation picked up and both seemed very comfortable in each other's company. Abby had to admit that she wondered how it would be away from the office. She remembered that Bob said he would take her home if she felt uncomfortable and that gave her some assurance.

Pulling up to the marina, Rob spotted his car and parked a few spots over. He couldn't help but check it out, and made sure Jeff was careful with his "baby". Abby noticed how he was eyeing the Lamborghini and couldn't help but ask what kind of a car it was. "This is a very sweet car. Rides like a cloud. Can go from zero to…" He immediately caught himself and simply finished his sentence with "must be nice from what I've read about it." After putting in the code at the gate, Rob quickly guided Abby to the end of the pier. He pointed to a small motor boat in the slip and helped her into it. He noticed the puzzled look on her face and said, "This is not the boat—she's out there". He then nodded his head to the left and pointed to an amazing boat out in the harbor. "This is simply the skiff we use to get out to the boat. Jeff usually brings her into one of the docks for us to board, but I think we can manage from the fantail."

They easily boarded from the fantail, and then climbed the several steps, not a ladder but actual steps. Abby noticed that there were steps leading up from both sides. "This is not a boat….this is a yacht!" Abby had never seen, let alone been on a boat this size. It was beautiful and breathtaking. Her eyes could hardly take it all in. After going through the automatic glass doors, they walked into a spacious living room; it had white plush carpeting throughout, a huge black leather sectional sat in front of a 65" Smart TV. Rob proceeded to take her towards the bow where a full galley was located. Before entering the galley, she saw the beautifully appointed dining room with a large polished black teak table and twelve matching chairs with white fabric. As they entered the galley, Jeff stood with his back to them evidently not aware they were on board. "Hey Jeff", said Rob. Jeff turned around taking a look at Abby right off.

From behind Abby, Rob shook his head at Jeff before he said anything inappropriate. "Well…hello", said Jeff.

Rob had learned after he first met Abby that she was different, and he knew she would never appreciate any kind of cussing. He was thankful that Jeff had caught on right away and hoped he would not have to run interference the next few days. However, he didn't appreciate the flirtatious look Jeff was giving Abby. "Jeff, this is Abby Sinclair; Abby, Jeff Anderson."

Abby extended her hand as did Jeff. "What an unbelievable boat or yacht you have. I have never seen anything like it."

"Thanks. I can show you around, but I think Rob would be more than happy to do that."

"Rob?" questioned Abby.

"Yeah", said Rob, scowling at Jeff. "My name is Robert and I go by Bob or Rob. Jeff's known me quite a while and can't seem to call me Bob like most."

Jeff simply mouthed the word, "sorry", as he rolled his eyes at Rob.

Taking Abby's elbow, Rob said he would give her the grand tour. They walked down a hallway on the port side, actually behind the galley, and into a beautiful appointed master bedroom with its en suite bath. It was hard to believe all this could be on a boat. "This will be your room, Abby", said Rob. "Jeff insists that you have this room as there are two more master suites down below. As you can see, there's a beautifully appointed master bath and walk-in closet." From the living room they walked down a carpeted circular staircase to the lower deck. Once below, he pointed out two master bedrooms with adjoining bathroom suites. Abby didn't think she ever closed her mouth the whole time. It was more than she could take in. Each of the bedrooms had a king size bed and lots of storage. All the woodwork was the same as the upstairs suite, with beautiful cherry wood that was polished to such sheen that she was sure she could see her reflection in it. As they walked past the plush carpeted circular staircase, Rob showed her another smaller bedroom with two single beds and another adjoining bath. Noticing her apprehension, Rob certainly wanted to put her at ease. "Hey, don't worry about a thing. I promise you'll have a good time...really. Remember you'll be up top and Jeff and I will each have a room down below. I don't think Jeff plans on pushing off until morning, so we'll have dinner on the boat in a little bit. If you decide you want to leave after dinner, we will."

Abby thought she better close her mouth but all she could do was nod at Rob. She was literally breathless.

"Let's go back upstairs and see what Jeff has planned for dinner tonight. He's quite the cook, and usually very creative."

When Abby finally did find her voice, she said she would like to change into some shorts. "Did you say my bag is upstairs?"

"Yes, I placed it in the master upstairs. Make yourself at home. I think I'll get some shorts on as well." Rob had already had Jeff move his boating apparel downstairs so it was no problem for him to change. "Do you mind if I stay down here and change? I'll be up in a minute."

"That's totally fine. I think I can manage to find my way back upstairs, although I can see where it would be easy to get lost on this huge boat."

"It's not that big. It's not a cruise ship or anything like that."

"Big enough and way more than I ever expected."

The three of them enjoyed an amazing dinner of shrimp scampi, delicious salad, and garlic bread. Abby knew her breath would not smell too good, but she had no plans of kissing anyone either. "The meal was delicious and I am absolutely stuffed. You're an excellent cook, Jeff."

Jeff sat with a big grin on his face looking like the cat that ate the canary. He was a good cook, along with the many hats that he wore for his boss and Stevenson Enterprises. The whole time Jeff was thinking, that hopefully, Abby would think that he was the billionaire with the Lamborghini and yacht, and maybe, just maybe, she would be attracted to him and not Rob. *A guy can always hope*, thought Jeff. "Let's have our dessert and coffee on deck," suggested Jeff.

"Great idea, I'll help with the dessert. What can I do?" Abby was more than willing to pitch in, and she certainly did not want this to be a weekend for her to be waited on. She also did not expect the guys to think that of her either. Rob offered to take the coffee out while Jeff and Abby dished up the dessert in the galley. Abby felt somewhat self-conscious being around someone this wealthy and having so much, after all, Jeff was probably a little bit of a snob. He was definitely out of her league. Still, it was very thoughtful of him to invite them out on his boat for the weekend. "Thank you so much, Jeff, for inviting me. I have never been on such an elegant boat, and dinner was fabulous."

"You're very welcome, Abby. I hope we can do it again sometime. I hope you enjoy yourself. Rob always enjoys coming out here, and we've had a lot of good times together."

Rob was getting a little anxious wondering what was keeping them so long. As Abby came out with the tray of dessert, she noticed a crooked little smile from Rob. He really was a handsome man. Jeff followed with three plates, and Abby helped dish up the delicious strawberry cheesecake. The three enjoyed sitting on the plush cushions surrounding the aft deck. *What a fabulous evening*, thought Abby. In her wildest dreams she could not imagine an evening like this under the stars... and in such luxury. The conversation was natural and Jeff was more than willing to answer all of Abby's questions about the boat. He certainly knew a lot about the Gulf Coast and the many yachts that were harbored here in Galveston and even the yachts harbored in some of the coastal marinas.

"So where did you and Bob meet, or do you want me to call you Rob?" Abby asked turning to Rob. Of course Jeff knew how he met Rob but telling the story reversed as to who was whom would take some doing.

"Hey whatever you want to call me. At the resort I guess most call me Bob but I go by either."

"Well okay. I'll try and call you Rob from now on since your good friend Jeff calls you that. How did you and Rob meet?" Abby asked again turning to Jeff who seemed more than eager to tell his story.

Jeff began with the story of how he practically grew up at the marina in San Diego and how Rob spent a lot of his time working on the dock. It wasn't long before they became fast friends. He left out how Rob was the very rich kid and he was the one who worked there every summer since he was twelve. Abby didn't seem to question any of it and thought it was sweet that they had been such close friends for so many years. Jeff knew it was because of Rob's friendship that he never got involved in the drug scene, especially growing up on the beach. Jockeying so many boats around made it easy for Rob to hire him on as captain of, *My First Mil.*

There was a time when Rob loved his father very much, in fact, he worshiped him, but he always felt like he had to prove himself to him. He enjoyed spending time on his dad's boat and felt a real sense of accomplishment when he could purchase a boat even bigger than his dad's. Rob's dad thought of him as nothing but a playboy and gave him little credit for his huge success; now he was a billionaire and Rob doubted his dad even realized this. They really had a very strained relationship once his dad remarried.

"The stars are breathtaking out here," said Abby gazing up into the night sky. "The moon is hanging so low I feel like I could reach up and pull it right out of the black sky… and the fresh air is simply intoxicating." She closed her eyes and took in a deep breath, enjoying the salty night air. "I'm sure I will sleep well tonight."

"Since it's only nine o'clock, I thought we could go in and watch a movie; how about it?" suggested Rob.

Abby was somewhat reticent in her reply wondering what type of movie he had in mind. Almost reading her thoughts, Rob said, "I have *National Treasure, Fools Gold, Overboard*—" Before he could finish, Abby quickly said, "How about *Overboard?* That's one of my favorite movies, and since we're on a boat, that sounds perfect." Abby was relieved to hear the movie suggestions he had, and that put her mind at ease for the evening. "I'll help clean up the dishes," as she began placing them on the tray. Jeff followed with the coffee mugs and carafe. Abby couldn't help but question in her mind how Rob never really seemed to pitch in, but he allowed his utterly rich and sophisticated friend do all the work. *Well, he must be used to his friend waiting on him.*

Quickly cleaning up the dishes, and putting them away, Abby was ready to sit and watch the movie Rob had already set up in the DVD player. The three sat down to watch the movie: Abby on one side of the cushy leather couch and Rob on the other. Jeff grabbed the matching overstuffed leather chair. In spite of it being a girly flick, the guys seemed to enjoy watching as well. She thought that they must be relating to the very macho male independence. Halfway through the movie Jeff took his leave stating they would be getting underway in the morning. Once again, Abby thanked him for a great evening. "May I finish your bowl of popcorn then? I simply love popcorn."

Since Abby said nothing of wanting to return home, Rob was not about to broach the subject. Oh yes, he was definitely looking forward to this weekend with Abby as he leaned back to watch the movie.

"Of course," said Jeff, "my pleasure. But I hardly left much at all." Abby sat enjoying the movie and the rest of Jeff's popcorn, but before long her eyelids seemed to be getting very heavy. After silence for some time, Rob looked over only to find Abby completely zonked out. *Now what, I can't very well let her sleep on the couch; not with Jeff showing up early in the morning?*

Rob went to her room and turned down the bedding. Going back to the living room, Abby lay with her head against the arm of the couch looking very uncomfortable. He took out the clip that was keeping her hair up in that loose twist she always wore; something he wanted to do for the last month. Her hair fell loosely over the side of the couch. It was much longer and fuller than he anticipated. He tried waking her but she didn't budge. She was totally out. There was only one thing he could do and that was to pick her up and carry her to the bed. She seemed to fit comfortably in his arms. He laid her on the bed and her hair splayed over the pillow taking his breath away. He stared at her long eyelashes and her amazing legs. Funny he never noticed her long lashes and beautiful long legs, but then she always wore a skirt or long pants. But those lashes he never noticed, perhaps he was always taken aback by her mesmerizing green eyes. Enough staring, he knew he had to get out of there. Abby wasn't just beautiful, but something about her made her different. He knew he could never take advantage of her, not that he ever would, but he couldn't take the chance. For some reason, so many Bible verses Rob learned as a young boy kept coming to mind. Just now he thought of John 3:16, the first verse he ever memorized. "For God so loved the world that He gave His only begotten Son, that whoever believes in Him should not perish but have everlasting life." *Wow, I never thought I could remember something from so long ago,* and it stabbed his heart. *What is happening to me?* Verses he had long forgotten were creeping their way into his head… no, more like his heart. After tucking in Abby, Rob quietly exited the room.

Abby woke with a start and could hear the hum of engines. Where was she? After adjusting to her surroundings, she realized she was still dressed but in this magnificent master suite aboard Jeff's yacht. She wondered how she got there. Somebody must have put her in bed, and it had to be Rob as Jeff had already gone to bed. *Well, that was embarrassing. What time was it anyway?* She thought. *Oh my, it's nine o'clock! I look a wreck, but I better go see what's up.*

Abby ran a brush through her hair, but it didn't help much. As she walked into the galley, both men were sitting at the counter on the bar stools having a cup of coffee.

"Hey sleepyhead, good morning," Rob said, noticing how adorable she looked all rumpled.

"Do I have time for a quick shower?"

"How about a cup of coffee first?" asked Jeff.

"That sounds good, but I look a mess."

Pouring her coffee, Jeff placed a mug in front of her. "Thanks. That does smell good. It'll help wake me up. I can't believe I slept this late. I think the fresh air really got to me," she said sheepishly eyeing Rob. "I hate to admit that I do fall asleep quite easily once I'm relaxed, and the amazing couch didn't help any. Where are we anyway? I heard the engines purring when I awoke."

"We're about twenty miles out of port and anchored in a secluded cove. The waters are deep but calm," said Jeff.

"You may not want a shower just yet" Rob interjected. "We happen to have a couple of wave runners down below. Have you ever ridden a wave runner, Abby?"

"No, I have not, and I'm not sure I really want to."

Rob chuckled as he continued to try and convince her how much fun they would have. "I promise we'll go slow and cruise around. Believe me when I tell you, you'll have a blast."

"Okay, I'll go get my suit on, and then we'll see. Just so you know I would be perfectly content to lie out and soak up some sun while you guys go on the wave runners." Abby left to get her swimsuit on.

Feeling self-conscious about her black bikini, Abby put on one of her husband's white dress shirts. The only clothing she saved of Thomas's was a couple of his shirts. She couldn't help the moisture pooling in her eyes as she sniffed the shirt remembering how good Thomas always smelled with his spicy cologne. It was never the expensive cologne but he always smelled warm and masculine. *I can't dwell on how bad my heart aches right now.* She realized this was the first she thought of her husband in several weeks. The loneliness and ache she felt in her heart were getting to be less and less. Abby thought she should have tried to get a new suit, perhaps a one piece, but considered it a waste of money when she had three bikinis that she purchased for her honeymoon. The cover-up she purchased for her honeymoon was way too sheer and she would never feel comfortable wearing it; at least Thomas's shirt really did cover her up. Now if she could simply keep this on over her suit until the guys went out on the wave runners, she could lay out comfortably while they were gone.

Abby walked out to the galley looking forward to some breakfast. She could smell the bacon, and Abby always loved a good breakfast whenever there was time to enjoy one.

Taking a look at Abby, Rob thought she looked adorable in the man's white shirt. Not having it buttoned all the way up it was obvious she must have on a black bikini. Jeff immediately handed Abby a plate of scrambled eggs and bacon, and asked if she wanted a cinnamon roll with it. "This looks absolutely delicious, and I'm starving. I'll have half a cinnamon roll please." Abby could easily eat a whole one but she certainly did not want to look like a little piggy.

Jeff tried convincing her that she would love going on the wave runner. He seemed way too insistent and she was feeling more and more uncomfortable. Rob quickly picked up on her uneasiness and realized it must be that she was self-conscious of wearing a bikini. "Abby, why don't you put on one of my T- shirts; it will help protect you from the sun. It can be brutal when you're out on the water."

Feeling relief, Abby was grateful for how sensitive Rob seemed to her uneasiness. "Thanks Rob, if you don't mind I think I would like that." *How did he know what was going through my mind?* Rob excused himself and went downstairs to his room and returned with a U of A T-shirt. After eating, Abby returned to her room to slip on the shirt. *Great, it's totally large enough and this will be a perfect cover up for the wave runner.* Only trouble, it smelled just like Rob, a rich woodsy scent. *It will smell like ocean once I'm in the water.*

The wave runners were off the fantail and ready to go. "I'm not going on one by myself," said Abby a little fearfully. "I've never been on one of these in my life."

Before Jeff could get in his offer, Rob quickly gave Abby a hand and told her to hop on behind him. "Jeff can go alone."

Abby sat behind Rob but did not feel comfortable putting her arms around his waist, so she carefully placed her hands on his shoulders and gave him the signal to go. She held his shoulders so tightly that she realized she was pulling him backwards and throwing him off balance. *This is not good,* so she slipped her arms around him. Abby couldn't help but notice his abs. *He must work out a lot to have a rock hard body like this. I guess if this is what people called ripped, he surely was.* More relaxed, they continued jumping over the waves, weaving in and out. They were the only two watercrafts in this secluded cove, and Rob was right...she was having a blast. The water spraying her face was refreshing and exhilarating. She never imagined it could be so much fun.

When they returned to the boat and tied up the wave runners, they all jumped into the water and swam around for a while. "It has to be close to lunch time," said Rob.

"I can't believe I'm hungry again," said Abby. "I thought after that big breakfast it would last until tonight."

"No way; when you're out on the water I think your appetite increases. At least I know mine does. How about it Jeff? What say we head on in for some lunch?"

Abby quickly offered to help with lunch preparations and headed for her room to remove her soaked T-shirt. She returned to the galley and immediately pitched in making a salad and preheating the oven for a gourmet pizza Jeff had taken out. She set the table on the aft deck and was thinking how she could easily get use to this kind of life. *No, not really,* she thought to herself. *This is way too rich for my blood. I think I'm really just a simple girl.*

After a very leisurely lunch, the guys were ready to go back out on the wave runners. Abby declined and said they should go and she would clean up. She did not want to admit to them that she planned on going to the forward deck where she had noticed several chaise lounges; a perfect spot to read and take a much needed nap.

The guys took off without hesitation, and Abby quickly cleaned up. There was not much to clean up when all they had was a salad and pizza.

Abby grabbed her Bible and study book as she had her lesson to do for her small group. Heading towards the bow, she was amazed how huge this yacht was. She had her choice of lounges and picked one facing the sun. Taking Thomas's big white shirt off, she quickly got comfortable. After lying on her stomach for some time, she rolled over and continued reading. It wasn't long before she felt her eyelids getting heavier than she expected, and thought a nap would do her good. Before she realized it, she was out.

Rob and Jeff returned only to find Abby fast asleep on the chaise lounge with her Bible and study book lying on the deck. Jeff stared with his mouth hanging open. "Hey man, what a beautiful body. She's gorgeous, isn't she?"

"Forget it Jeff. And you better close your mouth while you're at it. I tell you she's different and I don't want you looking at her like that."

"What do you expect when she's laying there in a black bikini? I'm not a priest."

Rob found himself rubbing her shoulder and calling her name, but first he put her shirt over her. Abby woke with a start shocked to see four eyes peering down at her. "I'm sorry. I guess I fell asleep. What time is it anyway?"

"It's almost four o'clock. We've been gone for over two hours. I hope you got some lotion on you or you're going to be fried." Rob really showed concern for her well being and that touched her. He must have been the one to cover her up with Thomas's shirt.

"I did get lotion on. I did lie on my stomach to begin with but I don't think it was for too long. If I have any burn it will probably be on my back as I couldn't reach to get any lotion there."

"I would have gladly rubbed lotion on your back for you." Jeff said a little too flirtatiously.

Abby let it go and quickly got up from the chaise grateful her shirt was handy to slip on. Rob helped her with it and she could tell he was careful where his eyes went, keeping them on her face.

Her hair was pulled back in a pony tail and he asked if her hair had dried. *Nothing like sounding like a complete idiot,* he thought to himself. *Of course her hair is dry she's been laying out here for over two hours.* He just hoped she hadn't noticed what a dumb question he just asked.

"Yes, I'm sure it is. I kept it down while I was on my stomach, and put it up when I rolled over. I wanted to keep it out of my eyes."

Abby went below to shower and change and was sure that's what the men were doing as well. She knew they would be heading back to the harbor in the morning. It had been a perfect couple of days.

As Abby walked into the living room, Jeff was seated in one of the cushy leather chairs and motioned for her to sit down. She sat on the couch and again thanked him for a fabulous time. Jeff couldn't help but ask if he could take her out to dinner some time. Abby thought this a little forward as she was really a guest of Rob's. "Thanks for asking but I really don't think so. I'm quite busy with work and church. In fact, getting adjusted to my new job takes up quite a bit of my time."

Jeff looked a little downcast but simply replied, "Hey, no problem. When you want to come back out for a boat ride let me know. It could be just the two of us... or with Rob if you like."

Abby knew he was too rich for her blood and didn't expect it to happen again anytime soon; they were from two different worlds. And she really was quite taken up with her new job. Rob came up and joined her on the couch. Looking at both of them he wondered if he was interrupting something; he chimed in, "I'm starved. What about you two?" Giving it some thought, he said to himself, *Wait a minute. Why should I feel uncomfortable? I own this yacht and Jeff's my employee.* Rob couldn't help but give Jeff a stern look and didn't bother to ask again, "How about we have dinner. I'm ready."

Jeff got the message and immediately got up and headed to the galley. He knew what was planned for dinner. Not wasting any time he started getting pots and pans out. Hearing the commotion, Abby started getting up to go help out when Rob suddenly stopped her. "Just sit and relax. I'm sure Jeff has it under control. He's really in his element when he's in the galley."

Abby reluctantly sat back down and somehow felt the tension between the two men. She hoped it wasn't due to her being there. She immediately tried to think of something fun to talk about. Rob noticed her discomfort as she leaned back on the cushion. "Your back is sunburned, isn't it?" asked Rob. "I can see the backs of your legs, and if your back looks anything like your legs we better get some lotion on you." He immediately got up and quickly returned with some Aloe Vera lotion. "Abby you have to lift your shirt up for me."

"Excuse me?" questioned Abby. "I don't think I'm going to lift my shirt for you or anyone."

"Abby you have to. Believe me this will make all the difference or you're just going to be miserable all night. I promise I won't look." Abby couldn't help but notice the little twinkle in his eye. She was wearing her white shorts and a fuchsia scooped tank top. "Lift it up enough so I can get this on you."

"Well all right." Abby carefully raised her top exposing her extremely sunburned back. At least her bra strap was in the same spot as her bikini strap. Feeling flushed, she was sure her whole body had to be as red as her back.

Rob carefully began to lather her with the aloe. She shivered at the coolness of the lotion. Abby couldn't help but notice how soft his hands seemed as he tenderly applied the lotion. *Not really hands of a maintenance man.* Just then Jeff walked in with a statement he could not resist. "Hey, some guys seem to have all the luck." Both Rob and Abby rolled their eyes at him, however, Rob really picked up on his jealousy. After a liberal application of the lotion, Rob pulled her shirt down and gave her the bottle to apply some lotion on the backs of her legs.

Wanting to keep things light and not dwell on her sunburn, Abby said, "You were right about the wave runner being such a blast. I had a great time. Do you get out on them often?"

"I love it and try to get out as often as possible." Remembering his role reversal with Jeff he immediately added, "And of course it depends on Jeff inviting me."

Jeff was busy running back and forth and it wasn't long before he announced "dinner is served". Rob got up and escorted Abby to the rear deck. The table was set beautifully. Jeff returned with a tossed salad followed by lobster tail with drawn butter, green beans with almonds, and baked potato with lots of butter and sour cream.

Abby was overwhelmed with the meal and Jeff's culinary skills. "This was a meal fit for royalty. It was amazing. Thank you so much."

Of course she was unaware that this was the meal Rob had selected for their last night on the boat.

Completely sated with the outstanding meal, they remained outside enjoying the night sky once again.

After an hour or so, Jeff came out with chocolate mousse and coffee for dessert. Abby was pleased Jeff joined them for dinner and for dessert. Once again she got up to help clean up the dishes but Rob, and then Jeff, insisted she enjoy her last night on the boat under the stars.

Rob suggested another movie or finish "Overboard" but Abby declined sheepishly, "I think I really need to get to bed early, at least before I fall asleep on the couch again."

Abby excused herself, turning in early. There was no way she was going to take the chance of falling asleep and having to be carried to bed.

When Abby left the room, Rob turned to Jeff and asked if he had asked Abby out. Something was nagging at him after he had walked into the living room earlier and saw the two of them together; he knew Jeff would jump at the chance. "Well, did you ask her out?"

Jeff had to admit he did, but had only asked if she would go out with him for dinner sometime. "And what did she say?" asked Rob.

"She thanked me and said she was too busy with her new job and with church, simple as that."

"Okay, but remember hands off. That's all I have to say, and hopefully, I won't have to keep reminding you who the boss is here."

"Don't worry boss. But haven't you wondered if she thinks I'm the one with everything, won't it be tempting for her to go out with ME?"

"I want her to like me for me. Not for my success, my yacht, my plane, and yes, my money. I'm just hoping it won't take too much longer before I can come clean and not have her furious with me." Rob was helping Jeff clean up the galley and wondered what had gotten into him. They were good friends and he certainly wanted to keep their friendship strong, even if he was Jeff's boss.

Abby woke up at eight feeling totally refreshed and grateful she went to bed early. She couldn't help but smell the bacon and quickly headed for the shower. She knew they would be in the harbor soon. She wondered if they already were as she did not hear the engines running. She showered, grateful once again for the very expensive body wash and lotion. There were a couple of different body washes, and she wondered how many women spent nights on the boat. She dressed for the day, putting on her navy blue, scooped neck, cotton dress with the little capped sleeves; sandals that she knew would go with her wide rimmed navy and white striped hat.

When she walked into the galley, once again she was welcomed with an amazing breakfast. This morning they had waffles with warm syrup, bacon, and fresh fruit. "This looks delicious and after last night's meal I can't believe I could eat even a morsel this morning; but looking at this beautiful spread I guess I was wrong. I feel like all I'm doing is eating."

"We'll eat and then pack things up here. As you can see," continued Rob, "we are back in the harbor."

"This was an amazing weekend, and I thank you both so much. I'm glad we didn't try and make it back early." Abby was pleased with the great time she had and berated herself for even feeling anxious about spending the weekend with two single men. She knew if she had told her mother what she was going to do this weekend, she would have heard such a sermon that she would have spent the whole weekend in guilt. The two guys were nothing but gentlemen and for this she was grateful. "I stripped my bed this morning and cleaned the bathroom. What would you like me to do with the linens?"

Both men simply looked at her with their mouths agape. Rob especially was surprised, and knew he shouldn't be, now that he had gotten to know her better. "Just leave everything. Jeff has a cleaning lady that comes on board, and she will take care of everything. By the way, you look amazing."

"Thank you," Abby said. "And I must thank Jeff for the selection of body wash and lotion. He must be used to having lots of ladies staying overnight. He certainly has good taste...and very expensive."

"I think he bought them just for you. It's hard to know what somebody might like to have for their shower. He wanted to know what I thought you would like and I told him to have a couple of choices for you."

"Well, they were lovely." Abby felt a little embarrassed that she implied Jeff had a lot of women spend the night. She was grateful Rob answered and that Jeff was not put on the spot. He had already walked away to serve up the food.

With the stairs being rolled up to the yacht, they were able to tie up to the dock. Before disembarking Abby put on her hat and also her big chunky sunglasses at Rob's suggestion.

Rob said Jeff would be staying back to button things up and then get the boat back out to the harbor to tie up. Abby leaned in and gave Jeff a hug and a kiss on the cheek, thanking him for the fabulous time. She did not notice when Jeff leaned over to whisper something in Rob's ear.

"Just so you know, Rob, there's a paparazzo on the other side of the gate." Acknowledging Jeff with a slight nod, Rob took Abby by the arm escorting her up the ramp. He also noticed the paparazzo that Jeff pointed out. Stepping through the security gate, Rob picked up the pace but not before a flash went off.

"What was that?" asked Abby.

Making light of her question, Rob simply replied, "I'm sure it's just a tourist. They like taking pictures of the bigger boats that come in; it's not unusual."

He quickly whisked her to the truck, and was thankful it was parked so close. He was also thankful he had Jeff's truck.

The ride back to the office to pick up Abby's car was non-eventful, even though they never lacked for conversation. Rob couldn't help but ask her one question that was eating at him. "So did Jeff actually ask you out?"

"He asked if I would go out to dinner with him sometime. I told him I was way too busy with my new job and also my church commitment. Anyway, there is no way I could go out with him."

"Oh, why is that?" asked Rob.

"I would absolutely die if someone like him were to even see my tiny house. It would be embarrassing to say the least; it's obvious we come from two very different worlds."

Feeling like an absolute heel, all Rob could come up with was to tell her there was no reason she should ever feel that way. Although he really didn't think she bought it.

Chapter 7

Before Abby got into her car, she asked Rob if he would like to come for dinner on Friday night. "It won't be much but I do love to cook, and I would love to have you come for dinner." Abby felt this was one small way she could reciprocate for the lovely weekend she had with him and the wonderful meals they shared since she started at the resort.

"Thanks I would love to, what time?"

"How about six o'clock? That way I'll have time to prepare after I get home from work."

"We have a date then, and I'll certainly be looking forward to it. Can I bring anything?"

"No but thanks for asking."

Abby stepped into her car with a bounce and a smile on her face. *Did I just invite a man to my house? I hope I didn't seem too forward.*

She cringed with the realization that tomorrow morning she would be heading out to the resort in California. This was something she really needed to pray about tonight. Even though she was ready, and the flight arrangements were made, facing someone who she knew was probably extorting company funds was not going to be easy.

After unpacking and starting a load of wash, Abby got ready for bed, but not before she spent some time reading her Bible and focusing on God's goodness and faithfulness to her. Abby put the clothes in the dryer and hopped into bed. She prayed, knowing she had to trust God for what would be happening in California. She prayed for His wisdom and guidance. Confident in not who she was, but confident in who God is, Abby closed her eyes and before long had a very peaceful sleep.

Waking at six, Abby had time to pack a light bag. She did not think she would be spending the night in California, however, she did not know what may transpire. Confronting a situation such as this was totally new to her. She knew she had to be confident and demand respect from any employee under her.

She still needed to stop by the office, pick up some papers, and check on her flight time with the crew. After a month of talking with the pilot and flight attendant on the phone, Abby felt like she knew them well. Doug, the pilot for the Leer Jet, said they would be ready for takeoff at half past eight as she had requested. The private air strip was only fifteen minutes from the resort, so it would be a quick drive.

Abby had never been on a private jet before and couldn't help but feel excitement over the prospect. She parked her car and walked into the private terminal that was beautifully appointed. Jenny, the flight attendant, was very gracious and personable; and Abby already felt like she had known her for years. Jenny was a beautiful woman probably in her mid thirties. She was tall and thin with naturally blond hair. Abby knew she was married, and she also knew that her mother had cancer and was not doing too well. After their greeting and some small talk, Abby asked Jenny how her mother was doing. "Not too good," Jenny was rather downcast in her response. "They started her on chemo and it seems to be taking a lot out of her. I'm so thankful for this job though. As you know Tyler (Jenny's six year old son) stays with my mom when I have a flight. At least her treatment was earlier in the week and she was feeling well enough to watch him today. When I worked for the airline, I had no choice but to leave him in childcare. My mom had a much greater responsibility when I was flying commercial. By the way, Doug and Len are doing the flight check and we should be leaving right on time."

For a small airport it seemed to have everything a municipal airport had. They had a service desk, a flight control tower, and a small airport crew. It was very impressive. She knew that many hotel guests flew their private planes to the resort. Jenny asked Abby if she wanted anything to drink while she waited, but she declined and thought it best to wait until she was on the plane.

Len, the copilot, came in to tell them everything was all set to go. Walking across the tarmac, the three of them continued up the stairs and onto the plane. As Abby walked onto the plane, she was totally taken aback at the luxury of the plane: plush navy blue carpet, white leather seats, and two white leather couches facing each other. There were also four regular leather seats, two on either side of the plane. Noticing Abby's expression, Jenny asked if she would like a tour of the plane. "Absolutely," Abby said. "I never imagined anything like this," as they walked to the back of the plane. Jenny pointed out the galley with everything in it, a beautiful restroom, and in the rear there were two extravagant bedroom suites. Everything was trimmed in walnut; she was sure it had to be real walnut. After the yacht this past weekend, and now this private jet, Abby had never been in such luxury. "Why would anyone need such an extravagant plane?" asked Abby.

"Mr. Stevenson really likes all the comforts of home and actually there are times when he uses the master bedroom to nap or for an overnight flight."

"I guess it's just overwhelming for me to imagine anyone having so much wealth."

Abby got comfortable in her seat, and Jenny was quick to bring her a cup of coffee. "Anything else I can get for you? As soon as we're in the air I will bring you some breakfast."

"Sounds wonderful; coffee is great for now, thanks." Abby no sooner sat back in her seat, when the two pilots came out to welcome her onboard before takeoff. She was pleased to put a face to the pilot, Doug, who she spoke with often. "I'm so pleased to finally meet you, Doug. By the way, how are your wife and kids doing?"

"They're doing very well. Thanks for asking. Abby, I want to officially introduce my copilot, Len. Len this is Abby Sinclair. Abby is the CFO for Stevenson Enterprises and the lady who makes sure we're paid and our flights get scheduled. Abby, this is Len Holmes. He's been my copilot for about two years now. You have to watch out for this guy: he's single and he's footloose and fancy free." Doug said this while slapping Len on the back. "Just kidding, he's really a great guy."

"How do you do ma'am...pleased to meet you." Len was certainly a Texan with an obvious Texas drawl.

"It's nice meeting you as well," responded Abby shaking his extended hand.

"We'll be taking off shortly, and if there is anything we can do for you, please let us know. I know Jenny will take good care of you." Len winked and returned to the cabin following Doug, who rolled his eyes at his friend and copilot.

It wasn't long before they were in the air, and Doug announced that the flight to San Diego would be about two hours. After a delicious breakfast, Abby got out her papers that she needed to go over. Feeling the tension once again, she knew she had to commit this day to the Lord and seek his wisdom.

Her rental car was waiting for her, and she was thankful it had GPS. She entered the directions to Hotel Furnishings; grateful she had plenty of time to make her appointment with the president of the company. Realizing she could have used her iPhone, Abby immediately felt the tightness in her chest; she forgot the phone call she had promised to make. *Oh my! I totally forgot to call Mr. Stevenson! As soon as I get to the parking lot of Hotel Furnishings I'll call him.* She was not looking forward to her phone call.

Abby had met with Hotel Furnishings in Houston the previous week, and they were able to find the Oriental rug that had been ordered in California. The identical rug was priced at $100,000, which to Abby was beyond comprehension, but evidently reasonable and a competitive price. Satisfied with her investigation, she would confront the president of the company in California. She was determined to find out why California's Hotel Furnishings was charging the outrageous price of $250,000 for the same carpet; fortunately it had not yet been delivered to the resort.

Rob was pacing the floor in his office wondering why he had not heard from Abby. She said she would call when she arrived in California. He had called Doug and he said they had landed a good hour ago. *Why hadn't she called? I hope she hasn't run into any trouble. She should never have gone alone.* So many scenarios started running through his mind. And why was he feeling so protective of her? He knew why, he was falling for her…big time. His nerves were frazzled, and he was definitely on edge. As he was frantically pacing, Wade entered Rob's office. "Man you look like a caged lion. You know you're going to wear a hole in the carpet pacing like that. What's gotten into you?"

"I haven't heard from Abby and I told her last week to call as soon as she arrives in San Diego; they landed over an hour ago, Wade. What do you think happened to her?"

"I'm sure she's fine, Rob. But you won't be when you take a look at The Buzz magazine."

"Why, what's up?"

Wade followed him to his desk, tossing the magazine in front of him. "How the paparazzi know where you are is beyond me."

Rob sat with his mouth agape as he looked at the picture and the headline. It was a picture of Abby and him walking through the marina gate with Rob's arm around her waist. The headline read: *Who is the unknown beauty with Billionaire Robert Stevenson?* The article went on to say that their sources believe her to be an upcoming foreign starlet. "I knew when I saw the flash go off that someone was taking our picture. Abby noticed the flash as well and commented about it. I told her it was probably a tourist and how they liked getting pictures of the large yachts when they came in. Wade, I know she doesn't read any of these magazines, but somehow I have to keep them from her. I can't blow my cover—not yet anyway."

"So what do you want me to do? Pull every magazine off the shelf?"

"Yes I do. At least within a five mile radius... buy every one of them."

"What about California? You know this is on every stand in America."

"Hopefully, she'll be too busy and have no reason to go to a store, and by the time she gets back here, the stores will be all out of them. You better get moving."

"I'm on my way."

Just then Rob's phone started to chirp. Looking at his phone, he saw it was Abby. He needed to sound a little stern as he did last week. There was no way he wanted her to identify his voice, "Stevenson here."

Hearing his voice, Abby's stomach tightened immediately. *I'm not going to let him intimidate me. I know my job and I'm doing fine, just take a deep breath.* "Hello Mr. Stevenson, this is Abby Sinclair."

"Hello Miss Sinclair. I expected your call earlier. Is everything okay?"

"It's Mrs. Sinclair sir, and yes, everything is fine." *Why did he sound like such a jerk?* "Actually, I was so taken up with getting my rental car, and finding Hotel Furnishings, that I forgot to call in. I'm sorry about that, but I am here now and in the parking lot."

"Well thanks for calling, and Mrs. Sinclair, please be careful."

Hearing him so pleasant gave Abby pause. He almost sounded like someone she had heard speak before. She quickly brushed that thought aside knowing she needed to concentrate on the task at hand.

Hotel Furnishings was located outside San Diego in a very upscale industrial park. After checking in at the front desk, Abby was escorted to the office of Joseph Macpherson, President of Hotel Furnishings. This happened to be Hotel Furnishings corporate office, and Abby was pleased she had already done some investigating of her own at the Texas store.

Shaking hands with Mr. Macpherson, he asked her to take a seat. "How may I help you, it is Mrs. Sinclair, correct? I understand you are the new CFO for Stevenson Enterprises."

"Yes it is Mrs. Sinclair, and yes I am the new CFO. Thank you for your time, Mr. Macpherson." Abby began explaining the information she had uncovered, asking about the specific Oriental rug that had been ordered from this particular location. Mr. Macpherson looked up the particular order and also the wholesale price to Stevenson Enterprises and Resort by the Sea. They both found this information quite disturbing as the cost to Stevenson Enterprises was nowhere near the $250,000 Abby had on her books. Mr. Macpherson was quick to point out that the $110,000 was not unusual. The additional ten thousand was due to it being purchased in California. This did not make any sense to Abby; however she agreed to go along with the cost. "But what about the $140,000 discrepancy," asked Abby? "This makes no sense at all when your original invoice is $110,000, and my invoice is for $250,000." Mr. Macpherson agreed and called for his sales rep to come to his office. Upon entering, Mr. Macpherson introduced Abby to Mr. Lloyd, their head sales rep. They shook hands, but immediately Abby felt uneasy; there was something disconcerting about this man. She was pleased to have Mr. Macpherson do the questioning, and found it very disturbing; it was obvious this man was hiding something. He was squirming, totally red in the face, and you could see the sweat beading under his collar. Mr. Macpherson noticed his discomfort as well. "Well Mr. Lloyd, do you want to tell us what this means, or do I need to call in the authorities? Something is not correct about the invoice that was sent to Stevenson Enterprises." Abby was shocked at how quickly this man came clean.

"Please Mr. Macpherson; I don't want to lose my job. This is the first time something like this has even happened to me. I got caught up in the opportunity Jeremiah Clark offered me."

"And what exactly is that, Mr. Lloyd?" asked Abby, unable to sit still any longer. After all, Jeremiah Clark was the financial officer for the California resort. Abby spoke with him often, but had never met the man. This certainly would change.

"He said if I would make out an "additional invoice", a dummy invoice if you will, he would submit that, and when the money came in to the resort, he was going to give me $25,000 for my effort." Abby removed a small tape recorder from her handbag and asked Mr. Lloyd for permission to tape his confession. He did so willingly.

"Mr. Lloyd, I am totally disappointed in you. I had great expectations for you and what you could contribute to this company. How could you be so taken in? You do know this is a punishable offense?" Mr. Macpherson was very shook up as well. His voice was trembling and Abby thought the man was going to have a heart attack right in his office.

Abby couldn't help but feel sorry for the young Mr. Lloyd. She had never seen a grown man cry. She saw the shame and regret that he could stoop so low in his new career. "Mr. Macpherson, since no money has been exchanged, I'm willing to allow you to handle Mr. Lloyd as you see fit. It's obvious the temptation was too much for him to pass up. And Mr. Lloyd, I would appreciate you keeping this conversation to yourself. If I find out you have contacted Mr. Clark, I will notify the authorities myself, even if Mr. Macpherson does not. Am I understood?"

Nodding his head, Dennis Lloyd was in total agreement with Abby Sinclair. "Thank you, Mrs. Sinclair. You have my word, nothing will be said."

Mr. Macpherson excused Dennis and told him he would be meeting with him later. Turning to Abby, he thanked her for coming and how much he appreciated the way she handled the situation. "You know how important your business is to us, Mrs. Sinclair, and I hope this in no way will hinder our partnership. Stevenson Enterprises has been a good customer of ours for over seven years; starting with the first resort here in California. As you can well imagine, I will deal with Dennis Lloyd personally. It's unfortunate that a young man possessing so much potential after graduating college could be taken up in such a scheme."

"He is young Mr. Macpherson, and if grace and forgiveness can be extended to him, I have no problem with that decision. But he is your employee, and if you deem otherwise, so be it. Thank you so much for your time. Oh, and Mr. Macpherson? I think it would only be fitting for you to charge us what we would pay in Texas for this ostentatious Oriental carpet."

"Yes absolutely Mrs. Sinclair. I will see to it that the correct invoice is submitted, and I will be happy to take off the additional ten thousand."

"Thank you so much Sir. Now for the difficult task I have ahead of me. I do not think Mr. Clark will be offered the same grace and forgiveness as Mr. Lloyd may be offered; embezzlement is a very serious crime, and no doubt there will be consequences for his actions." Abby extended her hand saying goodbye to Mr. Macpherson, thanking him for how well he handled the matter.

Abby took her leave and felt her knees still shaking. It went extremely well but still it was something she had never faced before in her career; now for Mr. Clark. Does she talk to him by herself or call the police. *I guess I better call Mr. Stevenson and let him know what's going on.* She was not looking forward to his twenty questions that she knew would ensue. *Why was he such an intimidating man?*

Returning to her car, she immediately cranked up the air conditioning. Taking out her cell she entered Mr. Stevenson's name. Now that he was in her contacts, it made the call much easier than looking up his number each time.

It was a couple of hours since Rob had spoken to Abby but to him it felt like an entire day. His phone chirped and he picked up his phone, "Stevenson here."

"Hi Mr. Stevenson, this is Mrs. Sinclair." Abby really emphasized the Mrs. hoping he would get the message. To her surprise he did.

"Abby, is that correct?"

"Yes sir, it's Abby Sinclair."

"How's it going? Did you meet with Hotel Furnishings?"

"Yes I did, and I know you will be just as disappointed as I have been when I tell you what transpired today." Abby began to tell him what took place in Mr. Macpherson's office. Mr. Stevenson sounded genuinely concerned and dismayed when she told him about Jeremiah Clark's actions.

"I can't believe Jeremiah would do such a thing. Why I hired him myself two years ago. However I never met much with him, as he seemed competent enough to be handling the California resort. I know he was disappointed not to get the CFO position here in Texas but to resort to something so despicable is beyond me." Rob sat stunned as he continued to listen to Abby.

"What would you like me to do Mr. Stevenson? Do you want me to talk to him alone or should I go to the authorities first, and have someone come with me?"

"No, I really don't want you going alone. Can you get yourself some lunch or something while I make a few phone calls? I'll get back to you as soon as possible. Find a really nice restaurant where you can sit and relax a little. This had to be quite tense for you. And Abby, thanks so much. I appreciate all you're doing." Rob was amazed to find out she even got old Macpherson to take off the additional ten grand. *She's all right; no she's better than all right.* Rob started to make his phone calls: first to the authorities and Sgt. Ferguson, who he had known for years. After that lengthy phone call, he called his stepbrother Steve who managed the California resort. He needed to fill both Bob Ferguson and Steve in on his charade and explained his reasons. "I found someone who likes me for me, not for what I have. I'm just hoping she doesn't find out before I can tell her. I don't think she would understand my reasoning now that I'm really getting to know her."

Steve was sympathetic of Rob's situation, although he couldn't quite understand how this all began. "No problem brother. She won't hear it from me. Do you want me to be in the meeting with her and Clark? I'll make sure he doesn't bug out before Bob gets here."

"Thanks Steve. I knew I could count on you. Oh, and remember, she's off limits."

"Yeah got it, but I haven't even seen her yet."

Abby found a cute little restaurant by the ocean in San Diego. She had no idea this was a hang out for a lot of Navy Seals. She found it a little uncomfortable with all the stares she was getting, but at least she was given a cozy table by the window overlooking the bay. *What a perfect place to have a cup of clam chowder and their famous cheesy bread.* She placed her order when the waitress returned with a glass of iced tea. She had no idea how long it would take for Mr. Stevenson to get back to her, so she didn't want to be in the middle of a huge meal when he called. Her soup arrived, and it was absolutely delicious. When she did make eye contact with a couple of the guys, she got a few smiles and winks from them. She knew they were harmless so she simply gave them a smile back. She had just finished her meal and was sipping her second glass of tea when her phone rang. "Hello, this is Abby."

"Hi Abby, this is Robert Stevenson."

"Hi, I've been waiting for your call. What's up?"

"I contacted Sergeant Bob Ferguson and also the resort manager there, Steven. I told Steve that I want him in on the meeting with Clark. He's going to meet you in the lobby along with Sergeant Ferguson. Steve said he would make sure that Clark is on the premises, and hopefully, he has not gotten wind of anything going on."

"I don't know how he would. I told Mr. Lloyd that if he so much as called Clark, I would make sure the authorities would be calling on him, no matter how Macpherson wanted to handle it."

"Good, that sounds good. Let's hope he was scared out of his wits." He was relieved he caught himself before he let a cussword slip out. He had been impressed with himself and how careful he had been in the past several weeks, even if he wasn't around Abby all the time. For some reason a Bible verse from his past popped up again. He could not remember it all but something to do with his words being pleasing to God. *Lord, that's what I want; for my words to please you.* Rob remembered his mom and Aunt Charlotte helping him to memorize the verses he would come home with from Sunday School or Awana. Feeling a sense of pain remembering his mom and aunt, he wondered what was going on in his head, or was it his heart. He hadn't thought of his childhood in almost twenty years. *Man, I haven't thought of that in years, and why now are these verses coming to mind?* He shook it off getting back to Abby on the phone. "Okay then, are you able to handle things at the resort? As I said, Steve will be expecting you."

"I'm heading there now, Mr. Stevenson. It shouldn't take us too long and then I'll be heading back to the airport and on my way home."

"After your meeting with Clark, give me a call. Should there be a big altercation, be sure and let Steve and Sergeant Ferguson handle it. Got it? And please call me Abby, immediately after your meeting."

"Yes sir, I will be sure to call." Abby couldn't help but chuckle to herself remembering how upset he seemed when she finally called after her arrival. If she wasn't mistaken, he was genuinely concerned for her. *I hope I get to meet this mystery man… and soon.*

Abby got back to her rental and entered the address to the resort. She started going east on the I-5. Traffic was horrendous and Abby wondered if this was common for California. She had heard talk of it in the past, but this was unbelievable. After driving about eight miles on the 5, she saw the turn off; it looked like she would drive a mile or so before reaching the entrance to the resort. To her relief she came to the entrance and found this to be a very winding road circling up to the resort. The grounds were beautiful with sculptured trees and shrubs lining the drive. There was valet service and since she did not even see a parking lot, there was no alternative but to leave her car with the young man. The semi-circle white marble steps were very impressive; there were two huge urns on either side of the entrance filled to overflowing with the most gorgeous flowers; in fact the flower beds and the flowers lining the walk were absolutely breathtaking. It looked like an English garden she had seen in a magazine. The fourteen foot clear glass doors had the letters SE in gold cursive. Of course the letters stood for Stevenson Enterprises. A little pretentious she thought. Abby's breath caught as she entered the lobby. It was obvious they catered only to the elite. She was pleased with her choice of attire for the trip and after the attention she received at the restaurant from the Navy Seals, she felt confident in her appearance; at least she did not feel out of place. Her pale yellow linen dress and four inch Mary Jane heels had her feeling confident about herself. She looked more like a guest than an employee of Stevenson Enterprises.

The lobby was opulence to the nines and Abby saw exactly where the Oriental carpet would fit. The deep floral sculpted carpet would definitely bring the beautiful flora from the outside into the resort lobby; it would be breathtaking.

Walking up to the concierge desk, Abby barely got out who she was meeting when a handsome man approached her. Extending his hand to her he introduced himself as Steven Stevenson. Steven couldn't help but notice Abby's eyebrows rise as she shook his hand. Abby felt he was holding her hand a bit too long. "I'm sorry but I was not given your last name by Mr. Stevenson. And you are Steven Stevenson?"

"Yes I'm Robert's brother, well actually his stepbrother." Not wanting to dwell on the relationship, Steven easily changed the subject. "Sergeant Ferguson is in my office and we'll meet in there first. I can't tell you how stunned I am to hear of this situation. I'm just glad I wasn't the one to hire Mr. Clark two years ago. Robert did that." Abby couldn't help but notice how pleased he was not to have been responsible for the hiring. She ignored the comment and followed Steven into his office.

Sgt. Ferguson stood to greet Abby when the introductions were made. "Do you have a plan of action when we meet with Mr. Clark?" he asked. "Mr. Stevenson gave me everything he had when he called but you can fill me in on the information you have. He thought it best you confront him with what you know."

Abby opened her leather portfolio removing the papers and the evidence she had. "I'm not sure how you want to handle this since I uncovered this prior to any monies being exchanged. I would like to be the one to speak to him and hopefully he will willingly confess his intent to commit a crime. I also have a tape of Dennis Lloyd's confession as we sat in Mr. Macpherson's office." Noticing the Sergeant's concern she quickly added, "He had agreed to my taping our conversation."

"Good for you. I'm impressed that this was something you thought of. That's great."

"Shall we head to Clark's office then?" asked Steve.

Entering Jeremiah Clark's office, Abby felt her legs shaking once again. She definitely wanted to appear confident, even with her shaky legs. She immediately straightened her back, and raised her shoulders—she could do this. Praying once again for God's strength, she entered with confidence.

Jeremiah stood from behind his desk, his look ashen. He certainly did not look like someone Abby would have hired. She thought he had beady eyes and a disheveled look. She reached over to shake his pudgy hand as she introduced herself to him. He was surprised to say the least, since he had only spoken to Abby on the phone a couple of times. When Sgt. Ferguson introduced himself, it was obvious the man knew why they were in his office. His voice trembling, he asked what he could do for them as he directed them to the chairs in his office. Taking their seats, Abby knew it was up to her to take the lead. She immediately opened her portfolio taking out papers and receipts. She did not show any hesitation in confronting Clark regarding her findings. He was considerably shaken but kept his emotions in check. He seemed rather cocky as she continued to question him. He denied all of her findings until she pulled out the tape recorder. Clark looked like the air was knocked right out of him. His countenance immediately changed and he began confessing that he did it because he felt he had been cheated out of the job Abby had. "Stevenson and Wade knew I wanted that position but they never even gave me a nod." Everyone caught the bitterness in his voice. Abby continued to tell him how unacceptable his actions had been and that this would definitely be grounds for dismissal if not legal action. She informed him that she would be taking his computer back with her. Sgt. Ferguson took over the interrogation after Abby. Although he denied any other illegal activity, Abby would definitely find out once she went through his computer. She realized Sergeant Ferguson was really there for back up and to give credence to the confrontation. There wasn't much he could do since no monies had been exchanged; unless things got out of hand. He did however escort Mr. Clark out of the building and to his car. This was grounds for immediate dismissal. Only after Mr. Clark heard the tape of Dennis Lloyd's confession did he show remorse and apologized for his actions. Before leaving the office, Sgt. Ferguson advised him not to leave town. When the two men left the office, Steve and Abby stayed there. Abby only hoped her nervousness was not too visible. Putting his hand on Abby's arm, Steve reassured her that she did an amazing job and thanked her for her findings. "I never would have guessed that Jeremiah Clark had it in him to be so deceitful. He said nothing to me about the cost of the carpet."

"It's amazing what greed can do. I'm so thankful that's over with. I need to call Mr. Stevenson and let him know what happened; we need to look for another financial officer for the California office." Abby felt good about the meeting, but had to admit she was uncomfortable with the cussing that went on between the Sergeant and Steven. This was something she was not used to but knew it was to be expected. She couldn't help but feel grateful that Rob never used such language.

Looking at his watch, Steve said, "It's almost five o'clock. What do you say we get something to eat? You can call Robert when we get to the restaurant."

"Is there a room available for me tonight? I told Mr. Stevenson I may not get back until tomorrow, and right now I am exhausted."

"Yes of course, and you need to let the crew know. They usually stay here anyway. I have Doug's number if you don't."

"Thanks that would be great. I'm sure once we have dinner it will be a late night for all concerned." Steve had the number in his phone and dialed for her. He also told Doug their plans and that he would be sending a car for them."

"Thanks, I appreciate you calling him for me."

As they walked to the dining area in the resort, Abby was grateful the decision was made to stay the night. Doug had told Steve that they would be bringing Abby's overnight bag with them. She knew she was emotionally drained from the stress of the day... starting with Joseph Macpherson and Dennis Lloyd. She couldn't help but wonder what would be happening to Dennis Lloyd. He was too young to mess up his life like that and as for Jeremiah Clark, Abby wondered what would come of him. She felt terrible having to let him go but there was no way he could stay in their employment. She was hoping she would find nothing suspicious on his computer. As she thought about it, he had all intentions of skimming $140,000 out of the company; even after giving Lloyd twenty-five thousand he would end up with a hefty $115,000. *Did he really think he could get away with it; now I wonder if he had gotten away with it before now?*

As Steve entered the exclusive restaurant with Abby, she was happy to finally sit and relax. Steve was every bit as polite and charming as Rob. Abby sighed as she wondered what Rob was doing right about now and she couldn't help but feel anxious about her dinner with him on Friday.

Noticing her deep in thought, Steve couldn't help but wave at her, "Hey are you okay Abby? You look like you're a million miles away."

Snapping her out of her reverie, and bringing her back to reality, Abby looked at Steve in surprise, "Yes sorry. I must have been thinking of something else." Just then it was her phone that rang. "Hello this is Abby."

"Hello Abby."

"Oh, no" said Abby as she held her hand over the mouth piece. "I forgot to call Mr. Stevenson. He's going to be furious with me." Steve couldn't help but chuckle and hoped she hadn't noticed. "Hello Mr. Stevenson."

"I haven't heard from you. I expected you to call and tell me how your meeting went with Clark." Of course he knew exactly how it went since he had already talked to his buddy Ferguson.

Abby quickly told him how the day went, and not wanting to sound like she was bragging, she left out much of it. Rob caught on and knew all the details from Ferg and was proud of her and how she handled the entire situation. "Sounds like you had everything under control. We can talk about it when you return. Will you be coming back tonight?"

"I'm staying here the night and will be coming home tomorrow. I'm having dinner right now with Steve, and the crew should be coming here soon. Steve called Doug and told him we would be returning tomorrow morning."

There was a long pause before Rob responded. "Yeah sure, that's a good idea to spend the night. Is Steve taking good care of you then?"

Abby noticed a little sarcasm to his tone and wondered why. "Yes he's taking very good care of me, and he also suggested we go for dinner. It's quite lovely here."

"Yes I'm sure it is. Well Abby have a good night."

"Mr. Stevenson hung up before I could even say goodbye." Abby felt a little offended especially after the day she had and saving him $140,000.

"He'll get over it." said Steve. "And our food should be coming soon."

Their conversation was light and Abby was enjoying her meal and grateful for the first time she had felt relaxed all day. Before they finished their dinner, the crew came in to the restaurant and quickly came over to their table. They were seated at the table next to them and Doug told Abby that her bag would be taken up to her room. They sat discussing what the crew did all day and Abby asked Jenny if she was able to talk to her mom, and if staying the night would be a problem. "I did call her and she said that it was no problem. Of course she had no choice but I always like to check in with her." Abby would not discuss the details of her day, and no one asked; confidentiality was of the utmost importance.

59

Abby looked over at Doug and asked what time they should leave in the morning. "You're the boss. You tell us when you want to leave, and as long as the weather holds out, and we don't have a lot of fog in the a.m. we should be okay."

Abby couldn't help but blush at Doug's comment that she was the boss, but continued to make her decision. "How about we leave after breakfast, say nine o'clock? Will that be too late?"

"No", said Doug "that should give the fog a chance to lift some before we take off."

"I think I'm going to turn in." said Abby. "I'm actually exhausted after the day I've had... like no other to be sure. Dinner was excellent, thank you, Steve."

"I'll walk you up to your room." offered Steve. "Do you happen to know Abby's room number, Doug?"

"I gave her bag to the clerk and he simply said they would make sure it got up to her room. You better check at the desk."

"Ok, will do," Steve pulled Abby's chair out and she felt his hand on her lower back as he led her out of the restaurant. Funny but there was absolutely no tingling up her spine as there was with Rob. Stopping at the desk, Steve picked up Abby's keycard and walked her to the elevator. "What time do you plan on coming down for breakfast in the morning?"

"Oh I don't know. I suppose I could have coffee in my room and then eat on the plane going home."

"Why not eat here? We offer a great breakfast, and who knows, you just may see a celebrity or two. Why not come down around eight and I'll meet you."

"Okay eight it is. Do you think the crew will be down by then as well or should I give Doug a call?"

"That's okay; I'll put a call in to him when I get back. They usually like to eat before they take off anyway."

Steve opened her door and Abby was quick to thank him for dinner and all his support. "My pleasure," said Steve. "I'll see you in the morning then."

"Yes that sounds great. I'll see you in the morning and thanks for everything."

Her door no sooner closed when Steve's cell rang. He knew he didn't have to check his phone to know who was calling. "Hey Rob. I knew you would be calling."

"And how did you know that?" Rob didn't even wait for a response. "I understand you've been taking good care of Abby and I told you she was off limits. How was dinner, and did you tuck her in?"

"Dinner was great, and no I did not tuck her in. Man, what's your problem? I have to admit she is beautiful...and pretty smart. One thing I don't understand is how come you're interested in a married woman? I thought that was a big no-no for you. You always said you would never date a married woman, so what gives? It sounds to me like you've lowered your standards, brother."

Steve could almost feel the tension through the cell connection. "I most definitely have not lowered my standards. For your information Abby, Mrs. Sinclair, is a widow."

Completely taken aback, Steve apologized but was quick to give his unsolicited opinion. "As difficult as it may be, you know you can count on me not to hit on her, but you also know that Lucas will be another story." Both Steve and Rob knew their younger brother's indiscretions. Although Lucas was Rob's stepbrother and Steve's brother, Lucas never made apologies for his behavior. Rob agreed with Steve and knew he would have to do all he could to keep Abby from ever meeting Lucas: at least not for a long time.

Lucas managed the Florida resort and Rob hoped Abby would never have a reason to make any trips there, at least if he could help it. After they disconnected, Rob sat contemplating not only his future, but couldn't help but reminisce. He was fond of his stepbrothers and knew he promised their mother before she died that he would always look after them. Giving the two brothers positions in his resorts, allowed him to keep a watchful eye on them. He also knew he paid them very well for their positions. Yes, he was labeled a playboy along with Lucas but since Rob was the one with all the fame and success, he got most of the attention—and he made all the headlines. Lucas was really the ladies man and not the least embarrassed to admit all the women he was involved with. Rob, on the other hand, never got that serious with any woman; however, that was not what the tabloids told. He figured no woman ever wanted to admit they never made it to third base with him, so when it ended, there was always another starlet or model that was willing to be by his side. Rob couldn't help but think of his mom, Caroline, and his Aunt Charlotte. Both women were committed Christians and he could still hear his mom's voice, "Bobby, never forget who you belong to, and sex is always something you wait for until you are married. You must always treat women with respect, and never take advantage of them." Those very words are what rang in his ears every time he got close to giving in. The memory of his mom always kept him focused and from making a huge mistake. She died when he was fourteen but she instilled in him respect for women and a moral foundation that he realized he took for granted. After his mom's death his Aunt Charlotte took over his spiritual instruction and was like a mom to him. She took it upon herself to pick him up for church each Sunday and also made sure he got to youth group.

Thinking of his youth group, Rob chuckled remembering his church high school camp experiences. He remembered with such clarity one of his youth pastor's talks. Pastor Mike held up two pieces of Styrofoam that were glued together. He had called Rob up to the front to help with the demonstration asking him to pull one of the foam pieces apart, and the pastor pulled the other. When they pulled the two apart, part of the foam stuck to the other piece. He told the kids that this is what happened every time you had sex with someone; part of you stuck to that other person. And each time, you left part of yourself with that person. When you finally met the person you would marry, you really were not a whole person anymore. *"Man, has this always been*

buried deep somewhere in my psyche and the reason I have waited?" Pastor Mike continued saying that God never gives us boundaries for His benefit but for ours. God is not some mean ogre; it's out of love for us that He sets these boundaries.

His father never really cared if he went to church or not but that never stopped Aunt Charlotte. When Rob was sixteen his dad remarried leaving him feeling a little indifferent and alone. His stepmother, Kathleen, was nice and loving towards him but she had her own three kids. Since Rob was the oldest, it was up to him to keep the peace with his new siblings: Steven twelve, Lucas ten, and Sharon eight. Rob was home for only two more years before heading off to college. He never saw too much of Sharon even now as she was married and lived back east with her husband and two children; with eight years between them, they never had much of a relationship.

Rob got up from the couch wondering where all this reminiscing was coming from. Heading for the bar he started to pour himself Bourbon. Looking at the golden liquid, he didn't have to look twice before dumping it down the drain. Instead of the liquor, he grabbed a Diet Coke from the fridge. *Why a Diet Coke? Ah, that's what Abby always has; either that or an iced tea when she's at a restaurant.*

Sitting back down on the couch, his thoughts continued to emerge from the past. When he was younger he wondered why Aunt Charlotte never really came in the house once his dad remarried. As far as he knew, she only talked to Rob and was only interested in keeping in touch with him. Aunt Charlotte was his mom's twin sister and he knew how close they were. They were identical, and from what Rob remembered, they did everything together. His dad, Robert Sr. was a wealthy man in his own right. Rob's mom and Aunt Charlotte came from old money and when his mom died he inherited her wealth. His aunt was also quite wealthy; she sat on his board of trustees and was also one of the main shareholders in Stevenson Enterprises. He always loved his Aunt Charlotte and knew he always would; she helped mold him into the man he was today. Oh, he knew he disappointed her in many ways, but she never chastised him, she simply loved him unconditionally. Sometimes she would give him that evil eye look when he cussed or said something inappropriate; she would even tweak his ear when she was really upset with him. Rob had to chuckle as he sat thinking of Aunt Charlotte with such fondness. He knew they had a board meeting coming up soon in California and he definitely wanted Abby to attend with him. She should anyway, as the new CFO for the company. He also thought of his dad who he really did love, even though their relationship was estranged. His dad was always after him for being such a playboy, and never thought he would amount to anything. He knew his dad continued to be in denial over Rob's success, and seemed to be waiting for him to really mess up. Why the competition he would never understand, but ever since his dad remarried and had another family their relationship was never the same. His dad had a lot of hardship, and all Rob knew of his mom's death was that she was in a horrible automobile accident when she and Aunt Charlotte were out shopping one day. She made it home after a couple of weeks in the hospital but was never the same for several months, and eventually developed pneumonia and died. It was his dad's secretary who stepped in bringing food for them almost every night, and to no one's surprise it was his dad's secretary who became his stepmom. Kathleen was a single mom and Rob knew her husband had died three years earlier. He always thought it strange that his Aunt Charlotte never filled that role. Deep in thought it wasn't long before Rob drifted off to sleep on the couch.

Chapter 8

Abby returned home Tuesday, and after landing drove immediately to her office. She was anxious to open Jeremiah Clark's computer and see if there was any other activity he may have been involved in. She certainly hoped not.

Abby's desk phone rang and she was somewhat surprised to hear it was Mr. Stevenson. She really expected to have a personal visit from him, but that didn't happen. He asked her a few more questions about her time in California; yet another day she went without meeting her boss. He was certainly a mystery man and perhaps that was for the best. He didn't seem to be a very warm or friendly person. Abby spent the afternoon peering through Clark's computer; mainly concerned with the financial reports. It looked like this was going to take some time and recovering all the data seemed incredulous, like she was digging for gold. She looked at so many numbers she was getting a major headache. Abby looked up and saw Rob staring at her from the doorway. "Hi, welcome back. How was your trip?" Of course he knew how it was but he could not let on.

"The trip was good."

"When did you get back? You weren't here this morning were you?"

"No it got to be late yesterday and I felt it best to spend the night. It's a beautiful resort and I was pleased I had a chance to see it."

"Did you have a chance to meet their resort manager?'

"Steven? Yes I did meet him. He seems to be a very nice man, although we didn't spend much time together."

"What was your trip about anyway? Want to talk about it?"

"I would rather not. Let's just say I got done what was needed."

Rob was very pleased with Abby's response. He wondered if she would disclose anything, and to his surprise she did not. He was more pleased that his brother Steve did not impress her, and for this he was grateful. "Are we still on for Friday night?"

"Absolutely," Abby couldn't help but notice the twinkle in Rob's eyes. She loved seeing that and wondered if it was because of her or something that came naturally. After a wink, he walked out of her office. She was grateful he never asked what she was working on. The incident with Jeremiah Clark was a confidential matter and not something to be discussed amongst other employees. Abby continued with Clark's computer but with her increasing headache, she thought it best to direct her attention to her own job for a while, however, not before she took something for her headache.

Friday came and Abby had not seen Rob since Tuesday afternoon. He popped into her office confirming the time he was to come for dinner and asked if she wanted to go to the grill for a quick burger. Abby thanked him but told him she had yogurt she was planning to have for lunch.

"Can I bring you a cup of coffee or something?" asked Rob. "I can run over to the café and get your favorite latte."

"That's thoughtful of you, and that does sound good."

Rob left immediately only to return ten minutes later with two cups of coffee. Abby thanked him and went to the fridge for her yogurt. Rob sat with her as she ate her strawberry yogurt. He enjoyed every minute of watching her eat. Before leaving her office he said he would be over at six.

Abby left promptly at five. She was pleased she had assembled her lasagna the night before and all she needed to do was pop it in the oven when she got home. She was getting the salad together when her doorbell rang. One thing she had to admit, Rob was punctual. He walked in with a beautiful bouquet of flowers and Abby felt the blush rise from her neck to her face. It had been a long time since anyone brought her flowers. Thanking him, she returned to the kitchen and got out a beautiful crystal vase, one of her many wedding gifts. She was delighted she not only could enjoy beautiful flowers but the crystal vase as well. Abby reached up and wiped the tear that was escaping from her eye; hoping Rob hadn't noticed. That's the last thing she would want him to see.

"Dinner is ready. All I need to do is pop the French bread in the oven."

"It smells delicious. May I help with anything?"

Abby got out her potholders and opened the oven door getting ready to pull the lasagna out. Knowing she was being watched, she felt her hands and knees shaking. *This is totally silly. What is wrong with me?* She knew it had been a while since she entertained anyone let alone a man, and told herself that had to be the reason for her nervousness. Rob walked over and took the potholders from her and removed the hot pan of lasagna for her. He placed it on the trivet set on the counter. Abby took the cookie pan with the French bread and placed it in the oven. Their hands brushed against each other and Abby felt the sizzle from his touch all the way to her toes. "Hmm, what would you like to drink Rob?"

"I'll have a Diet Coke if you have it." He waited while she opened the fridge and then helped get the drinks on the table. He wondered why he was helping so much. He was used to being waited on and this was a whole new experience for him. Helping out in a kitchen was never something he found himself doing. *I really think I could get use to this.* He couldn't help noticing how graceful Abby was as she maneuvered in her tiny kitchen. When everything was on the table, Abby offered Rob a chair. He immediately was at her side sliding her chair out for her. He automatically touched her lower back as he guided her to her chair. Once again Abby felt the tingling in her spine and couldn't ignore the flip her stomach made. Remembering that Steve's touch did not give her this same sensation, however, she knew the feeling, and knew she had to dismiss it. After all, Rob was a fellow employee. She sensed he liked her, but she also knew she would not allow herself to get involved with someone that did not believe as she did.

"This dinner is delicious, Abby. You're quite the cook."

"Thank you. How about we have dessert in the living room?"

Abby started cleaning up and Rob could not help watching her as she put the dishes in the dishwasher. Washing some dishes by hand, Rob found himself pulling the towel from her and drying the remaining dishes. Before he knew it, he bent down, and holding her waist, gave her a brief kiss on the lips. Feeling the heat from his lips, she felt like a stick of butter melting in the hot sun. "Sorry, I couldn't help myself." Rob, who was always in control, was taken aback himself.

She knew her face had to be as red as the dish towel Rob had used. Abby reached around him to get the dessert dishes and tray hoping this would be a distraction. Rob took the tray from her and told her she could bring the coffee. Thankful the moment passed, they went to the living room for dessert and coffee. Their conversation was a little awkward but still good as they talked about Jeff and his amazing boat. Just when Abby thought their conversation would end, the phone rang. It was her mother, Lois.

"Hi mom how are you doing and how is dad?"

Rob sat watching Abby; she looked a little upset as her mom continued to talk, with Abby saying very little in response. Finally she replied, "Mom, why are you doing this? I can't believe you. You know what happened between me and Jack, and you're letting him come out here? You have to be kidding. And I don't care how close you and his mom are. Mother, I'm sorry but I'm afraid nothing will come of it. I love you too mom and I'll talk to you tomorrow. Bye."

Her chest was heaving after she hung up the phone. As she sat back down on the couch, Rob noticed a few fat tears rolling down her cheek. "Do you want to talk about it?" Rob took his thumbs and wiped the tears away. His hands were so soft and he seemed like he genuinely cared. He started to gently rub her back and this gave some calm to her composure.

Abby began telling him about Jack O'Malley, the love of her life when they were in high school. "Although our parents were good friends, we really didn't hang out until high school youth group. I was fourteen and a freshman, and Jack was going into his junior year. For two years we were boyfriend and girlfriend. Everyone said we would end up together and I really thought they were right. I really loved him. Jack could never understand why I wouldn't sleep with him. He always said that we would end up together anyway and that he loved me so much and always would. We agreed to wait until we were married. It was a promise I had made to God and my parents before I went into high school. I was determined to keep that promise.

When Jack graduated from high school, he went off to UCLA and although we wrote back and forth quite a bit in the beginning, the letters came less and less from him. Finally my senior year, I received a letter that he had married and that I needed to stop writing. I was angry and devastated, but I got over it. I went on to the University of Arkansas and met Thomas, my husband, when I was a junior and he a senior. He went on to get his Masters in youth ministry and psychology; after graduation I went on to get my MBA and then eventually my PhD. I heard Jack had a baby girl and that his wife passed away two years ago leaving him to raise his young daughter. Now my mother and his mother think we should get back together and that I would make a wonderful mother for his little girl. Do you believe this? How can they even expect me to rekindle anything for him?"

"And he's coming here to see you?"

"Yes, he's coming here alone. She actually gave him my address and thinks he will be here tomorrow. I cannot believe this. I have no idea how long he plans to stay, but he will not be staying with me, that's for sure."

"He can stay at the resort. What does he do anyway?"

"The last I heard he's an attorney."

"Well then he can certainly afford staying at the resort." Rob said this with a chuckle in his voice. "Would you like me to come over tomorrow and stay with you? That way I can be here when he

69

arrives." He so wanted to pour his soul out to her and tell her who he was. *Tomorrow, that's when I'll tell her everything.*

"I think I would like that. Thanks."

Abby tossed and turned all night. She woke up Saturday morning feeling out of sorts, however, when she looked out her bedroom window her spirits lifted. The sun was shining, the birds were singing, and she even heard a blue jay screeching. That was her favorite bird, and seeing him fly into her tree made it even better.

Abby shuffled her way to the kitchen and got the coffee pot going. A cup of coffee on her back patio sounded good and would certainly wake her up. Taking her daily devotional with her, she set out for the back patio. She wished she could spend every morning like this, curled up on a chair in her soft comfy shorts and big T-shirt of Thomas's. She read from her daily devotional, Isaiah 26:3: *"You will keep him in perfect peace, whose mind is stayed on You, because he trusts in You." What a perfect verse for today.* Abby quoted that verse knowing today she was going to keep focused on Jesus and not dwell on Jack and what could have been. She really was thankful that she never did marry Jack, and was hoping he would feel the same way. Maybe he changed his mind about coming to visit her and he won't even show up. She would not waste her time worrying for nothing. Abby closed her eyes in prayer seeking God's wisdom for the day, and as every morning, she asked God to make her a blessing to someone. After her Amen, she looked up only to see Rob staring right at her. "Oh my, how long have you been here? And why are you here?"

"I told you I would come over and stay with you when Jack comes."

"But I don't even know when he's supposed to get here. I'm hoping he may have changed his mind and he won't show. Would you like some coffee?" Abby felt a little embarrassed still being in her sleepwear as she started to get up.

"Hey, don't get up. I can get my own coffee. I think I know where everything is."

Abby couldn't help but gaze at Rob as he sauntered up the patio and into the kitchen. He was wearing jeans and a white polo shirt showing off his muscled arms and great tan. She felt her heart pounding a little harder and her temperature rise. *What was getting into her?* Rob returned with his coffee and pulled up a chair beside her.

He noticed she had no makeup on what-so-ever and her hair was down and rumpled, even her freckles were visible. She looked adorable and Rob felt the urge to pull her into his arms and give her a kiss. It was certainly tempting but he knew better. He sat back enjoying his coffee along with Abby. Yes, he could get use to this.

Abby could not help but share her morning and how special it was to sit out in the yard, reading and listening to her favorite bird, the blue jay. She had to admit that after the week she had, it was good to relax and put the week behind her.

Rob thought for a minute she would talk about her time in California but she did not, and he loved her even more for that. Did he just admit he loved her? He never thought that about any woman. He knew he had feelings for her, that he couldn't deny, and he was certainly more comfortable with her than anyone he had dated in the past. She had been married and still wore her wedding ring and that alone made it difficult for him to get past. It was obvious she still had feelings for her dead husband. He had no idea how he died and never felt it was appropriate to ask. He was sure she would tell him when she was ready. Rob couldn't understand why her mother would encourage her to get together with her ex-boyfriend; it sounded like he was nothing but a jerk. *And to think he would even want to get back together after doing that to her.* Now he was eager to meet this guy, and he hoped he did show up today.

Sitting together seemed so right, but when the house phone rang both Rob and Abby jumped. Abby had the cordless phone outside and answered on the second ring. Rob could tell she was holding her breath even though she tried to remain relaxed. Sure enough, it was Jack. All Rob could hear of her conversation was when she ended the call telling him he should be there in about three hours. Hanging up, Abby looked at Rob with watery eyes and told him that Jack would be there in about three hours. "I guess I better go shower." Abby got up and told Rob to make himself at home. He noticed the grass in the back yard seemed long and offered to cut it while she got ready. He insisted on doing something, so she agreed, telling him her lawnmower was in the garage.

Abby really didn't care what she looked like for Jack, but for some reason she wanted to look good for Rob. Putting on a pair of skinny jeans and a blue and white ruffled top, she decided to put her hair up in one of her quick twists; leaving a few long tendrils hanging around her face. She slipped on her cute blue and white sandals and went out back just as she heard the lawnmower turn off. The lawn looked great and Rob had cut the front lawn as well leaving the air smelling of fresh cut grass. As Abby stepped out onto the patio, Rob was returning from the garage. "The grass looks great and it smells so good out here. Thank you so much."

"You're very welcome. Do you mind if I hop in your shower?" Rob's shirt was off and he certainly looked buff and very much in shape. She couldn't help but notice the beads of sweat on his glistening chest. "At least my shirt is clean so I shouldn't be too bad for your ex. You sure look beautiful. Is it for him?"

"Absolutely not, and please don't even think that."

Pleased with her response, Rob gave her a wink as he walked past her and into the house "I won't be long."

Since it was close to lunchtime and Jack wouldn't be there for another hour at least, Rob asked Abby if he could take her to lunch. "Are you sure? I could easily make us something here. I even have leftover lasagna."

"I think it would be good to go out. It would give you a chance to relax and we can have the lasagna for supper with Jack later. Give him leftovers, although the lasagna was delicious and I don't know if I want him to know what a great cook you became."

Abby giggled at Rob's comment and agreed it would be good to go out.

They were sitting comfortably on the couch when they heard a car pull into Abby's drive. Sitting where they were, they could still see the driveway; Rob saw a very handsome man climb out of a Porsche. He hoped there wouldn't be any competition here. Rob quickly grabbed Abby's hand and gave it a squeeze, giving her the assurance that he was there for her. Hopefully she wouldn't be sorry that she wasn't alone with the guy once she saw him. For what he did to her, how could she. "Hey babe, everything is going to be fine, you have nothing to worry about."

Abby couldn't help but notice his word of endearment in calling her babe. That alone gave her such warmth and she knew he was here for her.

Jack came to the door with a dozen roses and what looked like a bottle of wine. A real ladies man, thought Rob. He allowed Abby to go to the door while he remained seated on the couch. He had no problem seeing the front door as Abby opened it. Jack no sooner walked through the door and immediately pulled her into a very tight hug. "Sweetheart it's so good to see you. It's been way too long." Rob saw her back stiffen and he noticed she kept her hands against his chest. Jack seemed to ignore her distance and leaned in giving her a very deep kiss. She backed away, and Rob thought she was going to give him a good slap; something he thought of doing himself. *Who was this arrogant Casanova anyway?* Rob had all he could do from jumping off the couch and grabbing the guy by his shirt collar. Abby seemed to have everything under control as she quickly pulled herself away. Taking Jack's arm she led him over to the couch. Rob quickly got up as Abby started to introduce him to Jack. "Jack, I would like you to meet a very special friend of mine, Rob York." Rob couldn't help but notice the abruptness in Jack's expression as he glared at him. It was obvious the wind had been knocked out of his sails. Rob could play this game as well and glared right back at Jack. "Pleased to meet you, Jack. How long will you be visiting?"

Jack had given the flowers and wine to Abby after his "hello" kiss. He extended his hand to Rob and the two men shook hands. "I'm not sure how long I will be here. I think that will depend on Abby." Turning to Abby he told her about his mom and her mom working on getting them together. Like it really wasn't his idea at all but something he felt obligated to do.

Was Rob making him that uncomfortable? Abby hoped so. It was obvious that Jack assumed Rob was her boyfriend. *Good, let him think that.* By the looks of things, Rob didn't seem to mind. Abby sat on the couch next to Rob and Jack sat in the chair across from them. Jack definitely wanted to tell her about himself and how successful he was as an attorney and what he had been doing since their friendship in high school. After all his talking about himself, he began telling her about his wife, Gloria, and how he met her his second year in college. He confessed to Abby that he had gotten her pregnant and that's why he broke off their relationship. He told her that he found out after marrying Gloria that she was never pregnant to begin with but used that excuse to trap him into marriage. She could tell he was hoping she would have some sympathy for him but she felt nothing but pity for the man. He told her how his wife had died two years earlier from breast cancer leaving him to care for their two year old daughter, Molly, who was now four. Abby wondered why the need to tell her all of this. Pain stabbed her heart; not for Jack but for his four year old daughter. Abby's heart warmed as he showed her his daughter's picture. "She looks a lot like you, Jack. She has your eyes and your dark hair. She's a very pretty little girl."

"Thanks Abby. She can be quite the handful."

Rob sat feeling a little awkward as Jack and Abby settled into their personal conversation. He stood asking if anyone would like something to drink. He knew leaving them might not be a good idea but he also sensed they could use some privacy. "Thanks Rob, I'll have a Diet Coke. How about you Jack?"

"I brought a bottle of wine you could open."

"No thanks, Jack. I never became much of a wine drinker. Coke or iced tea is my preferred drink, right Rob?"

Rob was pleased with how familiar Abby seemed to be with their friendship. *Was she trying to make more of their relationship than what was there?* "Yep, that's my Abby. She's not much into wine or any liquor for that matter. How 'bout it Jack, want an iced tea or a Coke?"

"Diet Coke is fine with me then."

To Abby's amazement, the rest of the day went well. She offered to heat up the lasagna for dinner and had enough ingredients for another tossed salad and had the other half of the French bread left from last night. After dinner Rob suggested Jack follow him to the resort as he agreed that would be the perfect place to stay. Rob knew Abby was a little uneasy with what the plan was for the next day. Being Sunday, and Jack making it very clear he had no intentions of attending church with her, Rob suggested they go out on the boat. "Are you sure Jeff won't mind, Rob?" asked Abby.

"He won't mind at all. I'll give him a call. In fact I'll call him right now." Rob excused himself stepping out onto the back patio. Only Rob knew Jeff had no choice but to have the yacht ready to go in the morning. Rob walked back into the house announcing it was all set and they would meet Jeff at the pier the following morning.

Abby couldn't keep quiet telling Jack all about the beautiful yacht they would be on and what a good friend Jeff was to Rob. Jack wasn't about to be one-upped even if it wasn't Rob's boat but Jeff's. "I have a boat as well, Abby. Mine is strictly a speed boat and great for water skiing. I think you would enjoy going out with me sometime." Abby simply ignored his statement.

Jack agreed to follow Rob to the resort. As they said their goodbyes, Rob leaned over putting his arm around Abby and placed a tender kiss on her lips. "Goodnight babe. See you in the morning. We'll be by around eight." Abby caught the look of jealousy in Jack's glare as she reached up to meet Rob's kiss. She felt the sudden rush of butterflies in her stomach once again, to say nothing of her legs feeling like two noodles. Maybe it was an attempt for Jack to back off and leave Abby alone, but she felt that warm tingle all the way to her toes. Locking eyes with Rob, Abby said she would be ready.

"I'll pick Jack up at the resort and then we'll be by for you."

As he viewed Jack following in his Porsche, Rob was bummed that he wasn't in his Lamborghini instead of Jeff's pickup.

There was no way that Rob would reveal to either one of them that his apartment was at the resort. Rob would drop off Jack and drive to the back parking lot and go in the service entrance.

Chapter 9

The two men arrived promptly at eight in Jeff's pickup. Abby was ready with her beach bag all set to go. When they arrived at the dock, Rob once again eyeballed his Lamborghini. "Sweet car," said Jack. "A guy has to have a lot of bucks if he's going to drive that." Rob agreed but made sure they kept walking down to the pier. Entering the key code into the gate, they continued their walk to the end of the pier.

Abby noticed the boat was positioned at the pier with the stairs in place this time. Jeff came to the side welcoming them aboard. Abby was the first to board, she reached up to give Jeff a hug and a light kiss on his check. Jeff hugged her back and Rob noticed the smirk on his face and wishing he could wipe it off. Jeff was sure Abby could not be any different than all the women Rob and he had known. They were all gold-diggers and interested only in money and fame. It was only a matter of time before Abby would be falling for him. After all, as far as Abby was concerned, Rob was nothing but a glorified handyman and himself the billionaire.

It was obvious that Jack was very impressed and Rob knew this man was only interested in materialism and status. Of course Jack made sure that he bonded with Jeff immediately. Jeff shrugged his shoulders and as soon as he could get Rob alone he was going to ask him what was going on with this guy. Jack however seemed to stick to Jeff like glue as he followed him up into the wheelhouse to pilot the yacht out of the harbor. Jack had a lot of questions and Jeff was more than pleased to answer them.

Jeff found an alcove that they could anchor in allowing them to get out the wave runners. It was always best to be in a quiet and calm location and avoid the rough waters. At least they did not have to travel the twenty miles they did last weekend since they were only spending the day out on the water. Jack was excited to see the wave runners eased out from under the yacht as the fantail was lowered and then raised. This was an amazing boat and Jack was in awe of the wealth Jeff seemed to have. Jack tried convincing Abby to ride behind him on his wave runner but Rob noticed her hesitancy and immediately told her she could grab one of his T-shirts and ride with him. He knew she had had a great time last weekend and he wanted her with him, especially when Jeff said he would stay back on the boat. No way did he want Abby to stay behind with Jeff.

Abby went below and grabbed a shirt of Rob's. It was obvious that Jack was not pleased with their familiarity. Abby knew most of it was for show and Rob was only helping her not having to spend too much time with Jack.

The two wave runners were out quite some time and Abby had a ball holding on to Rob as tight as she could. She hated to admit how much she enjoyed her arms around his tight torso and bulging muscles. She chastised herself for the warm, unsettled feeling developing in her heart.

Rob dropped Abby off as she had enough for the day and also said she would help get lunch prepared. Rob wasn't too sure that he liked the idea of Abby spending any time alone with Jeff. No doubt Jeff would do all he could to flirt and seduce Abby in any way possible. His good looks and now his "so called wealth" would sound inviting for any gold-digging woman. But for some reason, Rob would bet his life that none of that mattered to Abby. She was special.

Rob asked Jeff to go out with Jack but he declined and not wanting to make it a demand, Rob let it go. He would make sure that they would not be gone too long this time. Abby sat on the plush cushion on the aft deck watching as the two men took off once again.

As Abby watched Jack, her mind drifted back to when they were teenagers. *Boy all the dreams we had back then.* Jack was still if not even more handsome than ever with his black hair and grey-blue eyes. He also had a very good physique and something she certainly was not allowing herself to even notice up until now. She could not imagine why he did not want to go with her to church today. In fact he was adamant that he would not be going. When they were kids they were always in church and never once missed youth group. They would sit and discuss what Pastor Adam shared in his talk and had no problem talking about the Bible. She even thought back to their week at high school camp and the pastor for the week talked about purity and the importance of waiting until marriage. It was after that particular talk that the pastor asked the kids to come forward if they wanted to make this commitment. She and Jack both went forward and it sealed their decision to wait until marriage. She couldn't help but wonder what ever happened to him and his relationship with God: was it his success, his wealth, the death of his wife, maybe having to raise a little girl all alone, or even worse, that he was an imposter when they were teens. Whatever happened to him, it was obvious he wanted nothing to do with God now. This really saddened her, and her heart ached especially for his young daughter. *Would he ever tell his little girl about Jesus?*

Jeff walked up to her snapping his fingers. "Hello Abby. Are you in there? You look like you're about a million miles away."

Abby looked up startled, not realizing how she was caught up in her memories. "Sorry, I must have been daydreaming. May I help you get lunch ready?"

"That would be great if you don't mind. I thought we could have corn beef sandwiches on rye, coleslaw, and chips. Does that sound like something everyone would like?"

"Sounds good to me, I'll help with the sandwiches."

As they moved to the galley, Jeff noticed that Abby had taken off the T-shirt but had also put on her big shirt cover-up. He retrieved everything from the fridge and Abby got out the fresh rye bread. "Do you want me to heat up the corn beef a little before I make the sandwiches? I think the guys should be returning soon and I'm sure if the sandwiches are warm they will taste even better."

"Sure go ahead." He said this while he intentionally brushed up against her.

He seemed to be getting too familiar holding her hand a little too long as he passed her the mustard and sauerkraut. If he was trying to get her to notice him, it was not going to work. "Did you happen to notice the Lamborghini in the parking lot?" asked Jeff.

"Well, I can't say that I noticed it but I know Jack was impressed with it. Why do you ask, is it yours?"

"Ah yeah it is. It's an amazing car. How would you like a ride in it? I could pick you up after work sometime. We could have a quiet dinner and then go for a ride."

"No thanks. I'm really not into cars so much, but thanks for asking. I'm sure Jack would like a ride."

Jeff didn't respond but kept right on getting lunch together with Abby. It wasn't long before they both heard Rob and Jack pull up with the wave runners. "Just in time", said Abby as she finished assembling the last sandwich.

The rest of the afternoon went by quickly. Abby was pleased that Jeff went out on the wave runner with Jack. She was really feeling uneasy being alone with him and she wondered why he was hitting on her. She knew she wasn't giving him any reason to. *Do I tell Rob or simply let it go?* Abby knew Rob and Jeff were such good friends; she thought she would do the latter—simply let it go.

They all agreed that they would head back and Rob suggested they go for pizza across from the marina. Pulling into the harbor, Jeff discreetly came up behind Rob and told him to look beyond the pier gate. "Looks like the paparazzi are waiting again; this time I count at least two of them." Rob simply nodded that he did see them and shrugged his shoulders.

Before they disembarked, Rob suggested that Jack and Abby go on ahead and he would help Jeff button up. He was hoping the paparazzi would be focused on Jack and Abby, at least until they got to the restaurant. Rob said that he would get their bags to the truck and then head on over. He couldn't tell Abby to put her sunglasses on as it was already getting dark.

Jack had his arm around Abby as they walked up the ramp and through the gate when a bright flash went off. In fact she was sure there was more than one. Ignoring this they immediately walked across the street to the restaurant. Jack was quick to take advantage of finally being alone with Abby, even if it was for a brief time. Perhaps if he sat next to her in the booth, Rob would get the message and lay off for a while. He continued to wonder what the real story was between them. He couldn't put his finger on it but something was amiss in their relationship. Abby still wore her wedding ring.

Rob watched them leave and also saw the flash from the cameras. When the paparazzi turned to follow Abby and Jack, Rob took this opportunity to put on his ball cap. He then picked up Abby and Jack's bags and immediately headed for the truck. Even if anyone was watching the car, they wouldn't expect him to get in Jeff's truck. Rob thought it best to move the truck from the marina parking lot to a parking spot in front of the restaurant. With no one suspecting who he was as he got out of the truck, he quickly entered the restaurant. He spotted Jack and Abby and immediately walked to their booth. He saw that Jack wasted no time in getting cozy with Abby. He sat opposite them and no sooner had he slid into the booth, Jeff arrived. Before he knew it more flashes were going off. "What's with the cameras?" Jack could not make out what was going on. As quickly as the flash had gone off the reporters were out of there. They finished their pizza and decided to leave the restaurant.

Rob didn't give Jack a chance to object but announced he would be taking him back to the resort first and then take Abby home. After saying their goodnights at the resort, Rob pulled out of the lot but turned in the opposite direction from Abby's home. "You're heading in the wrong direction, Rob. My house is the other way."

"I know that but I haven't had a chance to be alone with you all day and we're going for some ice cream."

"Okaaay, you know I can never pass up ice cream."

Rob pulled into an old fashioned ice cream parlor where he knew they could hide in a back booth for a while. Time passed quickly as it usually did when they were together. They finally left the shop after what seemed to be hours of bantering and light conversation. Seeing Abby relaxed brought a smile to Rob's face.

"What are you smiling about," asked Abby.

"Not what. Who. You make me smile, Abby. It makes me smile to see you so relaxed and happy."

Chapter 10

When Rob pulled into her drive, Abby froze and she literally felt her heart stop. Staring at her garage door was a very crude word written in bold red letters. She couldn't even say the word out loud: red paint ran down the whole garage door leaving them both with a sick feeling in their stomachs. Rob helped her out of the car and into her house. She shook so badly; Rob saw her eyes welling up with tears. "Why, why would someone do this to me? I don't understand."

Rob immediately took her in his arms and held her close. This was something he had wanted to do ever since he first laid eyes on her when she tried to fix the dumb cabinet drawer herself. He would rather it was under different circumstances but she smelled so good he never wanted to let go of her. "Baby, I'm so sorry. I don't understand either why anyone would do this but I do know I have to call the police."

Abby stood frozen, shaking in his embrace. She breathed in his amazing male scent as she snuggled into his chest. She couldn't stop shaking as he held her close. She also couldn't ignore the feelings that were welling up within her. Was she falling in love with this man? He was always protecting her and it warmed her heart to think about it: first when he gave her a T-shirt to wear on the wave runner, then how he covered her with Thomas's shirt as she lay on the chaise, and now holding her so close shielding her from this horrible discovery. She wondered if he felt the same way as she did.

Rob reluctantly released her and said he needed to call the police. "I have a detective friend who I'm going to call. I'm sure he will tell us to not touch anything. Make sure nothing is out of place." Abby nodded but also had no intentions of leaving Rob's side.

Rob and Abby sat quietly on the couch waiting for Lt. Jim Jansen. Rob sat with his arm around her continuing to hold and comfort her, unconsciously stroking her arm. He felt like she belonged nestled in the crux of his arm. She fit so well. The doorbell rang and Abby jumped in his arms. "I'm sure it's Jim. Stay here while I answer the door."

It felt like midnight but it was only ten o'clock. Abby was thankful that Rob was handling this as the two men went outside. While Rob stood in the drive he couldn't help but notice a car parked a little ways down the block—it looked like a Porsche. *I wonder why Jack would be here now.*

As Rob continued talking to Lt. Jansen, he mentioned Abby's week in California and having to terminate one of their employees. Jim said he would look into it and asked him to get all the info he could on Clark. Rob agreed but also told him he did not want Abby to know of this. He knew it would be too upsetting to her if she knew Clark was out for revenge after being terminated. It wasn't long before both men returned to the house. Rob introduced Abby to Lt. Jim Jansen. "Pleased to meet you ma'am. Mind if I have a look around?"

"Go right ahead. Do you need me to go with you? Rob and I went through the house earlier and nothing seems to be out of place."

"I'll call if I see anything suspicious."

Rob came alongside Abby and grabbed her hand. "Everything's going to be all right, babe. Did you know that Jack was coming over?"

Abby shook her head no but also wondered where he was. "Where did you see him?"

"His car happens to be parked down the street. I didn't know if you had made plans with him to come over. Maybe seeing cops here is freaking him out."

It wasn't long before the front doorbell rang; Rob immediately went over to answer. Jack stood there looking concerned and uneasy. "Is everything okay here? I saw the garage door and the cop here. After you dropped me off I thought I would come over for a while and visit with Abby."

Jim immediately began questioning Jack: his normal response when investigating a crime scene, and that's how he was looking at it. Jack had no problem answering his questions and Jim seemed satisfied with his answers.

Rob stood in the kitchen listening in on the questioning when Abby's house phone rang. His natural reflex was to answer and Abby gave him a nod to do so. "Hello. No, this isn't Jack. My name is Rob; I'm a friend of Abby's. Yes, she is right here." Rob walked into the living room handing Abby the phone. Jack remained in the kitchen with the Lieutenant.

"Hi mom, yes, Jack did make it. Listen I really can't talk right now. Mom, you have to understand, there is nothing or will there ever be, anything between Jack and me. It's been over for a lot of years. You tell Miriam that as well." Rob noticed how quietly she was talking to her mother and knew he was the only one that could hear the one-sided conversation. "Mom, you know I never read those magazines." Her voice started to rise as she looked at Rob in astonishment. Rob felt his stomach twist into the tightest knot imaginable. This was not the way he wanted her to find out his identity. "What are you talking about, mom? Yes I have a navy dress and a navy and white straw hat. Yes mom, I was on a yacht last weekend. I was NOT with Robert Stevenson. I have never even met the man." *Jeff, it has to be Jeff who is really Robert Stevenson.* "Mom, I really have to go. I'll call you back later."

Her face paled as she stood there in amazement; her voice but a whisper. "My mom said I'm on the cover of The Buzz magazine with the caption, 'Who is Robert Stevenson's Mystery Woman?' I've never even met him. How can I possibly be on the cover of the magazine? I was only with you and Jeff last weekend. Is Jeff Mr. Stevenson?" Abby asked as she looked inquisitively at Rob.

Now Jim and Jack were staring at both of them; Jim looking just as confused as Jack and Abby. Rob was quickly at Abby's side grabbing both her hands. "No, Abby, Jeff is not Mr. Stevenson. I am."

Abby felt like she had been kicked in the stomach and hoped she would not have to run to the bathroom. Clutching her stomach, Rob led her to the couch. She immediately withdrew his arm as she fell into the couch. "I think I've had enough for one night and I think you had better leave Rob, or whoever you are."

"No, Abby, I thought I would spend the night on the couch. I don't think you should be in the house alone."

Jack immediately came to Abby's aide. "That's quite alright, Rob, I'll stay with her tonight. I wasn't planning on going back until tomorrow and I'm willing to stay however long is necessary."

Rob's gut tightened along with the fists he was making. He couldn't help but notice the smirk on Jack's face and so wanted to go over and punch his lights out. "Fine, but Abby I would still like to have a chance to talk to you. And I certainly hope finding this out will not interfere with your employment with Stevenson Enterprises. I completely value you as an employee and I will do my best not to interfere with your career."

Abby saw the pain in Rob's eyes and wanted so badly to reach out to him and hug him; she also knew she needed time to think about everything that was happening.

Jim patted Rob on the back and motioned that he should walk out with him. Rob walked away feeling totally dejected. He so wanted to be here to protect Abby from what was a mean and disturbing incident; to say nothing of leaving her here with Jack. However, he knew it was best to leave with Jim.

Abby noticed the time and rising from the couch she told Jack she was going to bed. Jack stood with her and immediately had his arms around her. "Jack, what are you doing?"

"Sweetheart let's talk about us. You know we were always meant to be. We've always known it since high school. I've never stopped loving you. I want to build you that two story house with the white picket fence out in the suburbs we always talked about. You and Molly will never want for anything. Of course I plan on keeping my apartment in the city so I'll be close to the office."

Abby stood totally stunned listening to this man. "How can you say you have always loved me Jack? Don't you remember sending me a letter telling me how much you were in love with Gloria and how I needed to stop writing to you? And how is this acknowledgement honoring your dead wife and mother of your daughter? I stopped loving you, Jack, a long time ago. It may have taken me some time to get over you, but believe me, I am over you. I'm going to bed now and I'll get linens for the couch." Abby shook as she stormed off to the linen closet retrieving a blanket, sheet, and a pillow. "Here you can make the couch up yourself. I'm going to bed."

There was no denying that she was completely drained and exhausted as she walked into her bedroom and into her bathroom. She could barely wash her face and brush her teeth. She put on a pair of running shorts and a big comfy T-shirt. Climbing into bed she had no idea what was going on, in fact, no matter how tired she was she did not think sleep would come easy. She knew the best thing to do was to read her Bible. Turning to Isaiah 41 she had to re-read verse 10: *"Fear not, for I am with you: Be not dismayed, for I am your God. I will strengthen you, Yes, I will help you, I will uphold you with My righteous right hand."*

Abby knew it was amazing how God worked and to read this verse at such a time as this gave her peace and a sense of calmness. She could not be afraid of what she did not know. She thought about how close she was to removing her wedding ring tonight, and was relieved she had not done so. Her emotions were so jumbled. But how could Rob have deceived her so badly?

Abby felt the bed move and she froze. *Who is getting into bed with me?* She turned her head only to see Jack slide under the covers next to her. "Jack, get out of my bed!"

"Sweetheart, you can't possibly expect me to sleep on that couch of yours. I'm a big guy. And besides, I've been married, you've been married, and we're both consenting adults. You can't tell me that you still don't have feelings for me. We were made to be together. Our moms would be so pleased. Now come over here so I can make love to you; something I wanted to do when we were back in high school. I can't stand not being with you. You always did drive me crazy, Abby." His arm lay across her stomach holding her in place.

"Get your arm off of me! And who said I was consenting to anything?" Now she was screaming and didn't care who heard her.

"Sweetheart, you know you want this. It has to be a long time for you too."

"I'm not your sweetheart and for your information, Thomas and I never had a chance to consummate our marriage! He died on our wedding day! Please don't touch me at all!" Abby was sobbing and shaking uncontrollably as she kept kicking at Jack to get out of her bed. "If you're going to stay, sleep on the couch!" She screamed at him.

Jack stormed out of the bed but not before letting Abby know how great their time together could be. He slammed her bedroom door and Abby didn't know if he was staying or leaving her house; she really didn't care at this point. She knew she would never be able to sleep anyway. Especially knowing Jack may be in her living room. He was scaring her and she really did not want to be in the same house with him, but then she didn't want to be open to the wacko that may still be out there. No way would she sleep. *If only Rob were here.* She closed her eyes meditating on Isaiah 41:10. She would not fear. Abby never felt her eyelids close as she drifted off to sleep.

Chapter 11

Rob lay in bed staring at the ceiling what felt like the whole night. *Was Abby really safe with Jack?* For some reason he did not trust him, but then, Abby knew him even if it was years ago. Thinking of Jack and also the perpetrator still out there, gave him a sick feeling. He was pleased he had called Jim with the info on Clark. *Could this guy be so unstable that he would attempt getting even with Abby for terminating him?* What a night to have to admit who he was and he wouldn't blame her one bit if she walked out of his life and Stevenson Enterprises. *How could anything go so wrong?* He knew that once Abby read all the articles about him in the tabloids, she would no doubt believe he was nothing but a playboy having sex with every woman he was with. Nothing was further from the truth.

Rob woke with a start at the sound of his cell phone chirping. He didn't think it possible but he must have dozed off sometime in the night. He didn't bother to look at his phone and just answered it. "Hello this is Robert Stevenson."

There was sobbing on the other end. "Abby, is that you? What's wrong ba..?" Using babe may be a little too familiar right now so he stopped short.

"Oh Rob. I didn't know who else I could call; I need you to come over and... you better call Lieutenant Jansen."

"I'll be right over and I'll call Jim when I'm on my way. I'll be there in fifteen minutes." Abby's sobbing didn't stop and he couldn't imagine what happened; he also wondered what had happened to Jack. *Jack, he seemed so anxious to spend the night with her. A little too anxious if you ask me.*

Rob threw on a pair of jeans and a red polo shirt. Slipping into his canvas deck shoes, he was on his way. *If only I had my Lamborghini.* At least it helped knowing all the cops in town; driving the speed limit was not going to happen today.

Racing into Abby's drive, Rob pulled in thankful that Jim followed right behind him. Abby was sitting on her stairs waiting for them. Her garage door was open and as they exited their vehicles they both noticed the writing on the rear window of her car. 'He's not yours, he's mine'; with the same vulgar word smeared on the entire surface. Red spray paint was all over the trunk of her car.

Rob immediately ran to Abby wanting to pull her into his arms; however, he was afraid she would not accept his intentions. He wanted to protect her so badly but felt he couldn't. She was way too fragile. His heart broke seeing her like this: her face streaked with smeared mascara and her beautiful green eyes were rimmed in red. "Abby, when did this happen?"

"I was leaving for work and walked out to the garage to get in my car. I never even noticed anything until I looked out my rear view mirror and noticed the writing. How in the world did anyone get in my garage?"

Rob looked at Jim and they both acknowledged how dumb they were not to have checked the garage last night. "It's my fault. I'm the detective and I should have checked out the garage. I can't believe I never thought to do that. What was I thinking, or not thinking? I'm so sorry. May I take a look around?"

"Of course," Abby's response sounded numb as it echoed in Rob's chest.

"Where's Jack, Abby? I thought he was spending the night with you."

"He spent the night all right." Abby told Rob of her conversation with Jack and the house he was going to build for her and his daughter. She even told him of the unexpected visit to her bed and how she literally had to kick him out. Abby did not however tell him the part where she and Thomas had never had a chance to spend their wedding night together. That pained her too much and was too personal to share.

Rob had all he could do to keep from cussing as a few choice words that rolled around in his brain. He surprised himself that he could refrain from letting them slip out. Not only surprised, but he was actually pleased with how much restraint he had, knowing he no longer wanted that to be a part of his vocabulary. His rage for Jack was so great, he was happy for Jack's sake that he was gone.

Abby leaned into him and looking up at him with the most mournful eyes said, "Now that I know you're my boss, is it okay if I'm a little late for work today?"

Hearing that warmed Rob's heart as he gently put his arm around her. "Of course it's okay to be late—hey take the whole day off, Abby."

As Rob sat there looking at her car and the words written, he immediately jumped up and walked over to Jim. "Jim, we need to talk. I may have an idea who did this." The two men walked to the side of the house.

Rob asked Jim if he remembered the paternity test he took over a year ago. "Yeah, I remember, the one that showed that no way you could be the father of the baby that young girl was accusing you of."

"And you remember who she is, don't you? I think Gabriella has some serious mental issues. I'm afraid I've always thought that but I never imagined she could be capable of something like this. I need to get Abby out of here. Who knows what Gabriella may do? At first I thought of Clark, but now I think differently."

"I agree, but Rob you've always been close to the girl's family, right?"

"Yeah, her mom Maria has worked for me since I opened this resort five years ago. She's been like a mom to me. Gabriella was just a kid back then and was always infatuated with me I guess. When she got pregnant at seventeen, she insisted I was the father and I had never even been with her other than at her house for dinner with the family or at the resort when she started waiting tables for us. Her mom always knew it wasn't me and she was so embarrassed to think she would even accuse me. Her mom was relieved to find out that all along it was Jose who works in the kitchen. Jose loves her so much and even came forward confessing he had to be the father. After the baby was born, there has been no doubt that the father is Jose. For some reason she can't seem to let go of her infatuation with me. I offered to pay for therapy but she refused and to be honest, I was sure this infatuation she had for me was over. I'm going to try and get Abby to stay in one of the apartments we have. In fact it will be on the same floor as mine. I really want to keep her safe, Jim."

"Maybe if I talk to her she'll agree to move there for a while. You have to admit she seems pretty stubborn."

Abby listened in disbelief as Rob explained who he thought it might be and Jim confirmed everything Rob was saying remembering the accusation and Rob's attempt to help Gabriella. Jim carried on the conversation convincing Abby to stay at the resort for a few weeks. He said they may have to try and trap Gabriella in some way before she does anything really violent.

Abby had met Gabriella a few weeks ago and knew she worked at the registration desk much of the time. She always seemed like such a sweet girl. Abby did not know the history or that Gabriella was the daughter of Maria. She chuckled to herself when she thought of Maria and the first time she met this very loving, and always happy, Mexican lady. Maria was head of the kitchen staff and when she would see Abby she always patted her face and smiled with her huge brown eyes saying, 'I will take care of you, senorita.' And she did. Abby couldn't imagine her daughter being such a psycho but looking at Rob she could see the jealousy this young girl could have if he was even remotely interested in anyone. But what about all the other women he seemed to be involved with at some time or another? Why is she being singled out? She knew somehow she would be finding out; she hoped sooner rather than later.

Rob had convinced Abby to stay at the resort and was pleased she acquiesced so easily. They did not want to scare her but they did want her to know Gabriella could be capable of anything since she may be unstable.

Rob had waited while Abby got her suitcase packed, leaving many of her dressier work clothes on hangers. He assured her that he could easily send someone over to pick up the remainder of her things. He had already sent two of his men over to get her car washed and detailed. Both Jim and Rob wondered what Gabriella's reaction would be once she knew Abby would be staying at the resort. Jim questioned if they should let this information be known, they did want to catch her, and right now they had nothing to convict her of. Rob told Jim he really didn't want Abby to be used as a pawn thus making her a target, but he also saw Jim's point as well. "The minute she is in danger of any kind, Jim, she's gonna be out of there. Do I make myself clear? I'm not going to sacrifice her just to catch a psycho."

"I hear ya and I'll do my best to protect her."

"Your best may not be good enough. Fortunately I need to be in California for a board meeting and I want Abby to be there. In fact as CFO she has to be there."

"That sounds like a good excuse to me. At least it'll get her away from here."

Chapter 12

Abby walked into the apartment on the twelfth floor of the resort. It was in the wing that overlooked the woods and out to the beautiful lake beyond; it was a breathtaking view. Abby only wished there were different circumstances so that she could enjoy the view. Rob was having her suitcase and clothes brought up to the room and he should be arriving soon. Her apartment was absolutely gorgeous with furniture she could only dream of owning, even if it was way too formal for her taste. She had always liked the provincial style but also knew it was a little too stoic for her. The brocade couch and matching chairs in muted greens and blues matched the blue drapery. *How in the world am I going to feel at home in a place like this? I'm afraid to touch anything.* Rob came into the apartment and noticed Abby's concern as she looked around the room. "Please don't feel uncomfortable in here. We only have two apartments on this floor and two suites. Mine is the other apartment and believe me; it is not decorated like this."

Something had been niggling at Abby since last night, "Rob, who is Jeff? Is anything you and he told me on the boat the truth?"

"Jeff is really a good friend of mine even if he is my captain and all around guy for me. We did meet when we were just kids but we kind of reversed the story. My dad was the one with the money and Jeff was the guy that worked at the dock each summer. We've been close ever since we were kids. Abby, I'm so sorry I deceived you. I had no intentions of carrying it this far."

Abby was embarrassed and said rather sheepishly, "I didn't want Jeff to ever see how I lived because he was a snob and too rich for my blood. Why didn't you tell me who you were when we met?

Here I had no problem inviting you into my home and into my life. And then every time I talked to you on the phone you were so intimidating you scared the life out of me. I never even recognized your voice over the phone." Abby continued to sit in disbelief over her foolishness. "I've been such a fool. I don't understand why you did such a thing."

"No Abby, I'm the fool." Rob tried holding her hand but she pulled away and he understood he had to let her. He hated how distant she had become and realized that the more she was thinking about things the more she was questioning their relationship. "Abby, do you remember when I first met you in your office?" Her head nodded in response. "When I walked in to introduce myself to you, I couldn't help but notice how beautiful you looked. I really expected to see an older woman, since you are a widow. Wade never told me your age. And when you looked up at me with those beautiful green eyes and didn't recognize me at all, but expected someone from maintenance, all I could think of was having someone like me for me and not who I am or what I have. You looked at me as someone sent to fix your file cabinet."

"Why didn't anyone tell me who you are? I walked around here for over a month, even went out to California, and no one said one word."

"I made sure everyone called me Bob York until Jeff called me Rob and I thought for sure my cover was blown."

With a little chuckle Abby looked up into his beautiful dreamy sea blue eyes. No, she could not look at him. She felt the butterflies in her stomach and the shaking in her knees. She was not about to give in to her emotions. He was her boss and that's what their relationship would be—strictly boss and employee. She chastised herself for even thinking of taking her wedding ring off last night. But there was one more thing she needed to know. "How did you come up with the last name of York?"

Rob had such an irresistible twinkle in his eye and a very mischievous look. "When you introduced yourself to me, I knew I had to come up with a name... and fast. There was a nameplate hidden under the top of your desk that said York Brothers

Furniture. I immediately went from Rob / Robert Stevenson to Bob York. Wouldn't you agree that was pretty clever?" His little smirk never left his face and he looked like a little boy that had come up with the cleverest disguise. Abby wanted to reach over and give him a hug but she knew things had to be kept professional. There was much she needed to find out about this "stranger". Who was Robert Stevenson?

Before he left, Rob mentioned the board meeting in California. He also told her that she needed to be there and that they would be taking the corporate jet out Wednesday morning. He also expected Abby to take care of the travel details with Doug or Jenny. He said it would be best for her to be out of town for a couple of days anyway due to the circumstances. Abby simply nodded and said she would be ready. *Has he always been this controlling or is this the norm for him?* To Abby it seemed his persona had totally changed. She knew from now on she had to accept Rob, rather Mr. Stevenson as her boss.

After Rob left her apartment, Abby remembered that she had told her mom that she would call her back. "Hey mom, sorry I haven't had a chance to call back sooner. No, Jack left sometime last night." Abby started telling her mom of Jack's presumptiveness and how Jack just about attacked her.

Her mom was shocked. Jack seemed like such a nice young man; she was grateful that Abby was ok. "Abby, I'm so sorry that I even encouraged him to visit you. I had no idea and I'm sure his mom has no idea either how he is. He's had us all fooled."

"It's over now mom and I'm glad nothing happened." Abby wondered if she should tell her what had happened to her garage door and car. She decided she did not want her mom and Dad to worry, she knew they would. *My Dad would probably be on his way down here by now.*

"Abby, I was getting my hair done today and you know what I told you about that Mr. Stevenson. Well, all the ladies at the shop were telling me that Mr. Stevenson is such a playboy. They said he is always in those magazines. Maybe you should check some of the magazines out. They said you can find a lot about him online."

"Thanks mom. I think I just might do that. But mom, don't believe everything you hear or read. I really want to give Rob the benefit of the doubt. He has always been very kind to me. I need to get going mom. I'll talk to you tomorrow. Bye, I love you and tell dad I love him."

Abby hung up grateful for the loving family she had; even though they could easily overreact. She thought she would take her mom's advice and look up some of the magazines that headlined Robert Stevenson.

Abby had no idea how long this was taking her and was surprised at all the articles she found and from what she read, Rob was such a playboy. She realized she would definitely have to keep on her toes.

Chapter 13

Abby was ready when she heard the knock on her door. Rob was picking her up at eight and they would be driving to the airport. She quickly checked herself one more time and was pleased with what she chose to wear for the day. She wore a bright teal square neck sheath dress with a strappy pair of teal slings; she looked like a typical California girl. Grabbing her designer Cole Haan handbag and overnight bag, she headed for the door. Abby was surprised when she opened the door only to find an envelope on the hall floor in front of her door. Picking it up Abby wondered if she should open it in case it was from Rob or wait a few minutes more. No sooner had she had the thought, she saw Rob heading down the hallway towards her.

"Good morning, Abby. I see you're all set to head out."

"Good morning, Mr. Stevenson. Yes I am, except I just had a knock on my door and thinking it was you, I opened it only to find this envelope on the floor. I didn't know if I should open it now or wait for you to arrive. I thought perhaps it was a note from you with a change of plans."

"No, not from me, but may I open it? I think it best if we don't handle it too much."

"Do you think it's something I need to be worried about?"

"I hope not but to be safe, do you have a hanky or a tissue I can hold it with so we don't have a lot of fingerprints on it?"

"Oh good idea, I never thought of that. Yes, I'll get a tissue since I don't have everything moved over here." Abby went for a tissue and Rob followed her into the apartment.

Rob could see Abby was visibly shaken. He also knew she wasn't when he greeted her but it must be the concern she picked up in his voice and actions. "Abby, I'm sure it's nothing to worry about."

Abby returned with a tissue and Rob found the letter opener in the desk and proceeded to open the envelope. To Rob it appeared to be a nice card somebody may have sent her. But upon opening it, his face paled and he felt his knees go weak.

"Rob, what is it? You're scaring me. Please let me see."

Rob didn't know if he should let her see it or call Jim to get over there immediately and spare Abby from seeing it. "Abby, I don't know if I want you to see this. I need to call Jim."

"Please, I'm a big girl. I need to know what it is."

Rob considered her plea and carefully opened the card. Inside was a bleeding painted heart with the words, "your heart will be bleeding soon."

They sat together on the couch waiting for Jim to arrive. Rob was thankful he would be taking Abby out of there for a couple of days and he wondered if they needed to stay away even longer. Jim arrived in record time and immediately came up the back elevator. He did not want his presence known among the other employees.

"Hey Jim, thanks for coming so quickly."

"I guess you have something else for me to look at. What do you have?"

Rob directed him to the desk where he left the envelope and card. "I hope there are enough fingerprints on it to get a good match."

"I hope so too. Some of these guys, though clever, seem to mess up at some time or another." Putting on gloves, Lt. Jansen gingerly picked up the envelope and card and opened it cautiously. "Wow, it looks like somebody is trying to make a statement. Whether they are capable of murder or not, we have to consider every scenario possible. I need to get this to the lab. Rob, do you have security cameras in the halls and elevators?"

"Yes of course we do. Our security system is state of the art."

"Good. I'm glad you're taking Abby with you to California. You better head out and make sure your pilot has gone over that plane of yours with a fine tooth comb."

"Will do, but to my knowledge no one knows that we're heading out today. I haven't even told Wade, my resort manager. He's used to me traveling in and out of here all the time. Abby did you say anything to Wade or anyone?"

Rob had returned to the couch next to Abby and sat with his face in his hands. His hair was all rumpled from running his hands through it and Abby thought he looked adorable in spite of their horrible situation. Snapping back to reality, she shook her head. "No, I never thought of telling anyone I would be gone. I guess it was something I thought you would take care of."

"Grab your bag and we'll head out the back way. That's how I came in. I'm glad I know the back entrance and employee elevator. I'll keep in touch with you, Rob, so be sure and keep your phone on at all times."

"I will. Jim, I have my private elevator we can take down." Rob took Abby's bag and grabbed her elbow leading her out the door. "Let's be sure your apartment door is locked." Rob double checked the door and then led Abby down the hall. He was relieved that they were getting away from there.

They arrived at the resort's private airport behind schedule due to the horrific event of the morning and spending time with Lt. Jansen. The flight crew was there waiting and obviously concerned after receiving Rob's phone call to do more than their normal pre-flight inspection of the plane. "Mr. Stevenson, after receiving your call, not only did Len and I go over every detail but I had our mechanics check engines, wiring, and all the instruments."

"Thanks, Doug, I appreciate it. We had quite a scare this morning and I'll fill you in after we board. We really need to get up in the air ASAP. I have a board meeting to get to and I hate to have everyone waiting." Although the Texas resort was the corporate office, the board meetings were always held at the California resort as so many board members lived in the San Diego area.

They boarded and took off without incident. Rob felt guilty and somewhat embarrassed to hear Abby's interaction with the crew. She asked Jenny about her son and how her mom was doing after her chemo treatment. Why, she even talked to Doug like she had known him for years asking how his wife, Mary, and his two kids were doing. They were people that worked for him and he hated to admit that he knew nothing about them. That woman was something else and the more he was getting to know her the more time he wanted to spend with her. All Rob could do was to listen intently hoping he learned something from Abby and the interest she took in everyone she met. He wasn't too pleased however, when Len, the co-pilot, came out and sat next to her trying to engage her in conversation. He was a little too interested in her, as far as he was concerned. "Humph. I really think it's important you get back to the cockpit, Len. I have some papers to go over with Abby."

"Yes Sir, sorry, maybe we can get together some other time, Abby." Len got up tipping his hat towards Abby and giving her an obvious wink.

If he could help it, Rob knew there would be no way that she would be going out with Len any time soon, or anyone else for that matter.

The flight was smooth and Rob was grateful there was no incident. The limo was waiting to take them and the crew to the resort.

They no sooner pulled up to the resort and were greeted enthusiastically by the doorman. "Welcome Mr. Stevenson, it's so good to see you once again. I trust your flight was pleasant."

"Thank you Edward, it went well, as usual."

"It's so good to see you, Mrs. Sinclair. I did not expect you returning so quickly."

"Why thank you, Edward. It's good to see you as well. And how is Mrs. Foster doing? Has she gotten over her nasty cold?"

101

"Yes, thank you for asking. She is doing much better and on my way home I stopped and picked up some Ester C as you suggested. I actually think it may have helped her."

Again Rob felt out of touch with his own staff here in California. *How does she do it? I think she's an enigma.* "Edward, do you know if everyone has arrived for the board meeting?"

"Yes, I believe so and they are awaiting your arrival in the boardroom. Is there anything you would like me to do, Sir?"

"Yes there is, Edward." Rob looked at his watch, "Arrange for lunch to be delivered to the boardroom at one o'clock. That will give me an hour to introduce Abby, I mean Mrs. Sinclair, to the rest of the board members."

"I will see to it, Sir. Would you like the usual for lunch?"

"That will do. If there is any change, I'll give you a call. Thank you Edward."

A bellman took Abby's bag, however the crew took their own out of the trunk. It seemed they had their own routine and from what she understood from her last visit, they each had their own room at the resort. Before they parted, Jenny came over to Abby and told her to think about a date when they could all get together at Doug's for a barbeque. "We can discuss a date on our return trip."

Rob wondered what that was all about but Abby continued to puzzle him, and with that he just chuckled quietly to himself. He would find out soon enough. Nothing got past him.

Before they left the lobby, two very beautiful blond women came up to Rob expressing how happy they were to see him. However, the look and stare they gave Abby could kill a blooming rose bush. She wanted to tell them not to worry that she was not Rob's new flavor of the month, but another side of her wanted to scratch their eyes out. Instead of a word, Abby put her arm in Rob's and he simply nodded to the two women.

Could she be jealous? Yes, I think she's actually jealous. Rob chuckled to himself with the thought that Abby could be jealous of these two women Rob didn't even know. Of course everyone knew who he was, whether they had met him or not.

Abby felt remorse as she thought about her attitude and what she just did. She quickly pulled her arm out of Rob's as they walked to the private elevator. *He was her boss, what on earth was she thinking; more than that, what was Rob thinking of her right now.*

Chapter 14

The private elevator went directly to the conference room on the tenth floor. Rob wasn't sure how to respond to Abby but he had a good feeling that she was jealous of the two women in the lobby. He was chuckling as they walked off the elevator and Abby knew he was laughing at her.

As Abby entered the large conference room, she was greeted immediately by Steven, Rob's stepbrother. He could not resist giving her a big bear hug. "Abby, it's so good to see you again. You look beautiful as usual. I wish we could have spent more time together last week."

Rob gave him an angry look but wanted to stay as cordial as possible. "Hey Steve, I guess you've already met Abby?" He also knew that they had met last week and at that time warned him about Abby.

"We sure did meet last week, didn't we, Abby?"

Abby couldn't help but feel like she was suddenly in the middle of some brotherly tension; something she definitely wanted to stay clear of. Mr. Stevenson was her boss; something she would have to remind herself of continually. "Yes, we met last week, and thank you again for taking such excellent care of me. As brief as it was, I certainly enjoyed my stay here."

Steve had such a smirk on his face as he turned to Rob. "By the way, dear brother, Lucas will be joining us."

"What? I never told him about today's meeting since it wasn't necessary for him to attend. And besides, we can always conference him in if need be."

"I thought he should attend. After all, he should meet our new CFO for Stevenson Enterprises. I'm sure you'd agree."

"No, you know I don't agree. How's he getting here since I have the plane and had no intention of flying it down for him."

As the two brothers were in a somewhat heated discussion, Abby could feel the rush of blood to her face. Just when she was wondering how she could get away from them a very attractive older woman came to her rescue. "Hello, I'm Charlotte Livingston, and you must be our new CFO. But please just call me Aunt Charlotte, dear."

"It's very nice to meet you, Ms. Liv" – Aunt Charlotte gave her a pat on the arm and a sweet look of correction. "Aunt Charlotte. I've heard lots of good things about you from Rob, I mean Mr. Stevenson. It's good to meet so many of the people Mr. Stevenson has talked about so graciously."

"My dear, I would love to have you sit next to me at the table. Would you mind giving an old woman that enjoyment?"

"I understand we will be having lunch shortly; it would be my pleasure to sit with you."

"Great, and while the two, oh wait a minute, the three brothers are deep in discussion I would love to introduce you to the other board members."

Aunt Charlotte immediately took Abby's arm escorting her to the table where most of the members were already seated. They all stood as they approached the table and Aunt Charlotte started the introductions. It appeared that Aunt Charlotte was the only female on the board and the rest were all men, a few old codgers but most were in their thirties and forties. A few looked at Abby like she was way too young for the position she held; they seemed to be the older men. For the most part, they were all very pleasant and kind, doing their best to make her feel welcomed.

Aunt Charlotte motioned to the seat she would be taking and for Abby to have the seat next to her. Before Abby could sit down, someone grabbed her by the waist and twirled her around. It was Lucas, the other stepbrother. "Well, well, my brother sure knows how to keep a secret and I guess he wants you all to himself. My name is Lucas and I manage the Florida resort...what are you doing later tonight?"

Abby was stunned as she just stared up at yet another very handsome man. *What kind of pills were these three men given when they were younger?* Abby had never seen such gorgeous men. To Abby, Rob was still the most handsome of the three. He was taller, had the most beautiful ocean-blue eyes, and definitely not as arrogant as the other two. It was obvious that this brother thought he was God's gift to women.

"Hello. I'm Abby Sinclair; it's a pleasure to meet you, Lucas."

To Rob's chagrin, Lucas was quick to take the seat on the other side of Abby. Steve didn't look too happy with this either. Even though Rob knew he had to sit at the head of the conference table to conduct the meeting, he still didn't appreciate Lucas's boldness.

Rob asked if everyone had met Abby and was pleased that Aunt Charlotte had taken the liberty to introduce her. He knew he could count on Aunt Charlotte to make her feel welcome. "Lunch will be served momentarily."

He no sooner said this when the waiters came in with their lunch and it looked delicious. Abby was starving since they had not eaten since boarding the plane and after the stressful morning all she could eat was a muffin and a cup of coffee.

Abby bowed her head to pray before eating her meal and when she did so, Aunt Charlotte grabbed her hand and bowed her head along with her. Immediately Abby felt a kindred spirit with this precious woman. She would have no idea how close they would become in the months ahead. But Aunt Charlotte seemed to know.

The lunch and meeting went well and Rob asked Abby to tell a little about herself. He was hoping this would be an opportunity for him to hear how she became a widow so young. To his disappointment this did not happen. Abby talked about where she was from and all her college degrees; along with the fact that she had been married but her husband had died in an automobile accident. *Well at least that was something he didn't know.* Rob saw how difficult it was for her to talk about, and not wanting to cause any emotional stress on her, he quickly moved the conversation to something else.

"Thanks, Abby." Rob continued to tell the other members of Abby's encounter with Jeremiah Clark and how well she handled the disturbing situation even to the point of terminating Clark. Steve also expressed his admiration for Abby's strong tenacity in handling the very serious situation. Abby felt her face flush with all the compliments and thanked them for their confidence in her ability to handle the situation.

Rob excused several of the board members including Steve and Lucas. They seemed happy to be excused but not before Lucas patted Abby on the knee and whispered that he would be seeing her later. Rob continued the meeting after several men got up and left, "Sam, what do you have on the acquisition of my father's company?"

Abby was shocked to hear this announcement and had not seen anything come across her desk with any such information. Aunt Charlotte must have noticed her bewilderment as she leaned over and told her the company's name, Stevenson Freight. No, Abby knew she had never seen this name in any of the documents or spreadsheets; and she had studied everything quite extensively.

Sam seemed very knowledgeable of the acquisition and told Rob that everything was coming along and in a few weeks all would be finalized.

"Does my father know who's buying his company?"

"No, not at all; he seems pleased that he's getting out of it and is looking forward to retirement. He was concerned about his employees but we assured him we would keep as many as possible. He also knows the company is not earning what it used to and that it needs to be more diversified."

"Good. But I still don't want him knowing that I'm the one buying him out."

This was making sense to Abby as the puzzle pieces were coming together. She never saw anything regarding his father's company as it was done discreetly without his dad's knowledge. This was why he did not want Steve and Lucas participating in the discussion. Evidently they would have no problem telling their stepdad what was going on. Abby wondered what his father would think of the buyout and what exactly was the relationship between father and son? She knew Steve and Lucas were adopted sons; she also knew from Rob that he never felt that close to his dad once he remarried and had a new family. Abby was saddened that a relationship between a father and son could be so estranged. She wondered if his dad even knew what he was missing in not having a relationship with his son.

Abby and Aunt Charlotte talked for some time after the meeting and a loving bond was formed instantly. They shared their faith and it was obvious to each of them how much they loved God. Aunt Charlotte told Abby she had been such a blessing to her that day and was so grateful she was working for Stevenson Enterprises. Abby thanked her for allowing her to sit with her and how much she enjoyed sharing her life with her.

Rob shook everyone's hand and thanked them for attending and that he looked forward to the next board meeting. Abby saw Rob pat Sam on the back giving him a hearty handshake, evidently confirming how pleased he was with the progress being made in purchasing his dad's company.

Abby wondered if this would be something that Rob would be able to trust her with. If not, she understood how difficult it may be for him to talk about his relationship with his father. It was obvious that Aunt Charlotte was not going to offer any information this confidential.

When everyone had left the room, Rob came over to Abby and Aunt Charlotte. "Aunt Charlotte, it looks like you and Mrs. Sinclair really hit it off."

"Yes we did Robby, and what a lovely addition she is to Stevenson Enterprises. I do hope we have many more opportunities to spend together." Aunt Charlotte noticed that Abby had walked back to the table to collect her portfolio. Pulling Rob down, she whispered in his ear. "Rob, I certainly hope you do not let this one get away. Chase after her if you have to and don't let your brothers get the best of you."

"Thanks Aunt Charlotte, I'm really trying but right now I'm not scoring many points with her."

Aunt Charlotte raised her eyebrows as she gave him a stern look questioning what he meant by his comment. "Robert, you can expect a call from me. Right now I need to head on home." She immediately walked over to Abby giving her a hug and a kiss on her cheek. "My dear, I would love to have you visit me sometime. I live just outside San Diego, in La Jolla, and my house can be very lonely at times. Robby needs to visit way more than he does."

Abby returned the hug and told her how much she would enjoy visiting with her as well. "Thank you for your kind invitation. We seem to have a lot in common and I feel like I have known you for years."

Chapter 15

Rob and Abby were the last to leave the board room and stepped out of the elevator only to be greeted by Lucas. "Hey, I've been waiting for Abby. What kept you two?"

What was she a volley ball? Abby wondered what was between each of the brothers. They should be grateful Rob gave them employment.

"I thought we could go for dinner, Abby, if you have no other plans that is."

Abby began to answer when Rob immediately spoke up. "We already have plans, Lucas. And don't you have a plane to catch tonight?"

"Thanks to you I do have to fly commercial unless I go back with you and then I can take the company jet back to Florida. What do you say? Maybe we could all have dinner tonight and then I can fly back with you. You know I hate flying commercial. Come on bro, let me fly back with you and Abby."

Rob was tight jawed as Lucas was bulldozing him and he could see how uncomfortable Abby was getting. "Lucas, I want you to fly back to Florida tonight or early tomorrow at the latest. Is that understood?"

Abby was tempted to step in but also knew it was not her place to comment. Rob was the boss and not only boss but owner of Stevenson Enterprises. She saw the anger in Lucas's eyes but also the frustration in Rob's and she knew she could no longer keep quiet. "Mr. Stevenson, why don't we all have dinner together tonight? I think it would be good for all of us. And I think you should invite Steven as well. I like the idea of the three brothers coming together for dinner."

How could Rob argue with her? As much as he wanted to be alone with Abby, he certainly did not want to come off like some selfish jerk. Why was she insisting on calling him Mr. Stevenson anyway? Lucas and Steve will certainly have fun making this an issue. He definitely wanted them to know that she was his and for them to stay away from her. He knew his brothers could be ruthless, especially Lucas, when it came to women. The only problem, it was not going to be easy convincing her. Okay, he would play nice and hopefully this would attract Abby. "I'll make the reservations for dinner and Lucas, you invite Steven. We may as well eat right here in the dining room."

Dinner went well and Abby felt like it was a small victory. She was very impressed with Rob's gentle spirit with his brothers, as much as they tried to goad him. She never realized that calling him Mr. Stevenson would create the razzing it did. Finally Abby had enough, she put her hand on Rob's arm and looking into his beautiful ocean-blue eyes she said, "Rob honey, would you please pass the salt." Rob was elated and appreciated what she was doing to get his brothers off his back. With a little wink he passed her the salt. Abby thanked him but not without a response from Rob, "you're welcome, babe." Abby felt her stomach flutter. He hadn't called her that since the night Jack was at her house. She also knew why he had stopped. She didn't comment but knew things would have to go back to her decision to only consider him as her boss. For now it kept their comments at bay.

The decision was made to leave after breakfast in the morning. Rob agreed to let Lucas fly back to Texas with them feeling comfortable that his brother understood his interest in Abby. It also meant that, hopefully, Abby would continue with her familiarity and this would aggravate Lucas even more. One could only hope.

Sleep did not come easy to Abby as she had so much running through her head. She hated to think about the tension between the brothers, but more than that was the knowledge of the estranged relationship Rob had with his father. She wondered if God could use her to bring them together. *Lord, use me in some way to bring Rob and his father together. I don't know how, but you do.*

Rob stared at the ceiling for much of the night wondering what he could do to convince Abby he was not the man that she was reading about in all the tabloids. He may have been labeled a playboy, and yes he did have a different woman almost every month, but he never allowed himself to sleep with any of them. What always stopped him was how disappointed his mother and his Aunt Charlotte would be in him. *Never have I gone that far, but how in the world would Abby be convinced of this?*

They all met in the dining room at eight o'clock as prearranged. Abby was embarrassed to be the last to arrive but with the terrible night of sleep she got, she was lucky to be there at all. The three brothers, along with Doug and Len, stood as she walked to their table and Rob leaned over to give her a quick kiss on her cheek. She thought this awkward but then realized why he did it. It was all for show and especially for Lucas and Steven.

Abby greeted everyone at the table and sat down in the vacant seat between Rob and Jenny. She thanked Jenny for waking her up on time—well almost on time. Abby had met with Jenny for coffee last night and at that time asked her to give her a call when she got up. Abby told her she was always afraid when she traveled that her alarm would not go off. Sure enough, this morning it did not. Abby was grateful that she and Jenny had become such fast friends.

After breakfast the two women sat and chatted what seemed nonstop. Abby asked Jenny if she knew Aunt Charlotte. Abby wasn't surprised that she did. Jenny said Aunt Charlotte had used the company plane a few times when Mr. Stevenson sent for her. Jenny agreed that Aunt Charlotte was a sweetheart and when Abby talked

about their like faith Jenny lit up like a Christmas tree. "Oh Abby:
I thought you were a Christian but I was too shy to come right out
and ask. So am I." The two women giggled like two schoolgirls
catching the attention of the men who stood talking not far from
them. Rob's heart warmed hearing her laughter. *Yet another reason
to love her even more.*

Abby was so excited as she talked to Jenny. "I knew we had a
lot in common and it's so awesome the bond believers have. It feels
like we've been friends forever."

Jenny agreed and before they knew it the men were standing
right behind them wondering what they were giggling about.
Before either of the women could respond, Edward interrupted
informing them that the limo had arrived and was waiting out
front for them. Steve would be the only one staying so they said
their goodbyes to him. Rob kept his eye on Steven to see how he
was going to say goodbye to Abby. Abby approached Steve with
her hand out to shake goodbye but Steve would not shake hands,
rather, he reached out giving Abby a bear hug and a hard kiss on
her lips. "You better be good now and when you're tired of my
brother here, I'll be waiting." Abby felt slightly flushed but was not
going to let him get the best of her; she straightened, squared her
shoulders, and with the best smile she could muster, she looked
Steven square in the eye and said, "I wouldn't count on it if I were
you...Steven." With that said, she walked away from him. Leaving
Steve with his mouth agape, Rob went up to him and lifted his jaw
closing his mouth. Everyone around chuckled, except Steven, and
Rob gave him a pat on the back. "Keep in touch bro."

Abby, Rob, and Lucas sat in the private waiting area at the
airport while Doug and Len went through the pre-flight check.
Jenny went out with them to make sure all was ready when everyone
else came on board. As they waited, Rob's phone began to chirp.
"Stevenson." Rob was sitting across from Abby and although Abby
could not hear his conversation she could see his face, and watching

his reaction concerned her. His face paled and his eyebrows came together with such a stern, foreboding look.

Abby felt her stomach tighten and her hands begin to sweat. She couldn't help but think this had to be about her and the horrible nightmare they experienced before leaving for California: *was that just yesterday morning? It seems like a month ago.* Rob got up and walked away from her and Lucas.

"Jim, I was hoping you were calling with some good news."

"Sorry Rob, but it isn't good. I sent the envelope and card to the lab and it came back with two sets of prints. You said Abby never opened the envelope and that you took the card out using a tissue."

"That's correct. Abby and I both touched the envelope however, I did try and hold it on the edges but I guess both our prints would be on the envelope."

"Well, we have a man's prints on the card, matching prints on the envelope but the kicker is….we found a woman's prints on the card as well. Can't identify the prints but I really don't think the woman's prints are Gabriella's."

"Let's hope it's over and someone pulled a serious prank on Abby."

"Rob, there's more to this."

Rob sensed the hesitation in Jim's voice. "Give it to me straight, Jim."

"Rob, someone broke into her apartment at the resort."

"And? For crying out loud, Jim, tell me what happened!"

"They cut up her pillows and mattress. They trashed the apartment. But Rob that's not all. They also broke into her home and did the same thing: tearing up the bed and trashing whatever else they could."

"Jim, she's not safe at either place. Why is someone targeting her?"

"Rob, I want you to think, and think hard, if there is anyone that may be out to get you or Stevenson Enterprises."

"Why me, if you don't think it could be Gabriella, I have no clue as to who it could be. What about Jeremiah Clark? Think he's ticked off enough because he didn't get the CFO position?"

"I had him checked out and I uncovered something you may be interested in: Clark was in Texas two weeks before Abby started at Stevenson Enterprises."

"I had no idea he was in Texas. I can't imagine who he would have been visiting."

"Rob, until we know where this is going, I suggest you find another place for Abby."

"I'm already thinking about it Jim. I'm going to move her in with me. Don't get the wrong idea. I happen to have a two bedroom suite in my apartment at the resort."

"That's a good idea. And Rob, I think I'm going to have a female officer move into her apartment. We can disguise her to look pretty much like Abby. Well, not exactly. Abby's a beautiful woman Rob, in case you haven't noticed, but we can do a fairly close likeness. Now you just have to convince Abby the safest place to be is in your apartment. Rob, I think they're using Abby as a decoy to get at you."

"Jim, did you think of checking Abby's office?"

"Yes, and that's the other bit of news I have for you. We did check out her office and her door remains locked but I could see where someone tried forcing the lock and door. I think whoever tried was either spooked or didn't have the time and went straight to her home and apartment instead. They have to be looking for something, Rob, the way the two places were trashed. Call me when you get in later. I'd like to meet with you and Abby tonight."

Rob flipped his phone off and knew he had to hold himself together for Abby's sake. He had been running his fingers through his hair almost the whole time he talked with Jim and looked like he had been up all night when he returned to Abby and Lucas. Rob saw the worry on her face and knew there was no way he could keep this from her. "Abby, that was Jim. We'll talk about it on the plane."

All Abby could do was nod but Rob saw the tension and fear in her eyes and his heart ached for her. He wanted to take her in his arms and protect her from all of this, but he knew her feeling for him was not what it was a couple of nights ago. No, right now he was Mr. Stevenson, her boss.

115

As they boarded the plane, Lucas wasted no time in taking the seat next to Abby. She did not want him next to her but Rob didn't seem to take issue with it. Rob had stopped and briefly whispered something to Jenny before he took his seat opposite Abby and Lucas. He said he would tell her about his phone call; evidently he did not want anyone else to know what Jim had said.

Once they were in the air, Jenny came around serving drinks. Abby had a coffee as did Rob. Lucas however had a golden brown liquid. Abby wondered how many of these he would have before they arrived in Texas. When Jenny stopped by Abby she asked if she would come and sit with her on the couch. She wanted to talk to her about the barbeque they were all planning. Abby excused herself from Lucas as she slipped out. *This must have been what Rob was asking Jenny to do to get her away from Lucas.* She sat with Jenny on the couch and Jenny told her that Doug suggested they get together in three weeks. He had talked to his wife, Mary, and she thought that date would work best for them. Abby agreed and said she had no plans. She asked what she could bring and Jenny said she would give her a call later in the week. As they talked, Abby noticed Jenny's eyes glancing over at Rob and giving Abby a wink. She got the message and nodded. Jenny got up to return to the galley and Rob quickly came over to sit with her.

After a couple of drinks, Lucas was up and headed for the back of the plane. Rob noticed Abby's confused look but assured her Lucas was heading for the guest bedroom. "Lucas hates to fly and is really scared stiff. He thinks he needs a few drinks to relax and he finds the time goes by much faster when he can sleep a couple of hours."

"Jenny and I were talking about a barbeque we are having at Doug's in three weeks. Would you like to go?"

"Thanks, I would like that, and I'd like to go with you."

She hesitated a little but then agreed. "By the way, are you going to tell me about Jim's phone call? I get the feeling it can't be good."

"No it isn't good. But I assure you, we will get to the bottom of this."

Abby began to bite on her bottom lip and wring her hands, something Rob noticed when he sat with her at her house last Saturday night. "Well, Mr. Stevenson, are you going to tell me?"

Rob told her about her apartment at the resort and saw a couple of tears escape from her eyes. He couldn't help it but he had to reach up with his thumbs and wipe the tears away, holding her face in his hands. "Abby, I'm going to have you move in with me." He noticed the shock in her eyes and quickly added, "I have a two bedroom apartment at the resort."

"I can't do that. I'll just go back to my home."

"Abby, you can't go back home, not now anyway. They also trashed your house."

Shock flooded her face and she began to shake uncontrollably. "Why is someone doing this to me? I don't understand what I've done."

Rob didn't care at this point; he had to hold her as she laid her head on his chest. He rested his head on hers and took in the beautiful scent of her hair. *Boy she sure smells good! I could hold her like this all the way to Texas.* Rob assured her everything would be all right and that Jim would be coming over later to discuss the crimes. She asked him about the card she received and Rob filled her in on what Jim had told him. It wasn't long and he felt her body go limp and her breathing quiet and steady. She had fallen asleep on his chest. Rob spread her out on the couch and asked Jenny to bring a pillow and blanket. He first undid her hair clip and placed the pillow under her head, carefully pulling himself up from under her. He stood and gently put the blanket over her. *She is the most beautiful woman I've ever seen and I've dated some beautiful women.*

Chapter 16

Once again they entered the rear employee entrance heading for Rob's private elevator. His elevator opened directly into his penthouse apartment. Rob was relieved they had not been seen. After calling Jim from the limo, he expected him to meet them shortly. Rob did not want Abby to even enter her apartment but she insisted on seeing it. "Abby, I think it's best to wait for Jim and we'll go in with him."

Abby nodded her understanding and followed Rob into his apartment. She was overwhelmed with the opulence of his place. His apartment was completely opposite the ornate furnishings of her apartment. His was modern but still very luxurious. Rob explained that his bedroom was a suite to his left and hers was a separate suite on the opposite side. He walked her to her bedroom showing her the king bed and en suite bathroom with all the amenities. "I think you'll be comfortable here for the time being. I want you to think of it as your home for now. We will have to share the living area but I don't expect it to be a problem since I'm gone quite a bit."

Abby's breath caught as she eyed the beautiful ebony grand piano that sat in the corner of the living room. Rob couldn't help but notice the gleam in her eye, "Do you play the piano?"

"Yes I do, but I haven't played in quite some time."

"Well feel free to play it anytime."

"Thank you so much, Mr. Stevenson. Let's hope I won't be staying here for too long."

"Abby, will you please stop calling me Mr. Stevenson? I prefer you call me Rob."

"Yes sir. But I find it awkward and inappropriate when you happen to be my boss and CEO of Stevenson Enterprises."

"Don't think of me as your boss then when it's after office hours. Would this be acceptable to you?" He said this with such sarcasm that he felt remorse once the words left his mouth, but too late to take back. He saw her eyes flash and knew he must have hit a nerve.

"Yes that's fine. I'll try to remember that when it's after... office hours."

Rob noticed the bite in her words, so unlike Abby but he knew she was under a lot of strain right now and he also knew that his words probably did hurt her. She no sooner finished her sentence when the doorbell rang.

Lt. Jansen entered, shook Rob's hand and then reached out to shake Abby's. Rob asked if he wanted to sit at the dining room table or remain in the living room. "Either place you're the most comfortable. I hope we can look at some evidence: what we have and sadly don't have."

Abby took a seat at one end of the rather large black leather couch and Rob at the other while Jim sat across from them in one of the black leather chairs. He didn't look like he fit in such luxury with his crumpled suit and loosened tie.

"Abby, I need to know if you can think of anything at all that someone might be interested in: a letter, funds unaccounted for, strange phone calls, and anything that might seem out of the ordinary."

Abby shook her head and all she could come up with was her confrontation with Jeremiah Clark but that was in California. "Only Jeremiah Clark, I had to terminate him. I'm sure he was not pleased with me but I was representing Stevenson Enterprises."

"What happened after the termination? Was he escorted out of the building?"

119

"Yes he was escorted out by Sergeant Ferguson. I took his computer back with me."

"You did? Where is it now?"

"I locked it in one of the file cabinet drawers in my office."

Turning to Jim, Rob wanted his assurance that her office was not broken into. "It was obvious someone tried but with the door still locked I didn't want to raise any attention and go looking for someone to open it for me. Before I leave why don't we head to your office, Abby, and check it out."

"Okay. Maybe I can see my apartment and my home soon?"

"I wouldn't tonight but maybe tomorrow Rob can take you over. I don't think you will ever be prepared for what you are going to see."

Both Jim and Rob noticed how visibly shaken she was. Rob reached over and held her hand in his. "Abby, it's going to be all right. We'll get through this. You have to trust me. If you're worried about staying here, please don't be."

Jim assured Abby that it was best she moved into Rob's apartment. "I'll have an undercover officer staying in your apartment starting tomorrow morning. I thought it best to wait until you returned just in case anyone was aware of your absence. Let's wait until she arrives before you go over there."

Jim and Rob questioned if they should tell Abby that Jeremiah Clark had been in Texas before she started with the resort. As far as Abby was concerned, Clark was only connected to the California resort. They did not want Abby to worry any more than necessary so Jim looked at Rob before saying anything and Rob gave him the nod. "Abby, Jeremiah Clark was in Texas two weeks before you started with Stevenson Enterprises."

"Why was he out here? Does he have family here?" Abby's head was spinning and they could see she was deep in thought as she tried to come up with her own reason why Clark would have been there. "Could someone else be involved with the embezzlement? Someone connected to this resort?"

"I'm thinking the same thing. Rob, who did Abby replace as CFO?"

"This is a new position. We have had individual finance officers responsible for each resort separately. This was a position the board and myself created. We wanted someone to oversee the finances throughout Stevenson Enterprises. I'm sure there will be even more responsibility as time goes on."

"That's interesting. I'd like the name of the previous finance director. Was the director male or female?"

"She was a woman. I'll get the necessary info from HR."

"We need to check out your office, Abby. Do either of you have any questions for me?"

Shaking their heads in unison, Rob said, "Let's go."

Rob reached out for Abby's hand. When she took it, there was that charge of electricity shooting all the way up her arm and clear down to her toes. *What is wrong with me? My nerves must be so on edge.* But Abby knew this happened every time Rob touched her: no matter how subtle he was.

Abby got her keys and they proceeded to her office on the seventh floor. It was obvious the door was damaged but to what extent they were unable to detect. In fact if they were not looking for any damage it may have taken a while before anyone noticed.

Upon entering, everything in Abby's office looked in place. Her desk was neat as the day she left, her computer station looked fine, but then her eyes immediately took in the three drawer cabinet. The drawers were closed but something was askew. Abby noticed that although the drawers were closed the drawer that housed Clark's computer was not closed all the way. She immediately bent to open it when Jim abruptly stopped her. "Abby, do not touch anything!"

"I'm so sorry. I'm not thinking."

Jim proceeded to put on a pair of gloves and immediately opened the bottom drawer. The infamous bottom drawer, thought Rob as a smile curled the corners of his mouth.

When Jim opened the drawer, they were not surprised to see the computer missing—gone. Abby gasped covering her mouth with her hand as she was the one that had safely locked it in there. "I can't believe it's gone. Someone was in here after all." Suddenly she could not hold back a giggle and both Rob and Jim looked at her thinking she had finally lost it. "They got nothing but an empty computer!"

"What are you talking about?" asked Rob.

"I copied all the info onto an external hard drive and then completely erased everything from the computer. For some reason I decided it best to keep the external hard drive with me."

Rob picked her up by the waist and twirled her around. "Abby, you're amazing. Are you saying that you had it with you to California?"

Abby felt a little sheepish that she had carried the external hard drive with her their entire trip. "Yes. I had it in my purse the whole time. I really think it was God that had prompted me to take it with me. Otherwise it seems kind of silly, don't you think?"

"Nothing silly about it; that was the smartest thing you could have done." Jim was totally impressed with her astuteness as well. "This is one unbelievable CFO you have Rob."

"You're not telling me anything I don't already know." Rob didn't realize that he still had his arm around her waist but when he did, he gave her a squeeze.

Abby pulled away from Rob's hold and it pained him that she wanted to distance herself from him. "It's really late and I think I'm ready to turn in for the night."

Jim looked at his watch and agreed. "I'll be back tomorrow morning. I have a feeling there's something on that computer that somebody does not want us finding out about. And young lady, you better be extremely careful. Until we figure this out Rob, I want you with her at all times."

The three left together and Jim locked the door behind them. "I'll get forensics out here in the morning to pull prints. Abby, maybe tomorrow you could take a look at that external hard drive."

"Yes, I plan to. I could work from the apartment and then I won't have to go into the office until they're finished."

They said good night and Jim took the executive elevator down while Rob and Abby went to Rob's private elevator. Inserting his special key they rode up in silence to the twelfth floor.

Chapter 17

After entering the apartment, Abby told Rob that she was exhausted and would be heading for bed.

"Abby thank you for today and for thinking to back up everything from Clark's computer...that was brilliant!"

"You're welcome. I hope I can find something tomorrow that will help find the culprit. Good night."

"Good night, Abby, I'll see you in the morning. I hope you sleep well. Oh and Abby, please don't believe what you read in all the tabloids."

Abby was pleased that she had packed enough extra clothes so she had a fresh outfit for tomorrow. She never did like wearing the same clothes the next day. Taking a hot bath helped relax her tense muscles, especially the jets in the Jacuzzi tub. Sleep seemed elusive the past several nights and hopefully she would not have difficulty falling asleep tonight.

Abby awoke to the smell of fresh coffee and wondered how long she had slept. She glanced at the clock and saw it was eight a.m. *I must have really been out. Maybe Rob left already since it's so late. One could only hope.* Abby quickly showered but instead of dressing she put on the plush white robe that was hanging in her bathroom. It had the SE crest in gold letters. The robe alone had to cost at least a couple hundred dollars. Way too extravagant but she would enjoy it while it lasted.

Abby put her hair up in a loose twist and added a light touch of makeup. She was sure she would be alone and wanted to get a cup of coffee before getting dressed. She walked through the living room and into the fully equipped kitchen looking for the coffee when she heard the deep timbre of a baritone voice she would recognize anywhere.

"Good morning, Abby. I hope you slept well." All Rob could think about was how beautiful she looked in that robe.

Startled, Abby turned to see Rob walking up behind her. "Good morning, Mr. St....Rob. Yes, I slept very well. I can't believe it's so late. I thought you would be out of the apartment by now. I smelled the coffee and couldn't resist. Have you had some already?" She knew she was blabbering.

"Yes, I've been up quite a while already. I didn't know what you'd like for breakfast so I had a variety of breakfast foods brought up: bagels and cream cheese, an assortment of sweet rolls, cereal, bacon and scrambled eggs that we can heat up in the microwave. As far as me being gone, don't you remember the Lieutenant telling me I could not let you out of my sight?"

"I didn't think he meant it literally." *Why the twinkle in his eye?*

Rob's eyebrows raised but he ignored her response motioning to the food that lay out before her. Thanking him, she reached for a sweet roll and coffee and walked out to the dining room table. Although there were two bar stools at the counter, Abby knew with the huge plush robe wrapped around her it would be awkward for her to climb up onto one. If she were alone she would have but not with Rob right there watching her.

Rob decided to fill his cup once again and followed Abby out to the dining room. "Just so you know, I have twelve college buddies coming in Friday for a golf outing. We get together once a year, kind of a reunion of sorts."

"So you're telling me you won't be able to keep an eye on me the entire weekend." She could not help giving him a hard time over this.

"I can always have you ride in the golf cart with me." He said with a chuckle and a twinkle in his eye. "I'm sure we'll come up with something and I really don't want to make light of the situation at all. This is extremely serious and I do expect to keep you safe."

"Thank you, I appreciate it, I really do."

"So what are your plans for today? Will you be looking at that external hard drive?"

"I plan on doing that this morning. I think it best I work from here if that's okay with you."

"Absolutely. I need to run to my office for a time but after you get dressed I thought we could go over to your apartment and you can get what you need. I received a text from Jim that he and the undercover detective should be arriving within the hour. I'll make sure she gets set up and come back for you."

Abby finished her sweet roll and coffee; she then excused herself so she could finish dressing. Before entering her suite she heard the Lieutenant's knock on the door. She decided it best to dress and wait for Rob to return for her.

Abby dressed in the casual clothes that she had in her bag. She put on a pair of white jeans, a mint green tank top with a loose fishnet top in a darker green over it. With such plush carpeting throughout the apartment, the thought of going barefoot was tempting, until she remembered she would be going over to her apartment; she slipped on a pair of green sandals.

When she returned to the living room, the beautiful grand piano was calling to her. She thought it wouldn't hurt to sit down for a couple of minutes and play. She had never played such a magnificent instrument in her life. Adjusting the piano bench she began to play a couple of hymns she knew from memory. The first being "Great Is Thy Faithfulness" and the second "How Great Thou Art". The notes seemed to roll off her fingers; she played with such emotion and gusto that she was totally unaware that anyone had entered the apartment. But when she finished there was applause that emanated from the foyer. It was Rob and he stood with the biggest grin on his face. "Abby that was beautiful. When you said you hadn't played in quite a while, I never imagined that you could play like you just did." Rob recognized "Great Is Thy Faithfulness", although all the words seemed difficult to recall, he had tried singing quietly to the tune.

Abby couldn't help but blush and simply shrugged her shoulders thanking him for the generous compliment. "I didn't expect you to be back so soon. I thought you were going to your office after Jim arrived."

"I was but thought I would take you over while Jim was still there so he could introduce you to Detective Ashley. Are you ready to head over?"

"Yes I am. When I return I will start going through the external hard drive. Sorry I got so caught up with your piano... I thoroughly enjoyed it."

"And I enjoyed listening. I hope you feel free to play it anytime. And I hope it's when I'm here."

Abby was shocked when she walked into the apartment. The forensic team was there lifting what fingerprints they could and others followed putting things back together as each area was completed. Rob noticed a few tears escaping as she held her hand over her mouth. Lt. Jansen walked over and quickly took charge of the situation. He introduced Abby to Detective Rose Ashley. "Once she puts on her wig and is dressed in some of your clothes, I think we have a pretty good likeness. Detective Rose was the same height and weight as Abby although Rob couldn't help but think Abby was much more attractive. "We're hoping that when word gets around that Abby has returned to her apartment, the perp will try again to find what he or she is looking for. It's worth a try anyway."

"Great, so I can return to my apartment?" Abby said with some excitement in her voice.

"No, Abby, I'm afraid not. Rose will be staying here. I'm hoping that if anyone is watching her coming and going they will think it's you. We will coordinate the time you leave to go down to your office and that's when Rose will also head out, wearing your clothes and a wig." Rob asked Jim if he had a chance to look at the camera video from Monday. He said he had but wanted him to come down to the station and take a look at it. "It looks like there was a woman walking in the hall but it's difficult to make out her face. By the way, did you contact HR for the info on your previous financial director? Is it possible she could still have office keys?"

"I put a call in this morning and they're going to get back to me. I'm sure she turned in her keys, however, there was nothing stopping her from making duplicates." Rob noticed Abby getting some clothes together for Detective Ashley and also clothes to take to his apartment. He was pleased it was something she was doing without putting up a fuss. She seemed to be adjusting to the severity of the situation. Rose was pitching in giving her a hand carrying as much as she could in her arms. They left making the trek down to Rob's apartment since his entrance was down a ways from hers.

With clothes and toiletries put away, Abby got out her laptop and plugged in the external hard drive with Jeremiah Clark's computer info on it. After the short time she spent looking at it earlier, she knew it was going to be a time consuming task. She liked working from Rob's apartment but at some point she would have to spend time in her own office.

Chapter 18

It did not take long before Rob was accustomed to having Abby in his apartment. He had wondered how he would feel about sharing each meal with her and conversing throughout the day. Being this close to a woman almost twenty-four / seven was a totally new experience for him. He certainly was not looking forward to her moving back to her apartment and especially her home anytime soon. Abby always tried to maintain a professional relationship but he noticed there were a few times when she would forget and her fun and bantering side would let loose. Often she would catch herself and be right back to the serious Abby. He tried on several occasions to talk about his tabloid "exploits" but either Abby changed the subject or someone interrupted. It was Friday morning and the thought occurred to him that Aunt Charlotte would be the one person that he could count on talking to Abby. Aunt Charlotte has known his heart and intentions more than anyone. *I will give her a call right after breakfast and see if she could invite Abby and me out for a visit next weekend.* He knew he could count on her to do this.

When Rob walked into the kitchen, Abby was already making coffee and preparing breakfast. The previous two mornings Rob had an assortment of breakfast items brought via room service. "Good morning Abby. It sure smells good in here."

"Good morning. I thought having a homemade breakfast this morning would be a welcomed change for us. How do bacon and eggs sound? I also have some fruit and bagels."

"Awesome and I'm starving." Rob noticed the dining room table was set and OJ already on the table. "May I help with anything?"

"If you wouldn't mind taking the coffee carafe, I'll bring the rest. Would you like toast or a bagel?"

"Toast is fine, thanks." Rob smiled to himself thinking how he could easily get used to spending each morning like this with her.

While the bread was in the toaster, Abby found a tray for the bacon and scrambled eggs; and then she quickly buttered the toast and carried it all out to the dining room table. She couldn't help but feel proud of herself for not expecting Rob to wait on her continually. As great as room service was, it simply was not the same as making it fresh yourself.

Rob pulled Abby's chair out for her and then went over to his. At least she didn't set the table with him all the way at the opposite end. This table could seat at least twelve people. Abby sat to the right of Rob as she insisted he sit at the head.

Rob knew Abby would bow her head in prayer before eating and he sat patiently as he waited for her. Rob thanked her for the great breakfast she had made for him. Leaning back in his chair, Rob thought this would be a perfect opportunity to bring up all the tabloid headlines, but Abby asked when his buddies would be coming in for the golf outing. "They should start arriving about three o'clock. And Abby, I would love to have you join us for dinner tonight." Abby simply responded with a nod.

"By the way, have you found anything on Clark's computer that looks suspicious?"

"As a matter of fact I have. I need to do a little more digging but I have discovered some rather large purchases. I guess I never would have questioned the outlandish cost of some items if it wasn't something I was looking for now. I was waiting until I had more information before discussing this with you but if you would like to take a look sometime today I can show you what I have."

"Let's plan on this afternoon sometime. I think I'll give Jim a call and have him come over. I talked to HR and the previous finance director we had was Sarah Duncan. I can hardly place her as it was Wade that hired her and he was the one she was accountable to. I believe she was here for only a couple of years... if that."

"Hmm, a couple of years, I think I better go back even further than I am. If you can get me her exact start date, I'll go back to when she started. Or if you prefer, I can call HR and get that information myself. It sounds like you'll be having a couple of busy days."

"Thanks. Ask for Rebecca in HR and tell her that I've given you permission to do this. She will probably call me to verify but that's a good thing."

Picking up the dishes they both returned to the kitchen. Abby rinsed the dishes and Rob automatically started to stack the dishes in the dishwasher—so unlike him.

Once the dining room table was cleared Abby set up her computer and began the all consuming task of looking at numbers. Sometimes she thought her head would explode but she was determined to get to the bottom of this. She knew that the quicker the perpetrator was found the sooner she could return to her home. Living in such luxury was nice but something she knew was only temporary. Abby sensed there was something Rob was trying to talk to her about but she felt it awkward to ask if there was something he wanted to tell her.

She called HR and talked with Rebecca who said she would get back to her with the requested information. She knew Rebecca was going to call Rob; Abby told her she would be expecting her call.

As Rob sat in his study, which was off of his bedroom suite, the idea of calling Aunt Charlotte returned to him. Sitting with his feet up on his desk, he took out his cell phone. Aunt Charlotte answered on the second ring seeing that it was her nephew. "How's my boy doing? I'm so glad you called Rob. I never hear from you enough."

"Hi Aunt Charlotte, I have a huge favor to ask of you. You know everything there is to know about me Aunt Charlotte and you know how false all the stories are in the tabloids."

"That I do Robby. You can't imagine how it angers me to read those articles. I finally gave up reading them. In fact I don't want to ever see another one."

"That's what I'm calling about Aunt Charlotte. I was wondering if you would mind talking to Abby. I know you could be discreet about it. I have tried but something always comes up or someone interrupts, to say nothing of the fact that it's a little embarrassing talking about me. You of all people know my reasons and I think you would be able to talk to Abby about this. I know she believes much of what she has read, and well, our relationship this past week has been nothing but work related."

"Rob, why don't you and Abby come out here next weekend? I already told her that I would love to have her come for a visit. I'm happy to give her a call so she thinks it is all my idea."

"Sounds good to me, when would you like us to visit so I can arrange my schedule?"

"How about sometime Friday and you can stay the weekend. You know Robby, Abby will be going to church with me and I would appreciate you coming as well."

"We'll see Aunt Charlotte. I can't make any promises."

Aunt Charlotte hung up her phone with a twinkle in her eye. *Oh, we'll see about you attending church with us Robert. You will be there.* She would wait a little bit, but not too long, before she would invite Abby to her home in La Jolla. *This is going to be such fun.*

Rob hung up with a smile on his face knowing Abby could not refuse an invitation from his dear aunt. They both seemed to hit it off and he had the feeling Aunt Charlotte wanted to see them together. Although Rob was not so sure of a serious relationship with Abby at this time, he certainly wanted her to know more about him and that the stories she read were not in the least bit true. But why he cared so much about that now, he didn't know. Normally that would not have mattered one bit to him, after all it hadn't in all these years. He was his own man and to be honest, he really did like all the attention he got...up until now.

Abby sat transfixed on her computer screen. She was scrupulous in studying the books as she had gone back to the date Sarah Duncan was hired. In those years she discovered some very hefty purchases that she was unable to reconcile. It appeared the money was sent to the California resort but when it was put on Clark's books it was not the amount transferred. Nothing was making any sense. There appeared to be two sets of books. Rob came out of his suite and saw Abby deep in thought. "You look exhausted Abby. Can I get you something to eat or a cup of coffee?"

"A cup of coffee sounds good. Mr. Stevenson, I want you to take a look at what I just found."

Rob got close to Abby as he looked over her shoulder. *She smelled incredibly delicious. Maybe it was the Dior she was using that he had put in her bathroom.* Whatever it was, he was thoroughly enjoying where he was standing right now. Taking a few deep breaths before snapping back to reality, Rob looked at the screen Abby was pointing to. "It's Rob, Abby. Please I've asked that you call me Rob."

"Rob, do you have any idea why these highlighted items that were purchased here in Texas were even sent to the California resort?"

Taking a look at the items, Rob was as confused as Abby. She then pointed out how the amounts did not coincide with Clark's amounts that he entered. "Rob, it looks to me like Sarah was entering one amount and then when it went to Clark he entered another but it still doesn't add up as to what happened from point A to point B."

"Jim should be over soon and we'll see if he can make sense of this."

"Like I said, it simply doesn't add up. I get the feeling Ms. Duncan was in cahoots with Mr. Clark. I don't believe the carpet was the only purchase that was made and then a "dummy" bill entered.

When Rob came back in with the coffee, Abby was sitting with her head in her hands. He was immediately concerned and anxious for her wellbeing. He felt his chest tighten and knew he had to get control of his over protectiveness of her. He knew that he had never in his life felt this way for anyone. "Are you all right Abby?"

"Yes I'm fine. I do have a throbbing headache though, but I'm sure it's from staring at all these numbers."

Rob left the room and immediately returned with some medication for her headache. "Thanks Rob. This should do the trick along with the coffee you brought me."

Wanting to rid her mind of the task before her, Rob quickly remembered her mentioning the expansion of the resort. "Hey, how about we grab a couple of horses next week and take a ride around the property? I like the vision you have of a dude ranch being built."

Abby's eyes lit up at the thought of riding. This was something she always loved to do. "I didn't think you would even remember I had mentioned that...Bob." Rob could not help but notice the twinkle in her eye as he remembered she had told him that when he was Bob York, the guy from maintenance. He could not help but grab her two hands in his as he had pulled up a chair and was sitting beside her now. Abby's heart thumped and once again that spark went through her whole body. She pulled her hands out of his and brushed them against her pant leg. Suddenly her hands felt sweaty and her mouth dry. Grateful for the glass of water Rob brought her with the headache meds, she took a huge gulp. "I would love to go riding."

Abby was grateful for the distraction when her cell phone rang. "Hello, this is Abby. Oh, hello Aunt Charlotte. I'm fine how are you? It's so good to hear your voice as well."

Rob knew he was only listening in to a one sided conversation but he also knew why his aunt was calling. He could not keep the smirk from his face and had to immediately look away.

Abby continued her conversation with Aunt Charlotte and Rob knew she was inviting her to fly out for a visit next weekend. "I would love to come for a visit and it couldn't come at a better time. Thank you so much. No, of course I don't mind one bit if you invite him." She also knew she had no choice in the matter. "Thank you so much and I look forward to seeing you once again."

Rob tried to show his surprise that his aunt had called her and as far as he could tell Abby had no clue that it was all his doing. Trying to look annoyed, Rob told Abby that he could probably be expecting a call from Aunt Charlotte. "Yes she said she would be calling you. She invited me to come for a visit next weekend and asked if I would mind if she invited you as well."

"You won't mind then if I tag along? My aunt will probably expect you to attend church with her on Sunday."

"That would be lovely, and no I don't mind if you tag along. After all, what choice do I have?"

Rob appreciated the smile on her face as she said that. *I know I can count on Aunt Charlotte to set Abby straight.* He was not a playboy. He had been waiting for the right woman and marriage before he even thought of going to bed with anyone; but he also knew that Abby had been married and maybe sex to her was not such a big deal anymore. No, he could not believe that she would not want to wait until she was married again even if she was no longer a virgin. Rob chastised himself for having such thoughts.

There was a knock at the door shaking Rob out of the thoughts he couldn't believe he was having. "It must be Jim. I'll get it."

It was Jim and Abby began filling him in on what she had discovered. "Rob, I would like to get a subpoena for both Ms. Duncan and Mr. Clarke's bank accounts. Rob nodded but also felt like such a jerk that someone in his company, in fact two employees, were allegedly stealing right out from under him. *I guess being a multi-billionaire and treating your employees well didn't mean you couldn't have someone greedy enough to be capable of doing such a thing.*

Jim left quickly. He said he wanted to get going on the subpoena immediately and that it would take a couple of days to get it through.

Rob's phone chirped and he took it immediately thinking it had to be Aunt Charlotte filling him in on her phone call to Abby. To his surprise it was not his aunt, it was Wade. "Hey Wade, what's up?"

"Rob, I hate to tell you this but we do not have a concierge for this afternoon and evening."

"What do you mean we have no concierge? What happened to Lisa? Sick. What about Gabriella? Her baby's sick? Yes, I know it is Friday night but there must be someone who could fill in!"

Abby was taken aback hearing Rob raise his voice. She had never heard him raise his voice to anyone. Running his fingers through his hair she sensed he was having a difficult time finding a concierge for when all his friends were coming in.

Rob abruptly ended his phone call and breathed out a moan. "I can't believe we have no one to fill in as concierge tonight."

Abby looked at Rob with genuine concern for his predicament. "Rob, why can't I fill in? I'm sure I could greet the guests and direct them. Besides, it would give me something to do. I've been going stir crazy the past two days anyway."

"Abby, are you sure? That would be awesome and you would be perfect."

"I don't know about perfect but I think I could manage."

"You're perfect and this would be perfect because I can keep an eye on you the whole time. Like I mentioned earlier, I want you to join us for dinner anyway. This way you will be with me...and I'll know you're safe."

"What time do you want me in the lobby?"

"How about two thirty? I think most of the guys are coming in around three and they should all be here by six o'clock. Dinner is planned for seven. It would be about four or five hours is that okay?"

"Not a problem. I'll be ready then."

"Why don't I order some lunch before you get ready? How about a chicken salad sandwich and some fruit?"

"Fruit and a sandwich sound great."

As Rob was walking away he wondered if Abby noticed the spring in his step. He couldn't be more pleased that Abby would be right where he wanted her to be. She would be safe and that was his number one priority.

After ordering their lunch, Rob returned to the dining room. Abby was once again looking at her computer. "Abby, please take a break. We need to wait until Jim gets back to us anyway; I don't want you walking around with a headache all night."

"Thanks. Do you mind if I lie on the couch for a few minutes?"

"Not at all; I'll wake you when our lunch arrives."

Abby couldn't wait to lie down on the beautiful butter leather couch. She knew it would be utter comfort to sink into the cushiony leather as she grabbed one of the leather pillows equally as soft. No sooner did her head hit the pillow, she was out. Rob found a throw that he gently covered her with. Wondering if he should even awaken her when lunch arrived as she looked like she could easily be out for a while. He put that thought aside knowing she would want to have time to get ready for her concierge gig later today however, he did call room service telling them to wait an hour before delivering their lunch. He knew that when the boss called they made it a point not to let him wait…at all.

Rob was seated in one of the matching leather chairs not even realizing that he was in awe as he watched Abby sleep. She looked like an angel with her silky hair, beautiful long eyelashes, and plump juicy lips. *I must stop thinking like this. There is way more to Abby than how beautiful she is: her heart and her love for God are obvious; she's one amazing woman all right.* Rob's phone buzzed and showed it was Aunt Charlotte. "Hi Aunt Charlotte, it's really good hearing your voice too. Yes, I was sitting next to Abby when you called and I know she is looking forward to taking a trip out there. Aunt Charlotte, I know you will have a talk with Abby and tell her what I have not been able to. Lord knows I've tried but something always comes up. You know me better than anyone and I'm counting on you to explain things to her. Thanks for the invite. I love you too, more than you know." Rob ended the call and had no idea that Abby lay awake listening to his phone call.

Abby didn't dare move but lay there hoping Rob would think her still asleep. *What could he possibly want me to know about him?*

There was no way she was going to ask him what he wanted her to know. She lay perfectly still for at least the next ten minutes when she heard the knock on the door. She knew then it was safe to stir. She stretched and Rob figured this was the first of her waking up. "Hey sleepy head, our lunch has arrived."

Abby sat on the edge of the couch and stretched again; getting up she tried looking somewhat disoriented. "Wow, I must have really been out. Thanks for letting me sleep. I guess I needed it."

Rob opened the door for room service, and knowing it was their boss they were serving, they entered immediately. Heading for the dining room table they began setting everything out. They left as quickly as they entered and Rob pulled a chair out for Abby. "It looks delicious and I'm absolutely famished." When they finished eating, Abby excused herself to get ready for her new position as concierge. She had to admit she was looking forward to it.

Rob waited for Abby before heading to the lobby. He could not take his eyes off of her as she walked out into the living room. She wore an emerald green raw silk dress, four inch patent heels, and with her hair swept up in a loose twist, she was absolutely stunning. Her green eyes looked like deep sparkling emeralds shimmering behind those long eyelashes that he loved so much. "Abby you are breathtaking." Rob felt tongue tied and had no idea what else he could possibly say without sounding like a complete idiot.

"Thanks Rob. I hope I'm not overdressed. I really had no idea what I should wear, but when you mentioned dinner, I thought I had better dress up a little more."

Abby was thankful for the upscale retail job she had in college that afforded her the opportunity to purchase a couple of designer handbags and expensive shoes. As far as her clothes, she learned to shop from the sale rack. With her small size there was always a great selection; it also helped that she was right there when the sale started giving her first chance at designer clothing as well.

She only hoped that the boat-neckline on this dress wasn't too revealing. Abby had thought when she married Thomas, and being a pastor's wife, that she would one day have to sell her expensive designer wardrobe. She had told Thomas that she did not want him to feel uncomfortable with a wife having such an expensive wardrobe but he told her he would never feel that way and neither should she.

Chapter 19

Abby sat at the concierge desk waiting for the arrival of Rob's golf buddies. Of course there were others that arrived and Abby greeted them with grace and confidence. Rob kept his eye on her every chance he had.

It was half-past two when to Abby's surprise Steve and Lucas came walking through the lobby. She had no idea that they would be attending Rob's golf outing. They immediately caught sight of Abby sitting at the desk and just about tripped over themselves to see who would get to her first. Abby walked around to the front of the desk giving them each a hug and kiss on the cheek. Rob caught site of this and didn't know if he should chuckle or throw a punch at each of them. All he knew was his hands had automatically turned into fists as he watched the interaction between his two brothers and Abby. He managed to walk over and give each of his brothers a handshake and pat on the back. Steve asked Abby if she got a promotion as she was now the new concierge. Rob quickly answered telling them how grateful he was that she was willing to fill in on such short notice.

Looking at Steve, Abby commented how surprised she was to see both he and Lucas at the resort. "I had no idea that the two of you would be here. I thought this was only for some old college buddies of Rob's?"

"Rob always asks us to join him," said Steve, "I think it's just so we complete a foursome for him."

"We have four foursomes so I need them to help me make up the fourth."

Abby looked a little puzzled as she quickly added up the number of golfers.

"Okay, you need sixteen for four foursomes but you have fifteen. You're missing..." No sooner did the words come out when to her surprise, once again, up walked Jeff. "Hey, Abby girl, you look surprised to see me."

To her delight he leaned down and gave her a quick kiss. "Hey Jeff, it's good to see you too."

Jealousy rose up in each of the three guys standing there with their mouths agape. Rob especially felt a pang deep in his chest watching Jeff's familiarity. *Had Abby spent time with Jeff since they were on the boat? No, couldn't have as she's been with me all week. It's just that Jeff's personality always has a shock factor to it.*

It wasn't long after the four guys greeted one another and Abby that the flow of golfers started. Abby quickly excused herself along with Rob to greet each of the men attending. Rob could not help but notice how each seemed to gravitate more towards Abby than him. Only the married guys tried not to give too much attention to Abby. Rob couldn't help but think this was going to be a long weekend.

After the first wave of men came, and she had given each their packet for the weekend activities and directed them to the registration desk, Abby returned to her desk. She was grateful that most of the men seemed to know the routine and she realized that perhaps she was only there for the professionalism it added to the resort. By half-past six it appeared all the men had arrived and she had to admit she was exhausted. Her jaw was tired from all the talking she had done.

Abby never noticed that Rob had been watching her the whole evening making sure she was safe and that no one would show up unexpected. She sat back at the desk feeling a sense of accomplishment that the evening went well. Rob approached inviting her to dinner with everyone. "You look exhausted, Abby, I'm sorry it was so hectic for you. Are you hungry?"

"I'm starving and yes it was a busy afternoon. All your friends seem really nice and anxious for the golf game tomorrow."

Rob escorted Abby to the very exclusive resort dining room and to the table they would be seated at. Each of the men at their table stood acknowledging and welcoming Abby. Rob pulled Abby's chair out and with his hand on the small of her back guided her into the chair. Once again the electricity that always shot through her from the tip of her toes to the top of her head surged through her. *Why does this happen every time he gets so close or touches me?*

Dinner was delicious and dessert excellent, but Abby had a difficult time keeping her yawning at bay, even with all the conversation that ensued throughout dinner. She enjoyed listening to the stories that they all shared from their college days and it certainly sounded like Rob was the fair-haired child of their class. One of the men they sat with was Josh who had been Rob's roommate all four years of college. They seemed quite close even after all these years.

It was only half-past nine but to Abby it felt like eleven o'clock. "Rob, if you don't mind I think I'm going to head up to the room."

With all the attention the guys were giving Abby, Rob was surprised she was ready to leave, but she did look tired. "I'll take you upstairs. I don't want you going alone."

"I'm sure I'll be fine Rob. I don't want you missing out on anything."

Rob instead excused himself and Abby, telling his friends he would meet them at the pool in thirty minutes. Abby said goodnight as each of the men stood with them.

Rob walked out of the dining room with his hand once again on her lower back. Feeling flushed, Abby knew every eye was on them as they exited the dining room.

Rob made sure the apartment was clear as he checked each room. "We can't be too careful Abby."

"Thanks Rob, I never would have thought to check out each room but don't you think the worst is over and the perpetrator has given up? Detective Rose said that she had not had anything suspicious happen since she moved in."

"I would like to think so but until Jim tells me he feels it's safe, I'm not going to take any chances."

"Goodnight Abby. I'll see you in the morning." Rob wanted to kiss her goodnight but knew that would not be appropriate. Abby continued to think of him as her boss and continued to keep her distance from him even if they did share the same apartment. With his hand on the doorknob, Rob turned to Abby. "And do not, under any circumstance, open this door for any one. Do you hear me? No one."

Abby nodded and could not help but appreciate his genuine concern for her wellbeing. "Goodnight Rob and thanks for tonight. I really enjoyed meeting all your friends."

Abby went to her bedroom and changed into her sleepwear: flannel shorts and a cropped T. All she wanted to do was relax for a bit before heading for bed; it wasn't even ten o'clock. Looking through Rob's DVDs, Abby was sure there had to be a movie she would enjoy watching. After all, he had some good chick flicks on his yacht. *His yacht, and all the time I thought it was Jeff's.* Flipping through the DVDs she found *Fool's Gold.* She always liked Matthew McConaughey and even though she had seen it before, it was a movie like *Overboard* that she could watch over and over again.

Now for some popcorn and I'll be all set. Abby went to the kitchen hoping she would find some microwave popcorn. Letting out a squeal when she found the cabinet it was stored in, made her feel like an eight year old child again. As a little girl she would get so excited when her dad popped a huge bowl of popcorn for everyone to share as they watched a movie or their favorite TV show.

After popping the DVD in, Abby curled up on the couch with her bowl of popcorn. She had not been alone like this for quite some time and she almost felt a little guilty.

Half way through the movie Abby caught herself yawning; she knew it was no biggie. She told herself that she would go to bed as soon as she knew she could no longer keep her eyes open. *I just want to finish this movie and then I'll go to bed.*

She never planned on falling asleep on the couch, but it happened. Rob and his buddy Josh came in about midnight and once again Rob got a picture of Abby passed out on his couch sound asleep. She looked like an angel as he brushed her hair back and took out the clip holding her hair up. Rob knew his buddy was taken aback as he looked at Rob's very own sleeping beauty. "Man, Rob, what's with Abby sleeping on your couch?" Rob explained the whole situation and the fear they had been facing with a perpetrator on the loose. He told him about the destruction to her house and the apartment he put her in after that incident. "I understand the concern," said Josh. "Poor thing it can't be easy for her."

Rob excused himself telling Josh he was going to turn down the bedding on Abby's bed and would return to get her. "Hey, do you want me to carry her in?" asked Josh.

"Absolutely not," scowled Rob. "I'll be right back. It looks like she was watching a chick flick, and once again couldn't stay awake."

"What do you mean, once again?"

Rob explained how she fell asleep on the boat and he had to carry her to bed. "She seems to have a habit of not staying awake long enough to finish any movie she starts." The two men chuckled and Josh patted Rob on the back telling him he had it bad. "Is it that obvious?" Rob didn't wait for his response but quickly headed for Abby's bedroom. When he returned, he scooped her up in his arms and carried her to bed. Abby slipped her arms around his neck when he picked her up but he knew she was still asleep. He gently placed her in the bed and pulled the covers over her.

When Rob returned to the living room, Josh was sitting in the overstuffed leather chair with his head in his hands. For some reason he didn't look like the same guy Rob had known all these years. When Josh looked up, his eyes were watery and filled with such sadness. "Hey man, what's going on? I've never seen you like this and we've been friends for a very long time."

"Ah, it's nothing. I don't think I can talk about it anyway."

"You know you can talk to me, now spill it man."

"Thanks for inviting me up, I had to get away from the crowd."

"I know you and I know it's more than hanging with everyone."

Josh began to pour his heart out to Rob. He confided in him more than he ever intended. "I'm afraid I'm going to lose my company Rob. Things have been really tough and Mary Beth and the kids have gone to stay with her folks. She said she's gone if I can't make things work. I've really not been the best company for her or the kids. With the economy the way it's been, I'm afraid I'm going to lose it all. Construction sure isn't what it used to be."

Rob listened to his friend pouring out his heart to him. This was someone he had known all through college. He had been in his home in California many times; he was best man at their wedding seven years ago. What could have gone so wrong? This guy was a genius. Someone he had always admired and to Rob, Josh had it all: his own business, beautiful home, beautiful wife, two great kids. "What happened, Josh? You had it all."

"Yeah, I DID have it all. I made some really dumb investments hoping they would pay off and it would hold me over until the economy picked up. I should never have started the new development but I thought for sure the high-end houses would sell. Well, when everything tanked, people stopped buying houses. Now I can't even get a loan and the investors are on my back for their money. I could barely scrape enough money together to make the trip out here."

"So, how much are you talking about Josh?"

Josh sat quietly not wanting to sound like a charity case. "That's not why I'm telling you all of this, Rob. Somehow I'll make it through."

"I'm sure you will but I still want to know what you need: a hundred thousand, two hundred thou, or is it more? Come on, tell me man."

"Two hundred and fifty thousand is what I have to come up with for the remaining investors. I paid everyone I could with what I had but a couple of million can go pretty quick."

Rob stood quiet for a few minutes and then went over to his buddy. Putting his arm around his shoulder Rob told him that he would give him three hundred thousand. "And Josh if you need more I want you to come to me."

Josh sat there dumbfounded trying to catch his breath. "Why would you do this Rob? I don't know when I'll be able to repay you. That's a lot of money."

"Josh, I believe in you and I know you can turn things around when the economy straightens out. In fact, I would like to be a silent partner with you in your company. No one needs to know and instead of the three hundred I'm going to kick in a million. This should get those investors off your back, get Mary Beth back 'cause I know she loves you and has probably been under a lot of strain."

"I don't know what to say, Rob, except you know how much you mean to me and how much I love you man."

"You know I love you too and I'm glad we've had this talk."

"And Rob, I really don't care if everybody knows. We don't have to keep it a secret as far as I'm concerned."

"No Josh, I think I like it better that we don't tell anyone. Let's keep it between the two of us for now."

The two men hugged with such emotion.

Men were talking but whom, and where were the voices coming from? *I'm in bed, how did I get here? Oh no not again.* Abby realized that she must have fallen asleep on the couch and Rob once again had carried her to bed. *This is getting embarrassing. I can't imagine what he thinks of me now. Funny, but it certainly sounds like a couple of men talking.* Abby quietly walked out into her hallway and the voices grew louder. She listened intently, only really hearing the last of their conversation but it was enough for Abby to know what is was that Rob was having such a difficult time telling her. *He's gay.* Abby cupped her hand over her mouth. *I never saw this one coming.* But it didn't make sense. How could Rob have kissed her the way he did at her house, he seemed to genuinely care about her from the time she first met him. Although he waited a very long time before he told her who he was; really he didn't tell her it was her mother that told her and then he had to confess. *Maybe he has to maintain a good image for all the magazines that enjoy following him. But how do I get rid of the feelings I have for him? And how do I stop the feeling I get every time he touches me? From now on our relationship is strictly professional. I need my job.*

Abby heard the two men exchange their love for each other and Rob asked Josh if he wanted to spend the night. Not waiting for his answer Abby crept back to her room. She looked at her clock and it was two o'clock. She really needed to get some sleep, although she wondered how that would be happening after what she just heard. Abby lay for a long time wondering if sleep would even come to her. She prayed asking God how she would handle her thoughts of Rob and the feelings growing within. *I'm afraid I'm falling in love with him and now I have to let these feelings go completely.* Isaiah 26:3 came to mind. "You will keep him in perfect peace, whose mind is stayed on you, because he trusts in you." What a perfect verse for her to dwell on as she focused on God's love. She knew God's peace is perfect and her focus should be on Him. After all, she thought, she could never be serious with someone that did not believe as she did anyway. Abby wondered how she should react to Rob and realized that although she did not agree with his lifestyle choice, she knew he had to see Jesus in her. She would have to accept him just as he was. To her surprise she fell fast asleep not knowing what the morning would bring.

Back in the living room, Rob offered Josh his couch while he headed to the linen closet for a blanket and pillow. "This will be like old times, buddy."

Josh was grateful he did not have to go back to his room for the couple of hours left for sleep. "I'll get up earlier and head to my room."

"No need. We're the same size and you can shower and change here in the morning. I think breakfast is being served at six so get some sleep. I'll get you up at five-thirty."

"Sounds great; do you mind if I call Mary Beth in the morning before we hit the links?"

"No, not at all, I'm sure she will be happy to hear from you and give her my love while you're at it."

"I know she is going to be blown away just as much as I am. I know I won't be able to sleep much. I'm so excited. I can't wait to tell her the news."

Chapter 20

When Abby walked into the kitchen, to her relief both men were gone. However, Abby noticed a note on the kitchen counter:

> *Dear Abby,*
> *Josh and I left early for breakfast and then golf. I did not want to wake you. Please meet us for lunch at one in the Cactus Room. I will send Jeff to pick you up at 12:45.*
> *Be safe.*
> *Rob*

Meet for lunch? How do I act? What do I say? I know I have to ignore what I heard last night; there's no way I'm going to say anything. She knew that if she didn't show up Rob would think it strange and probably come looking for her.

Abby spent the time trying to focus on her computer and comparing what she was finding on her books to what Clark had on his. She felt like she was getting close but for some reason there was something she could not seem to put her finger on. It was obvious that Sarah Duncan and Jeremiah Clark were embezzling funds from the company but there was a missing piece. Before she knew it, it was twelve o'clock. She had forty-five minutes to get ready before Jeff arrived. Abby was comfortable around Jeff and felt she knew him better than Rob's brothers, even if he was quite the flirt.

Hoping she would not be underdressed, Abby put on a pair of white fitted dress jeans, an aqua and white floral silk top and a fitted aqua jacket. She slipped on a pair of aqua sandals. This was simply lunch so it shouldn't be a dressy affair and anyway, her first impression last night was what counted. Her makeup was minimal: enough loose powder to cover her freckles, a little blush, some mascara, lip gloss, and she was good to go. She could do nothing about her dimples and complaining about them never helped. She didn't have that much to be smiling about the past couple of weeks anyway. It wasn't that she didn't like her dimples; it was that so many people brought attention to them.

At exactly twelve forty-five there was a knock on the door: Jeff was definitely prompt, like his boss. When she opened the door Jeff just stood there with his mouth open and eyes roving up and down her body. "Please, Jeff, don't look at me like that."

"Sorry I can't help it. You look gorgeous, but then you always do."

"Am I dressed okay for lunch or do you think I should be wearing a dress?"

"Na you look great. The guys down there wouldn't care if you wore a baggy house dress. They still won't be able to take their eyes off you."

Abby giggled at his comment slapping him on his arm. She thought he looked pretty good himself. Jeff wasn't quite as tall as Rob but he had the broad shoulders and handsome looks. He knew he was handsome and it bothered Abby that he was so arrogant, and yet he was always fun to be around.

As they walked to the banquet room, she wondered if she should ask Jeff about Rob's sexual preference. If any one knew him well it was Jeff. She decided against it as this would really be uncomfortable for her.

Jeff took Abby's arm and slipped it in his before entering the room. The Cactus Room was one of the smaller banquet rooms. It was beautifully decorated yet still held a western charm. Rob looked up from the conversation he was having with a few of his friends; noticing Abby with Jeff made his stomach tighten in a knot. He didn't think he was the jealous type but evidently that was not the case. He felt this way every time he saw Abby with any other guy. As he watched the two of them enter the room it wasn't long before Steve and Lucas made their way over, even a few of his friends were quick to wander over to her.

Lunch was great and, as usual, Rob made sure that Abby sat next to him. After dessert Rob went to the microphone up front to thank everyone for coming and to give away the prizes that the guys won. Abby had no idea he did this and it was great fun watching the men light up when their name was announced for a particular prize. The prizes were not inexpensive at all: one was a Caribbean cruise for two, another a set of very expensive golf clubs and bag, an all-expense paid trip to Disneyland for an entire family, and the prize of all prizes was a new Lexus. It appeared that everyone won something even if they were only very generous gift cards. Abby was amazed at Rob's generosity even if he did have the money to do it.

Everyone was saying their goodbyes once all the prizes were handed out, with Rob getting all the attention and thanks from his peers. It was obvious to her that he was a very special man. Most had flights to make and could not hang around very long. Abby thought it strange how Rob knew so much about each of these college buddies and yet his crew he knew nothing about. *Perhaps if they're an employee they're not on the same level as his college buddies, so I wonder where that leaves me anyway. Oh well, I no longer have to think about that.*

Rob kept his eye on Abby for much of the afternoon that he felt a little bit like a stalker. His two brothers and Jeff stood with her laughing and talking much of the time. He could hear her laugh from across the room, and he loved it. She wasn't doing much of that lately. He was pleased she was having a good time and wished he were part of their conversation. Josh was the last man to leave but before he did the two men came over to join the others. Steve told Josh that it would not have been a problem having him fly out with him.

"Thanks Steve but I really wasn't sure if I would have been able to make it this year." Giving Rob a nod he continued. "I can't believe I won the cruise tickets. I really don't think I should accept."

"You won it fair and square. You made the one putt on the 13th hole: the longest putt of the game. You deserve it."

"I can't thank you enough, Rob." He turned to Rob giving him a hearty embrace and it looked like he was having a difficult time holding back the tears.

Oh brother, maybe he wanted to take Rob with him on the cruise and knows that would be impossible. For sure the whole world would know. Shame on me, I shouldn't even think that: not a godly thought at all. Abby felt bad and knew she would have to guard her thoughts from now on.

Lucas and Steve would not be heading out until morning and for this Abby was grateful. They would all have dinner together and she was sure the men would have something planned, if not, simply a relaxing evening together. Of course Jeff wasn't leaving any time soon.

Abby would have loved to go to church tomorrow and wondered how she could get away when a light bulb went off in her head. *I can call Millie I'm sure she would not mind picking me up for church.* Millie was a very sweet friend and a widow for many years and did not live too far from the resort. She was sure Millie passed the resort on her way to church. Now telling Rob would be a different story. She didn't know if this was something he would allow without making a fuss. *Well, it was her life and he couldn't control everything.*

Chapter 21

The evening went well and Abby was able to call Millie for a ride to church. Millie was delighted to pick her up and asked if she would mind going to the second service. She would pick her up at nine forty-five and told Abby it would be great fun to go out for Sunday dinner together. Abby rolled her eyes but agreed knowing Millie was probably lonely. At least it would get Abby out for a while and best of all, she was not going to miss church once again.

After everyone left the apartment, Abby approached Rob with the announcement that Millie would be picking her up for church at nine forty-five. Rob tightened his lips as he considered this. "You know I don't think it wise that you go off alone like that? We still don't know who's watching you or this apartment."

"But Rob let's face it. Detective Ashley said herself that every time she has gone out, when I've been locked up in here, no one has followed her anywhere."

"Hey, you make it sound like I'm keeping you a prisoner in this apartment. Is this what you think, because if it is… I'm sorry!"

Abby's face felt flush after the words escaped her mouth. She did not want to hurt him. She quickly walked over putting her arm on his. "Rob I'm so sorry. That is not what I meant at all. I know you're trying to protect me and I appreciate it more than you know. I hate to miss church and I know Millie passes the resort on her way; she was thrilled that I asked her for a ride."

"Abby, I could have easily had the limo take you to church."

"And then what? Alex waits outside for church to let out? Maybe you should just take me?"

"Yeah, I guess that wouldn't look too good, and no, I really can't take you. You don't understand what it would be like having me walk into a church."

"I guess I don't, Rob." Abby had no idea what he meant but she was not going to push the issue. It was his life and his conscience and maybe he could not deal with conviction.

Abby heard Rob let out a huge sigh, resigning himself to the fact that Millie would be picking her up. She was sure he had been holding his breath the whole time. They said goodnight to each other and walked to their respective suites. It was a long and a busy day for both of them and sleep sounded good.

Abby woke early, showered and got ready for church. She was so looking forward to it. She put on a floral sundress, a strappy pair of sandals, and grabbed a light sweater, just in case it was cold in church. She left her hair down and wondered if that was a wise choice. If it was really humid today, her hair would be way too curly for her own good but so far it looked like a sunny day and the forecast was for low humidity; she'd take her chances.

When she walked out to the living room Rob was already seated on the couch waiting for her. She couldn't help but notice the bright smile on his face when he looked up at her. *Man this guy can send all the wrong messages.* "Good morning Rob."

"Good morning Abby. You're looking beau…great this morning."

"Thanks. I thought I would meet Millie out in front of the resort after breakfast. I don't think I need to come back to the room." Abby grabbed her handbag and slipped her Kindle Fire into it. Although she preferred carrying her Bible so she could underline and write notes in it, using her Fire meant she would not be forgetting her Bible at church, or in Millie's car.

Abby hugged Steve and Lucas goodbye and said she hoped she would see them soon. Steve told her that he would be taking off in the company plane and when it returned they would pick up Lucas and take him to Florida. Abby knew Lucas's aversion to flying and understood his reasoning for not going with Steve to California.

Rob walked Abby out to the front and it was only minutes before Millie pulled up. Rob greeted Millie and opened the door for Abby; she felt like he was tucking her into bed. "Let me know when you're heading home and I will come out to meet you. Do you understand me?"

Abby nodded and said she would give him a call on her way home. She told him she and Millie would be going out for dinner after church. Rob looked a little downcast when she told him that and said she appreciated his concern.

Chapter 22

Monday morning came and Abby was in such a good mood after being in church yesterday. Rob wasn't anywhere to be found either in the kitchen or the living area. She immediately went to the piano and started playing and singing. She loved when her spirit soared along with the music. *What a perfect way to start the week!* When she stopped she heard coughing; looking up, there was Rob leaning against the entryway. "Please don't stop because of me."

"I'm finished, and besides, I really need to grab a cup of coffee." Once again Rob had a plethora of breakfast items set out on the counter for her. She couldn't hold back the smile as she thought of his thoughtfulness.

"After some breakfast do you want to take a ride around the property? We can drive down to the stable and pick out a couple of horses."

Abby's eyes lit up in complete excitement. "I would love nothing more than to get on a horse. Is that why you're dressed in jeans and cowboy boots?"

"Yep; I was pretty sure you would be up for a ride today. We can look at the property out back and you can give me your ideas for that dude ranch."

Abby gulped her coffee and quickly ate a bagel with cream cheese but Rob insisted she also have some scrambled eggs for some protein. She knew he was right as they would be riding and need the sustenance. Wiping her chin she ran off to put on her jeans. She was pleased she had taken her cowboy boots from her house knowing one day they may come in handy; remembering at the time what "Bob York" told her about having horses on the property.

She returned in no time, putting her hair up in a ponytail, then pulling on her boots—she was ready to go.

Rob stood chuckling at her excitement. She looked so cute he wanted to wrap his arms around her. In a matter of minutes they were out the door.

They drove to the stables and Abby could hardly sit still. Rob could not help reaching for her hand and holding it. She looked down at what was happening and tried to gently slip her hand from his. It broke her heart to do it but she couldn't let her feelings for him be damaged any more than they were already. With her heart racing she didn't know if it was from him holding her hand or the excitement of being on a horse once again.

Abby stood in awe at the beautiful horse flesh in each stall. She would certainly have a difficult time picking one out. "Rob, which horse do you think would be good for me?" She went from horse to horse nuzzling each nose and stroking each neck. One in particular stood out as she went down the shed row. An Appaloosa with the biggest brightest eyes she had ever seen caught her eye. "I think I like this one", she said as she stroked her between the ears. "Hey girl, ya gonna let me ride ya?"

Rob was impressed with the affection she was giving the horse. "She's a beauty all right. That's Princess and she really thinks she's an Indian princess. Not too many want to ride her. She's spoiled and can be pretty stubborn, but if you think you can handle her, she's all yours."

"I'd love to try. Give me a few minutes in the pen to get my bearings and get the feel of her. We'll see what happens."

Abby was surprised to hear Rob call someone up to come down and saddle the horses. She gave Rob a questioning look. "What? What are you looking at?"

"I'm looking at you. I can't believe you actually called someone to come down and saddle the horses. I can saddle my own horse and I can saddle yours too."

Rob felt a little embarrassed but it was something he was used to doing. He simply shrugged his shoulders, brushing off her insinuation that he was not even capable of saddling his own horse. "That's how it is when you have money."

"Yeah, too much money", Abby said under her breath.

It wasn't long before Ricardo, "Ricky", was there meeting them in the tack room. He took one look at Abby and knew exactly which saddle to put her in. Rob already had his own saddle and Miguel quickly went to work getting the blankets, bit, and saddles together.

Abby offered to bring her horse down to the tack room to make it easier to saddle and Ricky gave her a halter and lead. She found a candy dish with peppermints when she was walking down to the stall and put a couple in her pocket. *These will come in handy if I need a treat for Princess.* She made haste in getting the lead on Princess and began leading her down the shed row to the tack room; talking to her horse all the way. Abby took the lead and started to head back to the stalls to get Rob's horse. He mentioned that his horse was the black stallion named Midnight. As she walked she realized Rob had caught up to her. "I guess I can lead my own horse down."

Ricky gave Abby a leg up; it felt so good to be back on a horse. Princess stepped sideways a little but Abby quickly got her steady and never stopped whispering to her. Rob was impressed with her skills so far. He had no problem mounting Midnight and Abby's heart hitched as she noticed how truly handsome he was. His jean shirt fit him perfectly as it stretched across his broad shoulders and back. There was something about a man on a horse that got to her every time. She quickly shook off the feelings she was having, snapping her back to reality. Miguel opened the pen for her and she rode anticipating the antics Rob warned her about.

Abby rode comfortably for a brief time in the pen, pleased with how responsive Princess was to her commands. When she was ready she nodded to Rob who was waiting patiently for her as he talked with Ricky. Rob told her they wouldn't have enough time to ride the whole perimeter of the property so they took a trail that went through the woods leading to the lake beyond. Rob's heart warmed not being able to take his eyes off of her. She was quite the horsewoman and certainly knew how to ride; pride bubbled up in his heart. He had always said that his woman would have to love horses and be able to ride. *Could it get any better than this?* Yes it could because right now he knew she was pulling away from him. He hoped Aunt Charlotte would make things right. *She had to.*

They rode for quite a while through the magnificent poplar and oak trees only to ride out into a beautiful meadow. Just beyond was a beautiful crystal blue lake. It looked like sparkling diamonds glistening on the surface; it was breathtaking. "I never would have pictured this scene from my office window," said Abby as she looked up at Rob. "There is only a glimpse of the lake beyond all those beautiful trees from my window."

"I know. It is a beautiful scene. Tell me what you envision for all this property."

Rob saw the twinkle in her eye and thought it was the dude ranch she was thinking about but instead, her eyes were focused on a hill south of where they were standing. "I'll race you to that hill first", said Abby. "Then I'll tell you what I've been thinking about when I first mentioned my idea to… Bob York." She gave him the biggest smile and sure enough those adorable dimples of hers could not possibly hide.

Rob nodded as they lined up to take off. He could not believe she had enough confidence in Princess already to think she could beat him with his stallion. Midnight was one of the fastest horses he owned. "Okay, on the count of three we go. One. Two. Three."

They were off and Abby was riding hard. She was practically standing up in the stirrups and to Rob's amazement, she was flying. He did not let up either but was just as determined to win as she was. They rode neck and neck until Abby took the reins slapping them gently on the backside of Princess. She took off like a shot. Rob did the same but Abby still beat him by a nose. Both out of breath and panting, they dismounted. Abby had to hold her side she was so winded. Rob put his arm around her shoulders congratulating her for a great ride. "I never thought that horse could ever beat me like that. That was an amazing ride."

"Thanks. I think I've bonded with Princess: she's an amazing horse." Abby reached into her pocket un-wrapping a peppermint; she offered it to Princess. She took it anxiously but glanced at her partner, Midnight. Abby and Rob laughed as it was obvious Princess was looking out for her buddy. She un-wrapped another peppermint and offered it to Midnight who took it eagerly. Abby had a new friend.

Rob offered Abby a seat on the grassy knoll. They both lay back in the grass gazing up at the white puffy clouds. It was a perfect day and Abby was thrilled to be out of that apartment and enjoying God's magnificent creation.

She sat up noticing a herd of cattle way over to her left on the other side of a hill. "I never noticed the cattle before. Who owns them?"

"I do. I have about 200 head. Not a lot but enough to make me feel like a rancher."

"Wow, I can't believe it—they're beautiful Texas Longhorns. How much land do they have to roam?"

"I really don't know. Several hundred acres I guess. I have a few ranch hands that run this part of the property."

"Why is it that I've never seen anything on the books that deals with the ranch? I've never seen anything come in for feed or payroll, or any expenses for that matter."

"The ranch happens to be independent of the resorts. Ricky's dad, Miguel, is my foreman. Ricky's brothers, Juan and Pedro, are the other ranch hands. Miguel is Maria's husband. They've been with me for over five years now. Their sister Gabriella is the youngest. I think Miguel and Maria have been more like my parents than my own dad and stepmom. Other than Aunt Charlotte, they have been my family and I love them dearly. Miguel handles all the expenses and payroll for the ranch which comes from a separate fund... Now tell me what you envision for your dude ranch."

Abby sat wide-eyed listening to how much the Ortiz family meant to him but began explaining her idea of a dude ranch, a very exclusive dude ranch. She knew that with the clientele they catered

160

to, they would have no problem attracting the guests that would be willing to spend any amount of money for an unforgettable family vacation. At first she thought of using the lake for non-motorized water craft but now she wanted to see it remain pristine and a place where guests could simply relax and enjoy the beauty of it. Rob was taking it all in with interest and after Abby exhausted all her ideas she lay back down on the grass.

"What vision. That's a great idea and I have just the developer you can work with."

"Me? You want me to work with a developer?"

"Yes I do, and I want you to tell him exactly what's in that pretty little head of yours that you just told me." Rob leaned over and tweaked her nose before continuing. "That's what my friend Josh does, he's a developer, and I have an architect we can work with."

Abby stiffened at the mention of Josh's name. She knew this was not the right attitude but right now lying beside Rob, the race, the closeness, she was having a hard time reconciling her feelings with Rob's relationship with Josh. She willed herself not to dwell on this or allow it to cause a barrier in their friendship. Because that's exactly how she had to look at Rob: a boss and a friend, nothing more. Giving Rob a wry smile Abby started to rise. "Hey, I think the horses grazed enough. Want to ride over to the lake for a bit?" Abby needed to get her mind off of Rob and Josh.

Rob quickly noticed the change in Abby's countenance and the twinkle that she had all morning had dimmed. *What did I say? What did I do?* Rob wasn't aware of anything other than perhaps Abby was feeling a bit too comfortable with him and having too great a time. He ran his hand through his thick hair and wondered if he would ever figure her out.

They rode quietly side by side down to the lake. They dismounted and allowed the horses to drink from the bank. Little was said other than how beautiful the scenery was. Abby said she needed to get back and do some work. Rob only wished that returning would have been as memorable as their ride out.

Abby quickly showered when returning to the apartment and told Rob that she would be working in her office the rest of the day.

Chapter 23

Abby spent each day, since their ride, in her office focusing on her job. She saw very little of Rob and for this she was grateful. A couple of evenings they had dinner together but ate pretty much in silence talking about work and how the case was going.

Rob had talked to Jim on Tuesday and was told that they were going to remove Detective Ashley from the case as there had been no incidents to warrant her continuance. Jim also told Rob that Abby could return to her home or her apartment at any time whichever he felt the most comfortable with. Rob was not about to tell Abby she could return home. He knew she would jump at the chance. Lt. Jansen also told him that they expected the subpoena to come through any time and since they had arrested Jeremiah Clark in California and would soon have a warrant to arrest Sarah Duncan, they would have the two involved in this embezzlement scheme behind bars.

They would be leaving Friday afternoon for Aunt Charlotte's and Rob was hoping this would give them a chance to remove whatever barriers were keeping Abby so indifferent to him. They were friends but that seemed to be where the line was drawn as far as Abby was concerned.

Abby prayed each and every night for Rob asking God for wisdom and grace in how to handle their friendship. She needed to love him as Jesus loved him, unconditionally, and she was determined to do this. She also needed to guard her heart from a different kind of love that she was having for him: happy she had never expressed any of these feelings to him. He would probably wonder how in the world he could have led her on to feel this way.

It was early Friday morning and Abby hoped she was up before Rob; she grabbed a quick cup of coffee and bagel before she headed to the office. She was wrong as she looked up to see Rob leaning against the doorframe looking at her. "Good morning Abby. You're up pretty early."

"Yes I am. I thought I could get a few things done before our trip. My bag is packed and I'm basically all set to leave whenever you say."

"Good. Why don't we leave before noon and we can have lunch on the plane? Do you want me to stop by your office or meet you back here... say eleven o'clock?"

"I'll meet you up here at eleven. That way I can freshen up and pick up my bag."

"Abby you don't have to pick up your bag. I'll have a bellman come up for it; he has to pick mine up anyway." Rolling her eyes at him he continued, "I'll meet you here then. Hey, got some extra coffee in there?"

Abby was embarrassed that she never thought to offer him a cup of coffee and hoped the red flush in her face wasn't noticeable. "Oh, sorry, yes there's plenty of coffee," Abby said as she reached for another cup and filled it with coffee.

"Thanks Abby. Do you want me to walk you down to your office?"

"I'm sure I'll be fine but thanks anyway. I need to head down now so I get something done. I'll see you at eleven." Abby left but not without an ache in her heart. *I know I'll get over this feeling but how long is it going to take? Two broken hearts within the year would be unbearable.*

Rob watched Abby leave and once again it felt like he was punched in the gut when she walked away. *I sure hope Aunt Charlotte sets things right 'cause I'm not going to last much longer.* For some strange reason, Rob sensed the need to pray. He really didn't know what he was praying for but he also knew he hated when people used God as some Genie. If you rubbed the lamp he would grant you any wish you had. He desperately wanted Abby but he also wanted to pray for what God wanted for his life. It had been a very long time since Rob had prayed for anything. He remembered the last time he prayed was for God to heal his mom but that never happened. As a fourteen year old boy all he could think of was, "What was the point of praying when his mom still died?" Even though his Aunt Charlotte continued to take him to youth group and sending him to high school camp, the idea of praying for anything was something he could never bring himself to do. He walked into the living room and sat in the leather chair; holding his head in his hands he rested his arms on his knees and began to pray. He poured his heart out to God asking him to forgive him for all the years he had neglected Him. He didn't miss telling God how much he wanted Abby and asking what he could do to convince her that he was not the man she read about. When he finished praying he felt peace like he had not felt in a very long time. Of course he knew this did not mean that Abby would be dropped in his lap either – *only time will tell.*

Abby arrived back in the apartment at ten o'clock knowing this would give her enough time to freshen up and be ready when Rob arrived. After a quick change and fresh make up, she straightened her suite, cleaned her bathroom, and was cleaning up in the kitchen when Rob came back in. She knew he never liked her doing any of the cleaning but it was hard for her not to. He wanted her to leave it for housekeeping but she hated leaving dishes in the sink and a dirty coffee pot when it was just as easy for her to do it herself. She hated being waited on.

"What 'cha doing?" asked Rob, trying to be as nonchalant as possible as he walked into the kitchen. He noticed her cleaning up and gave her an inquisitive look. He bit his tongue refusing to be condescending; she was who she was and nothing was going to change her. "The crew is ready and the plane should be ready for take off at eleven-thirty."

"Rob, we both know that plane is not going anywhere without you. However, I am ready. I have to get my bag out of my room."

Rob told her that he would get it as he walked towards her suite. He looked around at her perfectly clean room and knew she had already made sure everything was spotless and in order. He could not keep the grin from curling around his mouth. *I don't think I could change her if I tried. Abby is Abby and that's all there is to it. She really is the girl next door.*

The flight to San Diego was non-eventful. Abby always loved spending time with the crew and especially talking to Jenny.

The crew would be staying at the resort until they returned. The limo was waiting for them and a car was waiting for Rob and Abby. "Another expensive car", thought Abby: this one was a red Ferrari. Rob opened the door for her and ran around to the driver's side. Sliding in beside her he gave her a wink as he started the engine. "You really like your fast cars," she said as she hung on for dear life. Rob chuckled but did not say anything until they were on the highway.

They drove for about thirty-five minutes before they arrived at Aunt Charlotte's house in La Jolla. This is not a house, thought Abby, this is a mansion. They pulled up to a huge gate before following the driveway leading to the house. Rob pushed a few keys on the entry pad and the massive gates opened. The driveway was incredibly long and lined with the most beautiful shrubs and flowers. The gardens were massive and welcoming, leading to the marble steps and entrance. On either side of the landing was a pedestal pot overflowing with flowers. Abby could see where this home must have been the inspiration for the San Diego resort because the design and gardens were very similar. Abby stood in awe in front of the massive double entry doors. Jackson, Aunt Charlotte's butler, answered the door, however, Aunt Charlotte was right behind him shooing him to get out of her way. Rob and Abby were greeted with the warmest hugs as they entered the beautiful foyer. There were two winding staircases on either side of the foyer leading to a balcony that overlooked the entrance. A beautiful crystal chandelier hung from the ceiling, the largest one Abby had ever seen in a home. Aunt Charlotte invited them into the parlor which in itself was breathtaking. Everything was light blue and gold. It was ornate but done with exquisite taste. Beautiful oil paintings lined the walls and Abby was certain they had to be originals. "Your home is lovely Aunt Charlotte. I have never been in a mansion."

Aunt Charlotte was humble as she took Abby's arm and gently led her to the couch in the parlor. "Thank you my dear. I know I have been very blessed and all of this is temporary. I know the mansion God has for me will far outdo this old place. My grandfather built this house in 1929. It has been renovated a few times and everything has been modernized so I think it will stay the way it is for quite some time. Rob can show you around if you like. I think you will enjoy the pool and gardens out back."

Rob asked Abby if she liked to play tennis and when he saw the glimmer in her eye he knew her answer. "I love tennis. I played in high school and loved it, although…I'm really not very good."

As they walked through the largest kitchen Abby had ever been in her entire life, it was hard for her to keep walking: marble and glass tile everywhere, two commercial stainless refrigerators, a gas stove with at least nine burners, two dishwashers, warming ovens, and even a wood burning pizza oven in one of the corners. The French doors opened to the formal veranda which Abby was sure could hold close to a hundred people; another patio was ten steps below—it was just as big but even more impressive was the array of colors bursting forth all around her as she walked down the steps. Breathtaking hardly described how beautiful the scene was. The swimming pool looked like it was transported from a Roman palace and to the right was the tennis court. The Pacific Ocean was just beyond the gardens and hedge of shrubs on her left. "This is so beautiful. Is that a private beach on the other side of the hedge?"

Rob looked to where she was pointing. "Yes it is," Rob leaned into Abby putting his arm around her shoulder showing her where the break was in the hedge and the path that led to the beach. He wondered why she stiffened but after a few minutes she seemed to relax as she leaned into him. The electricity she continued to feel whenever he touched her was still there and something she could not seem to control. She knew she had to get away from him; being this close was impossible. She was sure that once "his secret" was out in the open things would not be this awkward. Abby started walking toward the tennis court.

"So when do you want a tennis match?" Abby asked hoping the subject change wasn't too noticeable.

"What about tomorrow morning? Will you be up for it?"

"Absolutely. You're on, just let me know what time."

Rob chuckled as he thought about it for a moment. "Let's say seven o'clock."

"You have got to be kidding. Tomorrow is Saturday and my day off."

"Okay, how about eight then? We can have coffee first and then a game. We'll do breakfast after."

Down another beautiful flower strewn path Abby noticed another house. "Whose house is that? It looks like it's on the same property."

"Yes, it's part of Aunt Charlotte's property. That happens to be where the caretaker and his wife Rosa live. Rosa is Aunt Charlotte's cook. They've been with her ever since I can remember. In fact they worked for my grandfather. He died about eight years ago. With all my work, I never really saw much of my grandfather but he was a very loving man. I think that's why my mom and Aunt Charlotte are such loving people. I know God has always been the focus in their home, even for my grandparents."

Abby thought it quite interesting hearing him talk of God. "That's awesome, Rob, what a great heritage you have. I know I'm so thankful for my parents and grandparents and what they instilled in me from when I was a young girl. What was your grandmother like? Do you remember her?"

"Both my grandparents were very loving. My grandma died shortly after my mom died. I think it broke her heart to lose one of her girls. They were all very close. My grandpa went on but his laughter just wasn't the same. Aunt Charlotte always took me to visit him. He lived mostly at the New York residence. Aunt Charlotte lives here most of the time now but ever so often she goes back for a stay. I think the memories are too much for her at either house but she seems better now that the houses have been completely renovated."

"I can't imagine having that much. Owning my own home was always a dream of mine. I can't imagine owning two."

Rob wasn't about to tell her that he also owned a home on one of the islands in Fiji, a condo in Aspen, and that one day the two houses of Aunt Charlotte's would be his. *She will freak out if I tell her all that.*

They had walked back to the house almost out of breath for all the walking they did of the grounds. Rosa stood at the stove in the kitchen and Rob came up behind her giving her a big hug. "It's so good to see you again Rosa." Rosa gave his arm a pat and told him it was good to have him home for the weekend.

Aunt Charlotte came into the kitchen when she heard them walk in. "Dinner will be served in about a half hour. If this is too early let us know. I'm sure Rosa can put it off for a while longer." Rob caught the look Rosa gave his aunt and knew she wouldn't be happy putting dinner off.

Rob glanced at Abby and she nodded. "Oh no, that sounds great. I don't know about Abby but I'm starved."

"Robby you are always starved." Aunt Charlotte looked at Abby. "He was always "starved" as a young boy. Sometimes I wondered where that boy was putting all the food that was going into him." Rosa agreed and they all laughed at her comment. Rob felt his face flush in embarrassment.

"I hope this isn't going to be a "pick on Rob weekend." There are some things that should just never be shared."

Abby wondered if his "secret" was one of the things he never wanted shared with anyone. I guess this weekend would tell.

Abby was downstairs and in the kitchen before eight. The coffee pot was on and she helped herself to a cup. Looking out the beautiful French doors she noticed Rob sitting with his aunt having coffee. The outdoor furniture was without a doubt very expensive. Abby definitely did not need to see the price tag to reach that conclusion. She got comfortable in one of the overstuffed cushions and sat back enjoying her coffee with them. There was a tray of biscotti; Rob knew she could never refuse a biscotti. "You know me too well. Rob, it's not fair and you know they're my weakness."

Aunt Charlotte took one look at Abby. "Oh honey, with a shape like yours you have absolutely nothing to worry about."

"Thanks Aunt Charlotte, but I can't keep eating these or I will no longer have any shape."

"Are you ready for our match? Maybe you could burn off some of those calories." Rob said with a twinkle in his eye.

"Buddy you are on. You're the one that will be burning off the calories."

There game was fast and Abby knew she was giving Rob a real run for his money. She wasn't as out of shape as she was afraid she may be. Abby beat Rob two out of the three sets. She tried very hard not to rub it in but could not resist. Rob took it well and gave it right back to her how he had let her win one of the games. "Okay Rob, I'll admit it was a close game since I beat you by one point, but a win is a win and I won't believe for one minute that you let me win."

Rob picked up the phone that was a direct line to the house. "Hey Rosa, would you please have a pitcher of iced tea and a couple of glasses sent down to the lower patio? Yeah that would be good too, thanks." Rob noticed Abby laughing at him. "What? What are you laughing at?"

"I'm laughing at you. I can't believe you actually called Rosa to bring us some iced tea. You can't even walk up to the kitchen yourself?"

"Rosa loves it, and besides it is her job. Anyway, she'll have Jackson bring it down."

Abby rolled her eyes as she began the walk up to the house. Rob followed and as he did he found himself praying and asking God if he would please give him Abby for a wife. *What am I doing? Am I willing to admit I want her for a wife and if I want her for my wife what does that mean? That I love her?* Rob knew that something happened to him yesterday when he prayed. He had peace and joy that he really could not explain. And if Aunt Charlotte asked him to go to church tomorrow, he would not argue with her.

When they arrived at the patio, she did not want to admit that it was pretty nice to have their drinks and a bowl of fruit waiting for them; never would she give Rob the satisfaction.

Chapter 24

They each sat comfortably on a chaise lounge enjoying the tea and fruit. Abby couldn't help but ask about his sweet aunt. "I take it your aunt never married? She's still a fairly young woman, and very attractive I might add." Rob looked her way and started to tell Abby about his mom and aunt: "As I mentioned before, my mom and Aunt Charlotte were identical twins and extremely close all their lives. I guess when they were younger they pulled a couple of fast ones on their teachers and even my dad."

Abby gave him a puzzled look. "What do you mean they pulled a couple of fast ones on their teachers and your dad?"

"From what my grandpa told me they dressed the same but the bracelets they wore, when they were younger, to identify themselves for the teachers, they had switched. The teachers could never figure out who was who. When my mom had a date with my dad, my aunt took her place a couple of times. Rob chuckled as he thought about it. My dad was always at their house but as well as he thought he could tell them apart he really couldn't. I visited with my grandpa after my college graduation and I'm grateful for the time I spent with him then. I learned so much about my mom and aunt. Grandpa said that Aunt Charlotte was really madly in love with my dad but when she found out that my mom loved him she backed off and never got between them again."

"Awe, that's so sweet but at the same time very sad. So your aunt never found anyone else?"

"No, I think she has always loved my dad and continues to love him from afar. They have never talked since the accident. My dad allowed her to come and care for my mom after the accident but when she died my dad totally ignored her and said he did not want her ever in his home again. She insisted on seeing me and told him that I was like her own son and she would not abandon me. He conceded and said she could pick me up and take me to church and youth group or to lunch or dinner but that was it. I met her outside in her car. I know it broke her heart but she never let on how much he had hurt her. Whenever I look at my aunt I always feel like I'm looking at my mom and that's exactly how she would look now. I really love my aunt so much. She's been my rock."

Abby reached over putting her hand on his forearm. "Rob, I'm sure Aunt Charlotte feels the same about you. I think she's poured her life into you and is so very proud of all you have accomplished."

"Thanks Abby. I wouldn't be who I am without her. When I met with my grandpa ten years ago, he told me about my inheritance from my mom and what he put in a trust for me. Needless to say, that's how I got my start and much of it I have never had the need to use."

"Well, it sounds like God has really blessed you in so many ways."

"Yes he has." Rob stared into Abby's beautiful green eyes and then those luscious lips of hers. He had all he could do to not reach over and pull her into his arms and kiss her. *Some other time, man, just not today.*

Abby quickly turned her head feeling the heat rise all the way from her toes to her face. She hadn't realized that she had been staring into his beautiful ocean- blue eyes. She could drown in those eyes of his, they were definitely mesmerizing. She was relieved to see Aunt Charlotte walking down the stairs to the patio they were on. "I'm not disturbing anything, am I Robby? I thought you were going over to the resort this afternoon."

"Yes I'm planning to. I need to shower and head over there."

"Good, then we girls can have a nice visit."

Abby realized this would be "the talk" Rob had asked his aunt to have with her. She definitely did not want Aunt Charlotte to feel embarrassed or awkward in talking about his sexual preference so she would have to think of how she would respond when the subject came up.

Rob excused himself and started jogging up the steps. Abby felt flushed as she watched him; thinking what a handsome man he is. Aunt Charlotte could not help but notice the way Abby looked at her nephew. "He's a handsome man, isn't he?"

"Umm, yes he is. He's also a very kind man."

Rob came back down once he was showered and ready for the office. He looked gorgeous and Abby got a whiff of his cologne that was all Rob. She loved how he smelled. *Don't even go there.* Abby chided herself for her thoughts. *I'm about to get "the talk" from Aunt Charlotte and it's not about how much he may love me or cares about me. That really sounds caddy and I know I should not be like this. Lord, forgive me. I want to be Rob's friend and love him unconditionally as a friend. I know I keep saying this but I have to mean it. There is no reason why he should love me and I certainly should not be in love with him…we have a friendship.*

Abby smiled at Aunt Charlotte but excused herself to go shower. "I think I need to clean up a bit and then I'll be back down."

"You do that dear. Perhaps we can have a bite of lunch after you've showered."

Lunch was delicious and Abby knew this was a lifestyle she could never get used to. It was one thing living at the resort with all the wait staff and housekeeping but being doted on like this in someone's private home was so outside her element. They ate on the veranda and after the dishes were removed it didn't take Aunt Charlotte long before she mentioned Rob. "Abby there is something Rob has asked me to tell you. It's been rather difficult for him to explain and he really does not believe it's something you will understand."

Abby was happy she had rehearsed her thoughts while in the shower. She was pleased that she already knew what Aunt Charlotte wanted to say. "Aunt Charlotte, you don't have to tell me anything. I already know what you are going to say, and I do understand. I certainly do not want to make it difficult for you. I do know about Rob and one day it will all work out."

"You do?" Aunt Charlotte was a bit chagrined and confused but grateful she did not have to explain anything to Abby. *Perhaps Rob found a good time to tell her before the trip out here.* "Well dear, that sure made my job easy. Now let's have some coffee and dessert."

The afternoon went by quickly as the two women sat outside the entire afternoon sipping coffee, talking, more coffee, talking, then iced tea, then more talking. Abby loved spending time with Aunt Charlotte. They formed a bond that only one could share with a sister in Christ.

Abby was drawn to the crystal pool and hoped that Aunt Charlotte would ask if she would like to swim. Aunt Charlotte glanced at Abby and saw her gazing at the pool. "Did you bring your suit?"

"Yes I did. Rob told me to pack it, and if you don't mind I would love to try out your pool."

"Honey, you go right ahead. I think we have talked ourselves out anyway. I so enjoyed my time with you. I can see why Rob loves you so much. You are an absolute angel."

He loves me so much? Oh, I get it: he loves me as he would love a sister. That's okay; I'm trying to work through this. Lord, give me the strength to love him as you do—nothing more.

Abby quickly changed into her suit and when she returned to the patio Aunt Charlotte told her the bath houses by the pool had plenty of towels and a float mattress if she wanted to relax in the water. Abby thanked her and immediately left for the bath house that was situated a few feet from the pool. This too was gorgeous with beautifully appointed changing rooms. Each house had more than you could possibly imagine: a heated towel rack, a comfy couch and chairs placed in front of a fireplace, sauna, and shower. Abby grabbed a towel and a mattress and walked to the pool. She had put her hair up high so she could avoid getting it wet as much as possible since she had washed it just a couple of hours ago. Before slipping into the beautiful crystal blue waters of the pool her breath caught as she looked out into the Pacific Ocean; noticing a few sail boats not far from shore and a cruise ship out in the distance. It was a picture to behold and Abby wished she were an artist and could capture the beautiful scene. She began effortlessly swimming laps, now this was something she could easily get used to; the pool temperature had to be at least eighty-five degrees. After her fifteen laps she was exhausted and looked forward to relaxing on the float mattress allowing her to soak up a few rays before getting out.

To her shock there was a thud and huge splash almost tipping her off the mattress; taking her completely off-guard. Coming up out of the water right beside her came Rob with the biggest smile on his face, "hey, did I surprise you?"

"Of course you surprised me and you probably got my hair soaked. I have been trying my best not to get it soaking wet."

"I'm so sorry," said Rob, but as far as Abby could tell he wasn't the least bit sorry because the grin never left his face. "How about I race you to the other end of the pool?"

Abby always liked a challenge as she slid off the float. "You're on and no cheating this time and no dunking me under either."

"Hey, I don't cheat… and I can't make any promises."

Rob was impressed with Abby's swimming abilities. *Is there anything she isn't good at?* He tried coming up along side of her to dunk her under but she slipped under his arm and took off. She raced to the ladder and quickly pulled herself up and out. Rob followed right behind her and pulled her down into the grass; their laughter was heard throughout the entire backyard. When they came to their senses they both realized their situation and a sudden rush of awkwardness settled on both of them. Rob was the first to get up and retrieve a towel that he quickly wrapped around her. He hadn't noticed her black bikini until they stopped their innocent romp. Rob's chest tightened as he quickly covered her but not before he was once again consumed with her beauty. *She is going to be the death of me. Lord, give me the strength to be the godly man you want me to be.* Rob knew God was working on his heart and something incredible happened to him yesterday in his apartment. He didn't fully understand all that was taking place in his life but he knew God was doing something. Rob held out his hand for Abby, putting her hand in his, and pulled her up from the ground. The electricity that passed between them was still there.

Abby went over to the pool to take out the mattress but Rob quickly stopped her. "You don't have to put it away, someone will clean up." Once again Abby gave him that look as if he was incapable of doing anything himself. "Come on Abby let's go change. Believe me when I say they really don't mind cleaning up after me...they're used to it." He gave her a wink and they began their walk up to the house. Again Abby's legs felt like rubber as she made the long walk up the stairs, hoping in time all these sensations she felt when she was near Rob would burn out. Just when she thought she would never be able to fall in love again she meets Rob and now finds out he is gay. *How could this be?*

After dinner they moved to the veranda for coffee and dessert, Aunt Charlotte took this opportunity to invite Rob to church with them in the morning. She expected to hear all his excuses which she had heard on numerous occasions, and she was ready for them. To her surprise he asked what time church started and when they would be leaving. His aunt almost fell off her chair at his response but her delight was unmistakable. "Oh Robby, that's wonderful. Our second service begins at ten and that's usually the one I attend."

"Then we should be ready to go by nine-thirty?"

"Yes, dear, that should be plenty of time."

Abby was pleased to hear their conversation and Aunt Charlotte already knew that she would be attending. Abby was sure the gleam in her eyes was just as noticeable as Aunt Charlotte's delight. *Thank you Lord. This is certainly an answer to prayer. I know Aunt Charlotte has prayed this for many years. You are so good, God.*

Abby awoke early and knew she could never get back to sleep. She was too excited thinking about Rob attending church with them. And he even seemed anxious to go. Looking at the clock she moaned, it was only five-thirty…too early. She could sleep for another two hours. Abby knew this was not going to happen so she decided to go for a run along the beach. She threw on some sweat pants and T-shirt. After tying her gym shoes, she made her way down stairs being careful not to wake anyone else. *This house is so huge I doubt anyone would even hear me if I shouted.* To her surprise as she entered the kitchen, Rosa was already up and preparing breakfast. The coffee smelled great and she was pleased it was ready. Rosa reached for a mug and poured her a hot cup of hazelnut flavored coffee. "This is delicious Rosa. I did not expect anyone to be up this early."

"Early, I'm up at least by five every morning. I love being the first one up and taking my time getting everything prepared for breakfast and sometimes even getting dinner together. Then I can sit outside and enjoy my breakfast before anyone else is up. It is so beautiful sitting outside and watching the sun rise. God's creation is so beautiful."

"Yes it certainly is. And you can enjoy the beautiful ocean every morning; that's really a blessing."

"I love working for Miss Charlotte. My husband and I have been with the family for many years, before Robby's mom even married. In fact they were young girls when my husband and I started working for Mr. Livingston. Did you know Robby's mother and Miss Charlotte were identical twins?"

"Yes, I did know this. Rob told me they were very close and even pulled some pranks on their teachers and Rob's dad."

"They were really stinkers." The laughter in Rosa's eyes was unmistakable as she reminisced. "They even tried to fool me a number of times. I think when they finally went off to college they mended their ways. Rob's dad, Mr. Stevenson Senior, had his eye on Caroline from the time they were in high school. I think Miss Charlotte has always loved Mr. Stevenson but when Caroline, Rob's mother, fell in love with him she stepped aside. It was sad that she never fought for Mr. Stevenson even after the accident."

"Do you think that's the reason Aunt Charlotte never married?"

"Yes, I think she has always loved Mr. Stevenson. As far back as I can remember Miss Charlotte never even dated much. After Robby's mom died Miss Charlotte claimed Rob as her own son, although she never interfered with Kathleen, his stepmother. I do believe that Robby, being fourteen at the time, had a difficult time feeling part of the family that Ms Kathleen already had."

"Tell me Rosa, does Rob get along with his stepbrothers?"

"Oh yes, well enough I guess. You know Robby promised Ms Kathleen before she died that he would always look out for Steven and Lucas. I'm sure he pays them way more than what they deserve for the job they do, but that's Robby. He has always had a big heart."

"Well, thanks for the coffee and the visit. I'm going to go for a quick run along the ocean. It's a beautiful morning. I will probably be back by the time the others are up. We are all going to church this morning."

"That's wonderful. Is Robby going also?"

"Yes, he said last night that he was already planning on it."

"Oh, I'm so excited! You know he always has an excuse not to go and Miss Charlotte is so patient with him. I know she prays for him every day."

Abby gave Rosa a smile and took off down the steps and followed the path leading to the ocean. She wasn't sure which direction to run in but took the one that seemed open for quite a ways. Running always invigorated Abby and gave her time to clear her thoughts. She loved praying while she ran and this morning was not only a time for prayer but a time to praise God for what he had done in her life. She knew it was God that was healing her heart from the loss of her husband, something she thought she would never get over. Perhaps the hole would always be there but God was filling it and Abby was able to praise him. She was pleased she had her iPod and quickly had the ear buds in and her praise music playing as she began her run.

Abby ran for an hour and was surprised how quickly the time had gone. The sunrise was spectacular with the red, purple, orange, and yellow rays. The ocean sparkled as if God himself had scattered a million diamonds over it. Even the seagulls were awake and squawking. She was exhausted but in a good way as she slowed to a walk to cool down. She climbed the stairs and was surprised to see that Rob was already up and having coffee on the lower patio. "Hey good morning, you must have gotten up early to be out and running already."

"I couldn't sleep any longer and thought it would be great to go for a run along the ocean. I love to run and have not had the opportunity since moving out here. I think I may have gone a little longer than I should have for the first time."

Abby sat on a chair next to Rob feeling like her heart was about to pound out of her chest from running so hard. Rob handed her his orange juice and told her to drink up. "No thanks, I can wait. It's your orange juice."

"I want you to have it, you're totally out of breath and it will do you good."

Abby thanked him and helped herself to his juice thinking how thoughtful he was to share it with her.

Rob watched her drink and wanted so bad to pull her onto his lap and kiss her senseless. She was beautiful even if she was all sweaty and half her hair had fallen out of her clip. She had a freshness that always blew him away. The best part, not only was she beautiful; she was totally unaware of it. She was simply Abby. He also knew she could be a bit sassy when she wanted to but always in a humble sort of way if that was possible.

"Well, I better go in and shower. I think Aunt Charlotte said we would be leaving for church at nine-thirty."

Rob simply nodded as she got up and he had all he could do to not grab her and pull her close. *I just hope Aunt Charlotte had a chance to talk to her.*

Aunt Charlotte, Abby, and Rob arrived at church just before ten o'clock. Abby understood why Rob did not want to arrive any earlier; there were enough stares as they walked in trying to find seats near the back of the sanctuary. Several of Aunt Charlotte's friends turned and smiled at her showing how pleased they were that Rob had joined her. Abby knew he had to be on the daily prayer list of these dear ladies.

Abby was totally caught up in the worship and Rob had a hard time keeping his eyes off of her. He loved watching and listening to her sing. Not knowing any details, it had to be difficult for her to lose her husband at such a young age. *She was always so happy. Maybe one day she will tell me what happened to him. Were they married two maybe three years?* He had no idea other than a car accident. Quickly his attention was drawn to the pastor at the front of the sanctuary. "Open your Bibles with me to Revelation 2."

Revelation, I always liked that book when I was a kid. A lot to do with end times from what I can remember. Rob looked up at the pastor and to his surprise it was his former youth pastor during his junior and senior year in high school. He always liked Pastor Mike. Knowing who their senior pastor was caused Rob to sit straight, focusing on his every word. He listened intently to what Pastor Swenson was saying. Verse four of Revelation 2 got to him when he read: "Nevertheless I have this against you, that you have left your first love." Rob knew the Holy Spirit was talking directly to him. Pastor Mike continued to read verse 5: Remember therefore from where you have fallen; repent and do the first works..." He said, "Remember your passion for Jesus; get back to the Gospel when you were passionate about the lost." *Man I haven't been passionate about my faith or the Gospel since I was in high school.* His mind started to flood with memories of how much he had loved God and loved telling others about Jesus. Rob knew he had fallen: fallen from the relationship he once had with Jesus Christ. *College and success sure sucked all that from my life.* But then Pastor Swenson said something that gave him hope once again. "Even when you blow it, God is faithful!" Rob bowed his head at that statement. He knew God was speaking to him in his apartment the other day and he knew he needed to get back to the relationship he once had with Him. He knew how much he must have disappointed God and failed Him over the years but he could also see how faithful God had been to him. A peace flooded his soul like no other and hearing it explained so powerfully was almost more than he could hope for. After the message Pastor Swenson asked if anyone wanted to make a first time commitment inviting Jesus into their heart, or for prayer, to come forward. Rob knew all eyes would be focused on him but the tug on his heart was like a magnet. He was the first to move out from his seat, thankful it was on the aisle and he did not have to climb over anyone.

Aunt Charlotte grabbed Abby's hand and squeezed tightly. Tears were already running down Abby's cheek no matter how much she was trying to dispel them. Aunt Charlotte dabbed her eyes with her handkerchief; they were all happy tears.

Several other people had gone forward, including the prayer team, and once everyone was up in front for prayer, Pastor Swenson took Rob by the elbow and ushered him into another room. No doubt for some privacy. Many of Aunt Charlotte's friends came up to her after the service giving her hugs and praising God. They all seemed to be in her prayer group. Aunt Charlotte did not waste any time introducing Abby to her friends.

Pretty much everyone had left the sanctuary when Rob and Pastor Swenson returned. Pastor Swenson had his arm around Rob's shoulder and before Rob walked away from him he turned and embraced Pastor Mike as they said their goodbyes. It was a very touching moment and Abby wondered if it was too personal of a time. She felt somewhat awkward as she looked on, unable to keep her tears at bay.

Rob and Aunt Charlotte met in a warm embrace and it appeared they both shed a few tears. Rob came over to Abby giving her a hug; wishing it could be more. "Can you believe the senior pastor is my former youth pastor? And he remembered me from over eighteen years ago. He said he has been praying for me ever since I left for college... that just blows me away."

Abby was so choked up that nothing seemed to come out of her mouth; she simply held his arm looking into his face with watery eyes. Choking out the words she finally said, "Rob, I am so happy for you."

"Thanks, it has been a long time coming but I guess once God has a hold of your heart he really doesn't let go until you surrender everything to him. All I've known is success, fame, and making a lot of money, and all the while thinking I could manage my own life but the only one I've been fooling is me."

As they left the church, Abby walked between Aunt Charlotte and Rob when suddenly they heard a lot of clicking. Abby looked at Rob asking how anyone would even know they were at church. "Abby, they watch the house and as long as I leave the house alone they don't care but if I'm with anyone they follow me."

Rob escorted Abby and his aunt into the limo and was pleased James was waiting to pick them up. They quickly pulled out of the parking lot before the reporter could even make it to his car. "Hey James, I'm impressed with your driving skills," said Rob. He knew that not even a reporter could take away the joy he was feeling right now.

Rob told Abby they would be flying back to Texas shortly after dinner so she excused herself heading up stairs to change clothes. Rob took this opportunity to ask his aunt if she had a chance to talk to Abby about all the false articles in the magazines. "No Rob I did not. I tried but she told me she already knew and that it was not necessary to explain anything. I thought perhaps you talked to her on the flight over here."

Rob looked puzzled wondering why Abby would tell her such a thing. "I have not spoken to her at all about the articles and I can't imagine anyone else has either."

"Well Rob, I think this is something you will have to tend to yourself. I would think that your commitment today will make a huge difference to Abby."

"I hope so, but I also hope she knows this is something I had to do for me and not for anyone else."

"I know what you mean. There are so many relationships that are based on a false commitment only to win the girl, or the other way around."

"Aunt Charlotte, I know my heart is different and even though I invited Jesus into my heart at a young age, I really lost my first love as Pastor Mike talked about. You know it was really Abby and watching her life that convinced me I was not who I should be."

"I'm so happy for you Rob. And you can be sure that I will be praying for you and Abby. I think you belong together."

Leaning in to give his aunt a kiss he said, "Thanks Aunt Charlotte and thanks for all the years you have been praying for me."

Aunt Charlotte pinched his cheek as she so often did when he was growing up. "You know you have always been like my own son, Rob."

"I know and I love you so much for your unconditional love and patience with me. You put up with a lot: my partying, my language, I guess you could say my rebellion. Man, I really was living for self wasn't I?"

"Yes, we are all great sinners but we have a great Savior, Rob. Always remember that."

Just then Abby came down the stairs with her bag. She realized by the looks she received that she should have left her bag upstairs for Jackson to bring down. "Sorry, but it's no big deal. It's really not that heavy."

Rob winked at her, melting her to her toes. "You're fine, Abby, I could have run upstairs to get it after dinner." He met her on the stairs taking her bag from her.

Chapter 25

The flight back to Texas started out uneventful until Rob's phone chirped. Looking at his phone, Rob quickly answered. "Hey Josh, I was just getting ready to give you a call."

Abby could not help but overhear who Rob was talking to and although she stiffened upon hearing it was Josh she could not let this affect her mood. However, hearing Rob's invitation for him to fly in on Thursday to go over their plans for the dude ranch caused Abby to feel uneasy at this invitation. She did not hear any more of their conversation as her phone also buzzed. Answering her phone, she was surprised to hear it was Lucas. "Hi Lucas how are you? I'm good and we're on our return trip from visiting Aunt Charlotte. Yes, I think I can manage a flight out tomorrow. I'll check with Rob and the crew and if the plane isn't spoken for I can leave in the morning."

Rob almost forgot his conversation with Josh when he heard who Abby was talking to. He tried listening in to her conversation with Lucas. She seemed a little too anxious to fly to Florida. He quickly wondered if he had use for the plane tomorrow but could think of none. Finishing his conversation with Josh, he told him to bring Mary Beth out with him on Thursday.

Abby giggled at something Lucas must have said and as much as he loved hearing her giggle he did not like knowing that it was because of something Lucas had said to her. He could feel the jealousy bubble up and he needed to squelch this before it got the better of him. *Lucas must have a problem that he needs Abby to personally take care of.* He noticed her becoming quite serious as she nodded a few times. Before disconnecting the call, she told him she would get right back to him.

"What was that about? Is Lucas having a problem with his books?" asked Rob not wanting to sound too sarcastic.

"Yes he is. I have tried taking care of things over the phone but his financial officer is having a difficult time understanding some of the new procedures I have put in place. If it's okay with you I would like to fly out tomorrow morning. I should be back tomorrow night or Tuesday morning."

"You never return the same day." After saying this, he knew he was being condescending. "Sorry—I didn't mean it that way..."

"That's okay, and you're right. Things never seem to be as easy as I think they should be. Do you have plans for the plane tomorrow?"

As much as he tried to think of some excuse, even maintenance on the plane, he couldn't come up with anything. "No, that should be fine. Just let me know when you will be leaving, and I would appreciate a call when you arrive."

"Not a problem."

"And be sure to let me know when you will be leaving Florida."

"I will, sir."

Rob gave Abby a sidewise glance but let her "sir" comment go.

Abby was leaving at nine Tuesday morning. Rob was waiting with coffee and some breakfast when she came out from her room. She could not help but notice his concern for her as he insisted on accompanying her to the airport. "I want to make sure you're safe, Abby. I hate letting you out of my sight when things have not really been resolved."

Abby thanked him but assured him that she would be safe and for him not to worry.

"I'll be waiting at the airport when you return."

"Rob that's not necessary, if you have a car for me I'll be fine."

Abby was met by Lucas when they landed and they drove to Florida's Resort and Spa by the Sea. Another one of Stevenson Enterprises very upscale resorts: this was as breathtaking as the other two. *They certainly know how to build some impressive resorts.*

Upon entering the finance department, Lucas introduced Abby to Ben, their financial officer for this resort. She was pleased that she could put a face to Ben. Someone she often spoke with lately. Abby sat with Ben much of the day only breaking for a quick lunch when Lucas came in and whisked her away for a bite to eat. They ate in one of the resorts more casual restaurants and Abby ate as quickly as possible, anxious to finish and return to Texas as soon as possible. Lucas however, seemed to have other plans for her. "I have a room for you tonight so we can have a leisurely dinner later." He said this while raising his eyebrows up and down giving Abby an uneasy feeling.

"Thanks Lucas, but I think I'll finish up here pretty quick and be on my way."

"Okay Abby, but the offer still stands should it get to be too late for you to take off."

Abby returned to the office and continued walking Ben through the recent changes to their spreadsheets and record keeping. She could not understand why a smart man like Ben was having such a difficult time grasping the new procedures. Unbeknownst to her, Lucas had already asked him to take as long as possible.

The later it got, Abby found herself hardly able to think straight herself. By the time it was eight o'clock she was exhausted and it appeared Ben was getting a little anxious to get out of there as well. At nine o'clock Ben put Abby's fears at ease as everything she had shown him clicked into place. He seemed to breeze through the new procedure with ease and told her he didn't think he would have any problems in the future. Abby looked puzzled at his sudden understanding of the new procedures, but dismissed it that he wanted to leave as much as she.

Saying goodnight to Ben, Abby walked out of the office but remembered she left her jacket and quickly returned to the office. Upon entering, Abby overheard Ben on the phone with Lucas telling him he could not possibly stall any longer and that Abby had just left.

It was at this time that Abby realized it was all a hoax to get her to fly down to meet personally with Ben. She was furious but what could she possible do about it? There was no way she would give Lucas the satisfaction of even her anger. When Abby entered the office to pick up her jacket, she could not help but notice how red-faced Ben was when she entered. He looked like he had been caught red-handed…and he had. Abby ignored him as she picked up her jacket and walked out.

As soon as she came out of the office, Lucas was there to greet her. "It looks like you went late after all."

Abby noticed the smirk on his face and as much as she did not want to make this an issue her anger got the best of her. "This was a total hoax, Lucas, getting me to fly down here! How dare you take up my time like this?"

Lucas looked embarrassed but tried his best to look completely innocent. "I have no idea what you're talking about Abby."

"What exactly were Ben's words? Oh yes. 'I can't possibly stall her any longer?' Sound familiar, Lucas?" Abby was livid and Lucas noticed her beautiful green eyes getting darker by the minute.

"Abby I'm sorry. I only wanted to spend some time alone with you. I'm really attracted to you and it's totally unfair that my stepbrother gets all the beautiful women. I seem to get his leftovers and I didn't want that to happen this time."

"His leftovers, are you serious? I do not believe we are having this conversation!"

"Abby, I am sorry. Will you forgive me? I should never have done what I did and I don't blame you for being upset. If we could just have dinner together I promise you can go straight to your room after and leave first thing in the morning. It's too late to leave now anyway. The crew have already had dinner and checked in."

"Well, it looks like you leave me no choice."

"Forgive me?"

"Yes I forgive you but I still can't believe that you would do such a thing."

"Hey, please do me a favor and not tell Rob. He'll be furious with me."

"I hope you have learned your lesson. I'm not some pawn that can be played with and then discarded when the time is right."

"I know that and it certainly is not what I intended. May I start over and ask you to join me for dinner tonight?"

"Thank you…since I have no other offers." Abby said it teasingly and knew she wanted to get along with all three of the brothers. She did not want to come between them in any way. She knew how important family unity should be although the jealousy was unmistaken on Lucas's part, and she hoped she was not the cause of it. She sensed it was something that may have existed for some time.

Lucas held out his arm for Abby to take, and she did so. She noticed with Lucas, as with Steven, there was no unexplainable sensation as she had with Rob.

Dinner was amazing as they sat at the exclusive seafood restaurant in the resort. The theme was very tropical with the glass doors completely opened to the ocean. The beautiful palm trees and bird of paradise swaying in the warm night breeze added to the romantic atmosphere. Suddenly Abby wished Rob was the one sitting across from her.

It was half-past ten when Abby excused herself and Lucas thanked her for having dinner with him. He immediately got up with her and insisted on escorting her to her room. She was a little hesitant to accept his offer but after he cocked his head and told her she had nothing to worry about, she reluctantly took his arm as they headed to her room. "I need to tell Doug to be ready to leave at seven."

"He already knows. I know you're anxious to get out of here so I told him I thought you would want to leave early and he suggested seven. So if you would indulge me one last time for breakfast before you leave, we can eat at six."

"That would be fine. And thanks for a lovely dinner Lucas. I will see you at six."

As soon as Abby entered her room, she kicked off her shoes and took her phone out. She was not going to blow off calling Rob tonight. He would be furious with her and she did not need this on top of the night she already had.

"Hi Abby, I've been waiting for your call. It looks like you won't be coming home tonight. It must have gone later than expected."

"Yes. We finished up around nine o'clock and then I went to dinner with Lucas. Rob, the Sea Winds Restaurant here is absolutely amazing and dinner was delicious."

Feeling a twinge of jealousy in his gut and with clinched teeth Rob responded, "I'm glad you enjoyed it. Abby, I miss you. It's not the same around here without you."

"Umm thanks Rob. It has been a busy day for me. We plan on leaving at seven so I will be back in Texas in the morning." Abby sensed the awkwardness in their conversation. She did not know how to respond to Rob's comment. "Goodnight Rob. See you tomorrow."

"Goodnight Abby… and thanks for calling. Call me when you leave tomorrow?"

"Okay I will."

Chapter 26

No sooner had Abby ended the phone call that Rob's phone chirped signaling another call. He was hoping it was Abby calling back to tell him she missed him as well. Disappointment clouded his face when he looked at his phone and saw it was his aunt. He tried to cover up his disappointment with a cheery voice knowing his aunt would easily pick up on his current disposition. "Hi Aunt Charlotte, and to what do I owe hearing my favorite aunt's voice at this hour?"

"Rob, I'm your only aunt and exactly what are you trying to cover up with your cheerfulness tonight? Spill it Robby, I know you would never be this cheerful this time of the night."

"It's just that Abby's in Florida and I really miss her. I told her that when she called a few minutes ago and she didn't say that she even missed me at all; wouldn't that be the normal response?"

"Oh Rob, don't take everything to heart. I'm sure right now she has a lot on her mind and perhaps it really isn't the place she wanted to be the past couple of days. Anyway, I do have a reason for my phone call tonight."

"And what would that be?"

"Rob, your father called me tonight."

"And?"

"And, he is not too pleased with all the publicity he is seeing about you with Abby. He wants to know who this new "flavor of the month" is and what she is after."

"After? Why would he think she is after anything? And why is he calling you? How long has it been since he has even talked to you?"

"That isn't important Rob."

"Yes it is Aunt Charlotte. He didn't have the courtesy to say hello to you at my college graduation ten years ago." Rob felt his blood boil the more he thought about it. "I don't know if I can forgive him for the way he has treated you. And the more I'm thinking about it, the angrier I'm getting."

"Rob, please, if I have forgiven him, you need to do the same. And besides, he's coming to see you tomorrow." Aunt Charlotte had her eyes closed as she gave him the news knowing what his reaction would be.

"What? Why would he be coming here?" Rob ran his fingers through his hair and knew his blood pressure had climbed to an all time high.

"Rob, I tried telling him what a sweet woman Abby is but he would hear none of it. His exact words, 'I'm tired of reading about all his exploits in those horrible magazines.' It didn't matter what I said I could not make him listen. Rob I'm so sorry."

"It's not your fault he's such a jerk. I'm the one that's sorry for the way he has treated you all these years. Did he say when he's coming in?"

"Probably late in the day; he said he had some business to take care of first and an important lunch meeting."

"Oh yeah, he can't blow off a meeting to spend time with his son…even if it is to set me straight."

Aunt Charlotte could not help but notice not only the anger but more the cynicism in Rob's voice and her heart broke for the boy and young man that had wanted the approval of a father for so many years. No, Robert only saw his son as a playboy and someone that would never amount to anything; always taking risks and doing things his way. He never saw Robby as she did: a bright, extremely intelligent young man with so much ambition and a big heart. And now that he had recommitted his life to God she knew he would be more than she could have ever hoped for. Her prayers were answered and that's all that mattered to her. "Rob, your father will get over this. Let him know you love him because you know he will never be the one to say it."

"Thanks for calling, Aunt Charlotte. I will be praying tonight for my dad because I know that only God can get through to his heart."

"That's my boy. I love you Robby."

"I love you too Aunt Charlotte, more than you know. Aunt Charlotte thanks for always believing in me."

Rob knew that only God could penetrate his dad's hard and stubborn heart. *I'm sure that's where I get my stubbornness from…I guess I had a hardened heart as well. Lord, help me to be able to talk to my dad tomorrow without the anger that I have allowed to build up all these years. I give it all to you, Lord.* Rob fell into bed exhausted from his conversation with his aunt but saddened by his conversation with Abby. *Lord, I can't stop thinking about Abby and I want her so bad in my life. Please give her to me. Help me to know what to do.* Rob fell asleep wondering if his prayer for Abby was wrong but he really meant it. He wanted her more than anything he had ever wanted in his life. Rob fell asleep thinking about Abby and prayed for her safety and her trip home tomorrow.

Rob woke excited thinking about Abby coming home. *Home, I wish she really was coming home…to me and our home.* His emotions were conflicted as he thought of Abby and then thought of his father coming. He quickly showered as he did not want to miss her call and he refused to dwell on his father's visit. Abby did not call but sent him a text at six in the morning telling him they were on their way. He was disappointed not hearing her voice but understood she may not have wanted to wake him so early. She had no idea he was up at five and waiting for her call at six.

After spending an hour in his office, Rob could not concentrate on any work so he returned to his apartment. No sooner had he arrived than Lt. Jansen called giving him the news that both Jeremiah Clark and Sarah Duncan were arrested and would be in jail until their arraignment; it did not look good for either of them. Rob was relieved but also felt sadness as he thought about Abby going back to her house. *I really don't want to give her this information but I guess I have to. She needs to know.* It was not something he would be telling her immediately.

It was almost ten when Abby returned to Rob's apartment. She was hoping he was down in his office but she also knew she would be disappointed to find him not waiting for her. She was having a hard time reconciling her emotions and excused it as being tired from being up so early. She quietly entered the apartment and was surprised to see Rob lying asleep on the couch. He looked so peaceful, and handsome beyond words: wearing khaki pants and a black polo shirt he looked adorable even with his messed up hair. Thinking she could sneak past him and make it to her room, to her surprise Rob quickly opened his eyes. "Hi Ab, I'm not sleeping. Did you have a good flight?"

"I did thank you."

"How was Lucas?"

"Fine; I was pleased to get the new procedures in place."

Rob couldn't help but feel that Abby was keeping something from him but thought better than to push it. "Abby I would like to talk to you when you have a chance."

"Not a problem. I'll get my bag unpacked and be right back."

Chapter 27

As Abby unpacked she could not help but wonder if this was the "talk" Rob wanted to have. She really did not know if she would ever be ready to hear him confess his love for Josh and perhaps he was wondering how to handle this himself after totally committing his life to the Lord. Shaking this thought from her head, she returned to the living room.

Rob sat on the couch waiting for Abby's return, but when she did, she immediately sat across from him in one of the leather chairs. Rob felt disappointed that she did not join him on the couch. "Abby, after you called last night, my Aunt Charlotte called."

Abby's heart sank thinking something had happened to his beloved aunt and the woman she had grown to love in such a short time. She had never seen Rob looking so sad and forlorn. "Oh no, Rob, don't tell me something has happened to your aunt?" Abby's voice was raised as she searched Rob's face for an answer.

Rob wished Abby sat closer so he could grab her hands as he noticed how shaken she had become. "No, Abby, my aunt is fine; it's my dad and—"

"Oh Rob, I'm so sorry. What happened to him?"

"Abby nothing happened to him. He's coming to see me sometime this evening."

"Rob, that's wonderful... isn't it?"

Rob was not about to tell her the details of his father's visit. And yet it seemed like a perfect opportunity to tell her how untrue the articles had been about him. He could never deny the many women that were pictured on his arm and how, at the time, he really enjoyed all the attention. However he still could not bring himself to tell her.

"Abby I just don't get it. My father has not talked to my aunt since my mother died. I was fourteen years old then. He told her he never wanted to see her again. At my college graduation he wouldn't so much as say hello to her. It upsets me that he would even call her now and I'm sure that has to hurt her deeply."

"What did your aunt say? Was she upset with his call?"

"I think she was more upset for me than for her. She said she has forgiven my dad and that's what I need to do."

"Well, I think she's right, Rob, and I don't even know the whole situation."

"I never understood how my dad could have such anger for my aunt. The cops said the accident was unavoidable. Right after the funeral he became a different man, one I hardly recognized."

"Rob, have you ever heard of survivor guilt? It sounds like this may be something your father has been dealing with."

"No I haven't but you would think this was something my aunt would have had more than my dad, after all she was the driver."

"I believe the relationship your aunt has had with the Lord helped her get over whatever guilt I'm sure she had. And then she had you, someone I'm sure she felt responsible for. She wanted to pour her love into you more than anything. It became something your dad could not cope with. I read once that a person may feel guilty without being consciously aware of it. Conscious and unconscious guilt may act as an underlying factor in behavior, emotions and relationships."

"How do you know so much about this? Now you're sounding like a psychiatrist or something."

Abby took a deep breath and wondered if she would be able to get through telling Rob her story. She knew it would not be easy and immediately asked God to help get her through. "Rob, I know because of what happened to me and I know it was God that got me through."

"What do you mean? I have no idea what happened to you, Abby."

"Rob you do know that my husband was killed in an auto accident." Rob nodded and Abby began to tell him about her wedding day and the horrible accident that took her husband and his best man. Rob sat in horror noticing how difficult it was for Abby to talk about. Her hands were trembling and Rob wanted so badly to go over, put his arms around her, and hold her the rest of the day. He no longer even cared about himself or his dad coming to talk to him. She continued to tell him about how badly injured she was and how she had no idea that Thomas and Tim were killed in the accident until she had come out of the induced coma.

Rob could not bear to hear anymore but quickly went to her; kneeling in front of her he pulled her hands into his. "Abby I am so sorry. I had no idea that is how you lost your husband. I thought you may have been married a year or two but never becoming a widow on your wedding day." Rob reached up and with his thumbs wiped the tears off her cheek. "I can understand how difficult it is for you to talk about."

"I really don't know why I told you all this, but I think I understand how your dad may feel, and if he never trusted God to see him through, he has lived with survivor guilt all these years, conscious or unconscious of it."

"But why take it out on my aunt? She has only loved me and given me so much."

"It's your aunt that was driving the car, right? To your father she has always been the one responsible. But I think even more than that is the fact that your mom and aunt were identical twins and so much alike. Your dad has never been able to deal with that."

"Yeah I get it, but it seems like there has always been something more. I have never been able to figure it out."

Seeing the pain in Rob's eyes, Abby found herself reaching out to him. Holding Rob's hands Abby told him that maybe it was time he forgave his dad and try talking to him. She knew his stepmother had died a couple of years ago and his dad had to be a very lonely man. Rob wiped the tears from his eyes and he couldn't say if they were for Abby or for himself—probably a little of both.

196

Rob pulled Abby out of the chair and asked if she would sit with him on the couch; all he could think of was comforting her. Rob held her close as they sat in silence losing track of all time. Finally Rob broke the silence, "Abby, thank you for sharing your story with me. I can't imagine how difficult that had to be for you but I am very grateful you're here."

"Rob, you also had a great loss. I could never imagine losing my mom at such a young age. I can see how important Aunt Charlotte has been to you. Do you think your father has been jealous of your relationship with your aunt?"

"I never thought about that; however, I do know that when Kathleen and her three kids stepped in, I barely existed as far as my dad was concerned."

"It could be that in the beginning he was taken up with his new family but as time went on he realized he had lost you, and it became more than he could cope with."

"I doubt that. He has never given me credit for anything. Maybe when he finds out that I'm the one buying his company, he'll accept my success and that I have made something of my life."

"That's really important to you isn't it Rob…to outdo your dad?"

"Yeah, I guess it is. But after this past weekend, it doesn't seem like it matters that much anymore."

As Rob held Abby close, she felt such a conflict of emotions. She knew he was there to comfort her but the electricity between them seemed to be escalating, at least for her. She had no idea how Rob was feeling but sat waiting for him to confess his secret…it did not happen. After they sat together for what seemed like hours, Abby looked up into Rob's eyes. "Thank you Rob. I appreciate your comfort and strength more than you know. You must be hungry since we completely skipped lunch," she said with a giggle in her voice. She wanted to lighten the mood and not make Rob feel awkward wondering how he would let go of her.

She had no idea that he didn't want to let go of her. As far as he was concerned, he could sit with her in his arms the rest of the day, however, sensing her awkwardness, he removed his arm from his embrace. "Yes, I guess I could eat something. I'll call room service, what would you like to eat?" Looking at his watch he noticed it was already two o'clock.

"I'm fine with a chicken salad sandwich like the other day, but I can see what there is and make us something."

"I think ordering something would be best." Rob removed his arm that he had around her and immediately sensed the loss and warmth that they shared. He had no idea that Abby felt the same as he looked into her beautiful green eyes, still moist from earlier shed tears. *I know I love her but telling her now would scare her to death. I have to first know how she feels about me. She may still be in love with her dead husband for all I know.* Rob got up and went to the phone to call for lunch to be brought up to them.

There was a knock on the door and Rob thought that it was pretty quick room service as it seemed he had just ordered. To his surprise when he opened the door, there stood his aunt. "Aunt Charlotte what are you doing here? And how did you get here without my plane?"

"Robby you are not the only one I know with a private jet, and besides, I couldn't let you face your father alone. I listened to him eighteen years ago and never once stepped foot in his house but by golly he is not going to tell me I can't be here in your apartment." Aunt Charlotte leaned in to give him a hug and received a kiss on the cheek from him. Abby stood immediately but waited for their greeting to end before walking over to greet her. The two women exchanged a tight hug and Aunt Charlotte could not help but notice Abby's puffy eyes. *It certainly looks like Abby has been crying but I'm not going to pry. If Abby doesn't want to say anything, I know Robby will confide in me when we're alone.* Aunt Charlotte sensed that the less said the better.

"Aunt Charlotte, Abby and I just ordered some lunch. Would you like something to eat?"

"I'll have whatever Abby is having."

"I'm happy to share my lunch with you. I really don't think I have much of an appetite."

Abby no sooner said this than her stomach gave out an obnoxious growl. Four eyes peered at her stomach and she couldn't help but giggle. "I guess I am hungry."

Rob had already pulled out his phone and called for another meal to be brought up to them.

While they were eating, Rob thought it was best to tell Abby that Lt. Jansen had called and that Jeremiah Clark and Sarah Duncan had been arrested and would be spending a very long time in prison.

"Does this mean I can go back to my house Rob?"

Rob so wanted to tell her that he never wanted her to go back to her house but that was not going to happen. He knew this was a selfish thought on his part. "Ah…yeah, I thought perhaps we could get you moved back on Saturday. I want to make sure your place is clean and everything put back to normal. I hope you don't mind that I went ahead and ordered a new mattress. It should be delivered by the end of the week."

"Rob you didn't have to do that. I could have purchased a mattress."

"I wanted to. I want to make sure everything in your house is as good as new."

"Thank you Rob. That's very thoughtful of you."

As Abby cleared the lunch dishes, Rob's phone started chirping. "Stevenson here. Okay, thanks for the heads up." Rob turned to his Aunt Charlotte and Abby. "My dad just arrived and should be up shortly."

Abby wanted Rob and Aunt Charlotte to spend time alone with Mr. Stevenson, so she excused herself telling them she needed to get some work done in her office and that later she would probably go check on her house. Rob looked as if he wanted to run off with her and not have to face his father but Abby gave his arm a squeeze and told him everything was going to work out. "I hope so, Abby. I really hope so." He had such mournful looking eyes that it just about broke Abby's heart to think a son could not want to face his father.

Abby quickly went into her room for her purse and keys before leaving for her office. "Oh Rob, I just realized that I have no car here if I'm going to my house later."

Rob tossed her his keys and told her to take his car. Abby just stood staring at him. "Abby it will be fine. It drives like any other car."

"But it's a Lamborghini Rob. I have never driven anything that expensive."

Rob so wanted to tell her to get use to it but refrained from doing so. "You'll do fine Abby, believe me."

With that Abby was out the door and on her way to the hall elevator. The handsome older gentleman walking towards her had to be Mr. Stevenson. She could see where Rob got his good looks. He simply nodded and she was sure he never even looked at her. He was awfully anxious to meet with his son.

Chapter 28

No sooner had Abby walked out the door than Rob felt the tightness in his chest. She would be leaving his apartment and he missed her already. He looked at his aunt who must have known what he was feeling; never giving thought to what she must have gone through with his dad. His dad really did shut her out.

There was a heavy knock at the door and Rob knew it had to be his father. He opened the door and they just stared at each other. Rob nodded to his father not knowing if he even wanted to embrace him it had been so long. "Hello father. It's been a long time."

"Yes it has Rob. I take it your aunt called warning you of my visit."

Hearing this, Aunt Charlotte stood up from the chair she had been sitting in and walked from the living room to the foyer over to Robby and his father. "Hello Robert. It has been a very long time, and yes, I did warn Robby that you would be visiting him."

Mr. Stevenson was obviously unsettled and bristled at Aunt Charlotte's presence. He stood staring at her for the longest time, checking her out from head to toe. She was a very beautiful woman and as he looked at her he felt his heart stir but not without a rush of sadness as he thought of his wife Caroline. He could not push away the guilt he felt for how he treated his sister-in-law all these years. *That must be how my wife would look right now if she were still alive.* "Charlotte you're looking well."

"Thank you Robert. I am quite well, thank you. And how have you been? I was sorry to hear of Kathleen passing. I'm sure it was very difficult for you."

Mr. Stevenson all but ignored her as he turned to his son. This only angered Rob even more. "Dad I will not stand by as you ignore Aunt Charlotte. It's been eighteen years since my mother died and since then you have not so much as acknowledged her twin sister. What gives you the right to harbor all this anger for so many years? Let it go!" Rob was surprised at how much his voice had raised to his father.

It was Aunt Charlotte that stepped between them putting a hand on both their arms. "Please Robby it's not necessary to defend me." She spoke with calm and sweetness; with eyes that held nothing but love and almost pity for Rob's dad.

Guilt stabbed at Robert's heart and he needed to discuss what he had come all this way for. "Junior, I came to find out about this new "flavor of the month" woman that I have been reading about. The latest picture I saw happened to be of her walking between you and your aunt."

Rob was taken aback hearing his father call him Junior. He had not heard this since he was a kid. Brushing this aside, Rob explained the picture to his father telling him they happened to be leaving church. "Dad, the so called "flavor of the month" has made me the man I never thought I could ever be. I have nothing but respect for her and… I think I'm in love with her." Rob noticed his aunt's eyes sparkle with delight giving him the confidence he needed to continue. "She has been living out her faith and love for God ever since I met her. She is not at all like any of the other women I have dated."

"I'm sure she knows what you and I happen to be worth and she is nothing but a gold-digger as far as I'm concerned."

Rob's hands turned into fists as he stood in front of his father. "I will not stand here and let you talk about her like this. She has been through a lot: she lost her husband on their wedding day for crying out loud, and now her life has been threatened because of her working for me. I refuse to stand by and have you trash someone you do not even know!"

"Robby I had no idea that was how her husband died. She never told me," said his aunt.

"She told me today; that's why her eyes were all puffy when you came. I'm sure it had to be the hardest thing in the world for her to share with me."

Rob's dad looked confused and wondered what was going on between him and Charlotte. "What in the world does this have to do with anything?"

"It has to do a lot with what we are talking about, Dad. Abby believes you have been living with survivor guilt all these years."

"Nonsense, if anyone should be living with guilt it should be Charlotte here."

Charlotte clutched her chest and tears began to slide down her cheeks. "Oh Robert, you have no idea the guilt I lived with. If it wasn't for knowing Jesus and allowing him to take away the guilt I had, I don't know where I would be."

"And besides Dad, I happen to know the cops said the accident could not be avoided. You of all people should be able to handle facts. That's all you ever live by."

Mr. Stevenson's countenance changed and the anger and fire in his eyes was beginning to soften. He reached for Charlotte's hand and quietly whispered, "Charlotte will you ever be able to forgive me?"

"I already have Robert...a long time ago."

Looking at his son, Mr. Stevenson asked Rob if he could find it in his heart to forgive him. "Son I haven't been the father I should have been to you. Can you forgive me?"

The two men embraced in the most beautiful way a father and son could and Rob had only wished that Abby could have been there to see the three of them together. "Dad, you need to know how much Aunt Charlotte has meant to me all these years. She has loved me unconditionally and instilled in me what Mother did: to make the right choices. Dad, I have not had an intimate relationship with any woman from those magazines, in fact I have never had an intimate relationship with any woman. I hope you can believe me."

"But all those women you were seen with... and your picture plastered all over those magazines —"

"Dad, believe me when I tell you nothing happened. Do you think any of those women would admit they never went to bed with me? I won't lie; I really did like all the publicity and all the charity balls I attended. I even loved the women hanging on me every chance they had. Believe me, I came very close to giving in to the natural male urges a guy can have but I never did. I've changed and there's only one woman I want more than anything… and that's Abby Sinclair."

"Well what are you going to do about it?"

"I have no idea. Right now she has distanced herself from me and I have no idea why other than I know she is not comfortable with all my money and my way of life. I should say, my past way of life."

Robert looked at Charlotte with such longing in his eyes that Rob wondered if these two were destined to be together after all. His dad reached over and held his aunt's hands in his. "Charlotte we have to help our boy here, would you agree?"

Charlotte winked at Robert and felt the flush rise to her cheeks. "I'm sure you will come up with something Robert."

"Where is your Abby now, Son?"

"She went to her office to work and then she said she was going to check on her house. We have had a couple of very stressful weeks but I think the worst is over. I'll fill you in later."

"Hey why not give her a call and see if she will have dinner with us. I would really love to meet her. After all, she may be my future daughter-in-law."

"I sure hope so."

Rob pulled out his phone and immediately called Abby. He had no idea if she was still in her office or at her house. "Hi Abby, where are you?"

"I just pulled into my driveway. I thought I would check on my house."

"Can it wait until later? My dad wants to meet you and the three of us thought it would be great to have dinner together."

"It sounds like your meeting with your dad went well."

"Better than you can imagine."

"I have been praying for you ever since I left your apartment."

"Thanks Abby. I'll tell you all about it later. Can you meet us for dinner?"

"Yes, I'll leave right away. I can always check on the house another time."

Dinner was amazing but even more amazing than dinner was seeing the sparkle in Aunt Charlotte's eyes. The way she and Mr. Stevenson looked at each other certainly looked like love to her. Several times Mr. Stevenson reached over to hold Aunt Charlotte's hand. *Will I ever have someone to love me like that again? It's a shame it has taken them so long and wasted all these years.*

It had already been settled, Aunt Charlotte would have Abby's apartment for the remainder of her stay and Rob's dad was to have one of the suites. When Abby protested trying to insist she go back to her house, they would not hear of it. "It's all taken care of Abby. There's no need for you to move anything out of my apartment. We can wait until the weekend like I said previously."

They all agreed to meet for breakfast but Abby really wanted Rob to spend as much time as possible with his father. They had missed a lot of years together already. "I need to spend time in the office tomorrow. Being gone two days this week, I have a lot to catch up on." It was after ten when Abby excused herself telling the others she needed to get to bed. They agreed with her that they too needed to get up to their rooms. To Abby's surprise, Mr. Stevenson gave her a hug goodnight.

Abby did not break at all from her work until Mr. Stevenson came in at five o'clock and asked if she would join them for dinner. Aunt Charlotte and Rob were already seated at a booth at Abby's favorite restaurant in the resort…the Texas Grill. She was pleased that dinner was not at the exclusive Black Stallion. A warm feeling came over her as she remembered the first time she ate here with "Bob York". She wondered if Rob felt the same as Mr. Stevenson escorted her to the booth to join the others. Rob stood up allowing her to slide to the inside of the booth sitting across from Aunt Charlotte.

Conversation flowed well and it was obvious to Abby that Rob and his father had enjoyed their day together. She was pleased that she stayed busy all day as CFO of Stevenson Enterprises. Abby did not want Rob to think that she in any way would neglect her duties and the responsibility she was entrusted with.

Abby was looking forward to a quiet night in the apartment where she could relax, do her Bible study, and spend the rest of the evening reading or playing the piano as long as Rob was spending the evening with his father. She knew they had a lot of catching up to do.

Chapter 29

Abby woke early, showered and dressed, hoping to make it out of the apartment before Rob was up. No such luck. Rob sat at the dining room table. As soon as she entered he was up and returned with a cup of coffee for her. "Thanks so much Rob. I thought I would get down to the office early so this is all I'm going to eat this morning."

"That's really not enough to go on."

"I'll grab something a little later, thanks."

Rob shrugged his shoulders and Abby knew he wasn't too pleased with her decision. She did not forget that Josh was coming in this afternoon and she did not want to spend any more time today with Rob than necessary. She knew she had to protect her heart. After Thomas she did not think there would ever be another man she could love but spending time with Rob had become almost unbearable. He made her feel in ways Thomas never had and she never imagined that could be possible. Getting away from Rob today became her priority.

Not long after Abby had entered her office, Wade knocked on her door. "Come in Wade. I haven't seen much of you in a long time."

"Yes I know. I've been kept busy." He seemed extremely casual for someone Abby never spent much time with as he tried to keep their conversation light. "Rob told me how much you loved riding and I was wondering how you would like to go for a ride this afternoon."

Hearing the words "go for a ride" was music to Abby's ears. "Oh Wade, I would love to go. It looks like a beautiful day for a ride as well. Let me know when you would like to go and I'll make sure I'm ready."

"How about twelve-thirty or one?"

Abby agreed with great enthusiasm and of course Wade had no idea she was anxious to be away when Josh came in. Although she knew she could not avoid the meeting that was scheduled with Josh for tomorrow. "That will give me time to change and I can meet you back here at twelve-thirty."

Wade gave her a big smile and said he would see her later.

Abby knew she still had a lot to do however, was pleased she had spent all of yesterday catching up on her work. She was going riding and nothing could interfere with the great mood that put her in.

She took off early to go change into her riding clothes. As she was returning to her office, Aunt Charlotte was walking towards her. "Abby dear I've been looking for you. Would you like to have lunch with me?"

"Oh Aunt Charlotte I would love to but Wade invited me to go for a ride with him. He said that Rob told him how much I love to ride so he offered to take me today." Aunt Charlotte looked somewhat puzzled but Abby dismissed it; she was too excited to think of anything else.

"Rob went to the airport himself to pick up Josh and—"

Abby interrupted quickly, "I'm running late Aunt Charlotte. I told Wade I would meet him at twelve-thirty and it's already past time."

"Sorry dear. You run along and I'll see you tonight."

"Thanks Aunt Charlotte. And I'm so sorry I can't have lunch with you."

Abby was practically out of breath when she arrived at her office. Wade was waiting for her and looked a little unsettled. "I'm sorry I'm late, Wade, but I'm all set to go."

"Good. I was at the stable earlier and got our horses ready. Ricky said you like riding Princess."

"That's right. She is such a sweet horse and very responsive. We seemed to hit it off right away."

They rode silently to the stable and Abby was looking forward to getting on Princess once again; she really claimed that horse as her own.

Wade pulled up to the stable and Abby saw the two horses tied at the hitching post. They were a beautiful sight. "I don't believe I have ever seen your horse before Wade. But then I didn't have a chance to get acquainted with any of the other horses other than Princess and Rob's stallion Midnight."

"This is Chester and I've been riding him for a couple of years now."

"Well he's beautiful as well." Abby said this as she stroked Chester down his neck and rubbed his muzzle. Princess looked a little miffed that she was being ignored and Abby quickly walked over to her giving her equal attention. She had picked up a couple of mints and gave each horse a mint. With that she knew she made another new friend in Chester.

"Ready to mount up?" asked Wade who seemed rather impatient to get going.

"Of course; I can't wait. Where are we headed?"

"I think we should ride out to the north rim. What do ya say?"

"Sounds good to me," Abby quickly mounted her horse and started walking Princess out away from the stable. Wade quickly followed.

Once they were out of sight from the stable hands and in the open, Wade challenged Abby to a fast run to the rim. "Are you up for a race Abby?"

Of course Abby didn't have to be asked twice. She loved the competition. She remembered her ride with Rob and it brought a smile to her face. She had won that race hands down... even if it was by a nose.

Rob had picked up Josh and Mary Beth and returned to the resort. He would have sent the limo but he wanted to meet them himself. Josh was too good a friend to simply send a limo. Upon returning to the resort, Lt. Jansen was waiting for him in the lobby. "Hey Jim to what do I owe this pleasure? I hope it's not business that brings you here."

"Sorry Rob but it is."

"I thought the arrests have been made and it's safe for Abby to get back into her house?"

"Well, I thought so too but we got the results of the other prints on the card Abby received; to say nothing of Sarah Duncan singing like a bird."

"Anything we should be worried about?"

"How well do you know Wade Jenson?"

"What do you mean how well do I know Wade Jenson? He happens to be my manager here. Why, what do you have on him?"

"We now know that he's the kingpin in this whole scam operation. Sarah Duncan happens to be his girlfriend, or she was his girlfriend. I need to take him in for questioning. I also have a warrant for his arrest in case he refuses to come willingly. Where can I find him?"

"He should be at the desk or in his office. Have you been here very long?"

"No, in fact I arrived shortly before you pulled up so I haven't asked about him."

Rob turned to Josh and Mary Beth and told them they would be in the other suite on the top floor. Josh said he would stay with him but sent Mary Beth up to their room so she could unpack.

As they approached the front desk, it was obvious that Wade was not there but Gabriella was. "Gabriella, do you know where Wade is? Is he in his office?"

"No Mr. Stevenson he's not in his office. He told me he was going for a horseback ride this afternoon."

"Really, why on earth would he be doing that?"

Gabriella merely shrugged her shoulders as she responded, "I have no idea, but I think he asked Mrs. Sinclair to join him."

The bile rose in Rob's throat and fear gripped him as he fled to Abby's office on the seventh floor. *She has to be there. Why would she even consider going for a ride with Wade?*

The three men flew into Abby's office but she was not to be found anywhere. Rob went to the office next to Abby's and asked Rae if she had seen her. Rae was their reservation manager and he knew Abby and Rae ate lunch together many times. Rob was completely out of breath but tried to keep calm. "Rae, do you have any idea where Abby is?"

"Yeah, she said Wade invited her to go riding with him. She was so excited. Wade told her that you had told him how much she loves to ride."

"I told him no such thing. Let's get out to the stable." Rob said this as he looked at the other two men who seemed to grasp the concern and fear in Rob's eyes.

On the way to the stable, Rob gave Ricky a call and asked that he get his horse saddled. He looked at the other two men and they both nodded. "Also get two other horses ready to ride."

"Hey boss, what seems to be the problem?" Ricky couldn't help but notice the stress and tension in Rob's voice.

"Do you know if Wade is out riding with Abby?"

"Yes, they rode out about forty-five minutes ago. I saw them leave. Wade called this morning and asked me to get Princess and Chester brought down. I offered to saddle them but he insisted he do it: said he needed to keep in practice."

Unbelievable fear gripped Rob and he couldn't get to the stable quick enough.

Princess took off at a full gallop and Abby enjoyed the thrill of riding so fast. She was standing up in the stirrups when she heard a strange sound erupt from the saddle. It creaked as if she was climbing up into it. Something was not right. The saddle felt loose as her feet seemed to slip back and forth. To Abby's shock, she felt the saddle slipping away. She tried slowing Princess but knew if she pulled back too hard on the reins she would slide off and risk splitting her head open or breaking her back. No, while she had a chance, she had to quickly push herself off the side of the horse and roll on her shoulder and side. It would hurt but it would be controlled. She noticed the saddle fall off Princess as she pushed herself off. She saw Princess begin to slow—then everything went black as the wind was knocked out of her.

Chapter 30

Coming to, Abby moaned and groaned wondering what happened to her horse. And where had Wade gone? She grabbed her right arm noticing the horrible throbbing pain shooting through it. She opened her eyes only to see Wade standing over her. *Is that a gun in his hand? It is, and why is Wade aiming the gun at me?* Fear immediately gripped her and she knew all she could do was pray... and pray she did. As she prayed, she experienced a peace that flooded her soul. A peace that she knew she could never explain to anyone. "Wade what are you doing, and what in the world have I done to you?"

Wade snarled at her and his face contorted into an evil unrecognizable look. "What have you done? You ruined everything for me. My girlfriend's been arrested, my friends are in jail ...and it's all because of you."

"Me? How have I done anything to you?"

"It wasn't enough that Sarah couldn't be promoted to CFO or Clark, but no, that arrogant, spoiled brat, Rob Stevenson, had to have someone with a fancy degree."

Abby knew she had to keep Wade talking in order to try and disarm his defenses. "But you're the one that hired me, Wade. I don't understand why hiring me can have you this angry."

He growled at her, shaking her to her core. "You have no idea do you? For two years I had the perfect plan. We had so much money coming in and Mr. Fancy Pants had no idea. Why we could have robbed him for many more years to come and he would never have known...except for you. You had to come in and discover our scheme. I thought hiring a woman would give me an advantage and eventually I could win you over to my side. And now you're going to pay. I thought I could scare you off, but no, he protected you by moving you into the resort and then taking you to California with him. Wherever you were, he was at your side. I searched all over for Clark's computer but you even took care of that, didn't you. If you had only gone into your house the other night, you would have had a nice surprise...me."

Abby shuddered to think that Wade was in her house when she went to check on things. That was certainly God's protection when Rob called and invited her to dinner with his dad and aunt. "Why would you have to be so greedy to want more? Rob takes very good care of all his employees, and he has taken very good care of you, Wade."

"Why? I'll tell you why. Because he has it all and it isn't fair. There's no reason why anyone should have all that he has. That's why he would never miss what I was taking."

"But he's earned everything he has. He built Stevenson Enterprises into what it is today. He knows how important all his employees are to him and he could never have been such a success without you Wade."

Abby had no idea that Rob, Lt. Jansen, and Josh had ridden up and were hidden in some bushes behind Wade. Rob's heart was pounding so loud in his chest that he was sure the other two men could hear it. The whole ride out, Rob was praying that Abby would be all right and that God would keep her protected. Relief washed over him when he saw her on the ground, but when he saw the gun Wade had pointed at her, his stomach twisted into knots. *God please keep her safe and keep Wade from pulling the trigger. God I need her and love her so much. I don't know what I would do without her.* Tears clouded his vision as he tried controlling his emotions. Before he knew it, Lt. Jansen was walking out into the clearing with his gun drawn. *What is he doing?* Panic rose in Rob's heart.

"Drop the gun Wade."

Hearing the Lieutenant's voice startled Wade and he quickly turned around and fired at Lt. Jansen. The shot rang out but not without hitting the Lieutenant in the shoulder. Jansen fired back but missed his mark. Abby winced in pain as Wade grabbed her injured shoulder. Holding the gun against her temple, Wade hollered, "I swear I'll kill her Stevenson. Now back off."

This was the first Abby saw Rob as he started walking towards Wade. Abby shook her head not wanting Rob to come any closer. "Let go of her, Wade. You want me not Abby. I'm the arrogant spoiled brat, remember?"

"Yeah… but now I can take care of both of you."

"What do you have against me Wade? I have been nothing but good to you, man. Who helped your mom out when your dad died? As I remember your mom didn't have enough money to bury him."

"Don't talk to me about helping my mother. You have plenty of money as it is. That was nothing for you."

"Maybe it wasn't, but I know it meant a lot to your mother."

Rob noticed Wade's hand begin to shake and was hoping he had unnerved him. What Abby didn't realize was that Josh had gone around and was sneaking up behind her and Wade from another direction. Rob kept a sharp eye on Josh and prayed Wade would not notice his friend.

Suddenly and without any hesitation, Josh plowed into Wade full force knocking him to the ground. Wade's gun went flying and Rob took this opportunity to run up and grab the gun. He immediately found his way to Abby; bending down and holding her close. He heard her moan and realized then that she was hurting. "Babe your hurt, I'm so sorry."

"I'm okay now Rob. I fell on my shoulder after I jumped from Princess and rolled. I have no idea why the saddle was loose."

Rob gave her a skeptical look acknowledging the fact that Wade must have cut the saddle strap and as she rode it didn't take much for the strap to break all the way.

It wasn't long before Lt. Jansen and Josh had Wade handcuffed. "You're under arrest Wade Jenson for embezzlement and attempted murder. You're going away for a very long time."

215

Abby could not help but feel sorry for the man. As far as she could tell, he had bigger issues than going to prison. His heart was black and he needed help.

Rob cautiously kept his arm around Abby. "We need to get you checked out." Abby had no idea that an ambulance had been sent for. It wasn't long before the paramedics were there and had her on a back board. "What are you doing? I'm sure it's nothing. Rob please, tell them I'm okay."

"No Abby. I want you checked out. You may have a broken collar bone or something minor but we need to know. I want the doctor to take a look at your arm and shoulder."

Abby noticed that Lt. Jansen, who only had a flesh wound, had already left with Wade, after being bandaged and checked by the paramedics, but Josh, was still there with Rob. *Josh, was she still to meet with him tomorrow?*

Chapter 31

After several x-rays and MRI, Abby lay comfortably in a hospital bed. However it only brought back memories of her last hospital stay. She wondered what had happened to Rob. Was he at the hospital or with Josh? She knew he wanted to ride in the ambulance but the paramedics talked him out of it. She just wanted to get out of there. She was sure she was fine. Abby lay with her hair splayed on a white pillow with her eyes closed trying not to think of her last hospital stay. If only she wasn't so alone here. She wiped at the tears trickling down her cheek. *Quit feeling sorry for yourself...you're alive aren't you?*

There was a knock on her door but before she could even answer, it opened wide and Rob, Mr. Stevenson, Aunt Charlotte, Josh, and another woman she did not know, entered. Rob was carrying the biggest bouquet of roses she had ever seen in her life. Walking over to her side he leaned down giving her a kiss on her forehead. "Hey babe, how are you feeling?"

It sounded like he was back to his endearing name for her and she wondered how Josh felt about that. Before long they were all standing around her bed and she felt a little embarrassed over all the attention. Aunt Charlotte and then Mr. Stevenson bent down to give her a quick kiss on her cheek. Rob acknowledged Josh. "You remember my friend Josh don't you?"

"Yes of course. I have you to thank for saving my life."

"Nonsense, I was happy to be there at the right time."

Rob motioned to Mary Beth to step up and began to introduce her to Abby. "Abby I would like you to meet Mary Beth. Poor thing, she's married to Josh." He said this while slapping his good friend on the back.

Abby wondered if her shock was evident. "You're… married to Josh? I didn't know Josh was married."

Rob spoke up. "Yeah they've been married for seven years and have two great kids."

"Why that's absolutely wonderful." Abby had the most euphoric look on her face and they all thought it must be the meds kicking in.

Everyone had left the hospital leaving Rob alone with Abby. The doctor came in and told them that nothing was broke but he wanted to keep her overnight for observation and she would have to keep her arm immobile for a few weeks. From the MRI it looked like a few ligaments may have been torn and would need to mend. Rob was relieved but wondered why Abby seemed so anxious to leave. He saw genuine fear in her eyes. "What's the problem Abby? You're awfully anxious to get out of here. One night won't hurt. You however, look like you could claw your way out if you needed to."

Abby hesitated not knowing it was that obvious. "Rob the last time I was in a hospital was after the accident. The memories are too overwhelming. It may take time, and I know in time I'll be okay, but right now I can't help but feel restless. I just can't spend the night here."

Rob put his arm around her and gently pulled her to himself. "Then let's get out of here." He called for the nurse and had her released in no time. She was thankful for his influence.

Rob thought the ride back to the resort was awfully quiet and when he glanced at Abby he saw why: she was sleeping. *Must be the drugs they have her on for pain.* He could not hold back a smile as he thought of how easily she could fall asleep: on his yacht, on his couch, on his plane, and now in his car. He loved watching her sleep and looking at her beautiful lips he couldn't help but remember how sweet she tasted when he kissed her that first and only time at her house shortly after meeting her. He knew then that he loved her and wanted to protect her; but when she found out who he really was from her mother it ended everything. Somehow he had to make her realize who he was: he was not some arrogant playboy. And certainly not the man he was a couple of weeks ago.

Believing he would need help getting Abby up to his apartment, Rob thought he better give his aunt a call. Simply speaking her name automatically connected him to his aunt's cell. Modern technology was amazing. "Aunt Charlotte, I'm heading to the resort right now with Abby and I'm going to need some help with her. She happens to be out cold and I'm not sure how well she'll be able to walk even if she does wake up. Can you give Josh a call to come and help me with her?"

"Not a problem Robby. We'll meet you outside."

"Thanks. I'll be using the rear entrance; it's a lot closer to my private elevator."

"We'll be waiting."

As Rob pulled up to the rear entrance, there was Jeff waiting with his aunt. *Why is Jeff waiting with Aunt Charlotte? There is no way I'm going to let Jeff touch Abby. He's a good friend but that's where I draw the line. I'll carry her up myself.* "Hey Aunt Charlotte, what happened to Josh?"

"I couldn't get a hold of him. He must be with his wife. When I told Jeff, he was more than willing to come and help out."

"I'm sure he was." Rob said under his breath. "Well, I think I can manage," Rob said as he lifted Abby from the front seat.

"I don't mind carrying her up for you Rob."

Rob took one look at how eager Jeff was to take Abby from his arms and immediately refused. "She's not heavy at all and once I get in the elevator it will be easier, but it would help to keep her right arm still. Aunt Charlotte do you mind getting her bed turned down?"

"I'm right with you Rob."

Upon entering his apartment Aunt Charlotte went immediately to Abby's suite. *Leave it to Jeff to offer to help undress her.* Of course he got his answer by the piercing look in Rob's eyes. "I think my aunt can handle that by herself."

As soon as Rob laid Abby down, her eyes fluttered open but only long enough for her to take one look at Rob, and with the most beautiful smile on her face she said, "You're not gay." This was all she said and then she was out again.

Rob scratched his head and wondered where that came from. Aunt Charlotte also heard the comment and simply shrugged her shoulders. Neither had any idea why she would say such a thing and chalked it up to her being somewhat delusional from the drugs. They left her to sleep peacefully.

Rob dismissed Jeff thanking him for his help and asked if he would take care of his car. He thanked his aunt for all her help and told her he would be staying with Abby until she woke up.

Chapter 32

When Abby did wake, Rob was right by her side. Instead of waiting in the living room, Rob took up residence in the chair in her room. After the scare he couldn't seem to get close enough to her, why he even thought of climbing in bed with her but knew that would not be a good idea. "Oh Rob, you're here with me. How long have I slept and what time is it anyway?"

"It's almost eight; you must be pretty hungry by now."

"My mouth feels like it's stuffed with cotton."

Rob immediately went to the kitchen to get her a glass of water. When he returned Abby was admiring the beautiful roses that he had given her in the hospital. "Rob, the roses are beautiful. I've never seen anything so beautiful, thank you."

"Abby what would you like to eat? I'll have something brought up for us."

"I'll eat whatever you choose. You know I'm not picky." Holding her arm Abby winced but started to get up. She immediately fell back onto the bed. Rob grabbed her in time before she had a chance to hit too hard. "I never thought I could be this dizzy."

"I'm sure it's the pain meds they gave you that has knocked you out." And with a twinkle in his eye he continued, "I have never seen anyone fall asleep as easily as you…even without drugs."

Abby grinned shyly at him. "I know I've always fallen asleep easily." Seeing her wince with pain, Rob handed her a couple of pain pills. "Thanks. You must really want me to stay knocked out." She couldn't help the giggle that escaped.

"Just try and stay awake long enough to eat. Our dinner should be up any time now."

Eating with her left hand was difficult however she was able to manage with a little help from Rob. Abby stayed in bed as they ate together and it wasn't long before the pain meds kicked in. Rob let her sleep and went out to the living room to watch some television.

There was a rap on the door and Rob was pleased to see Aunt Charlotte and his dad coming to check on Abby. They stayed for a while keeping Rob company. "Rob, I've given a lot of thought to the comment Abby made about you not being gay. All I know is when I tried talking to her as you asked me to, she immediately told me she already knew what I wanted to say and that it wasn't necessary that I explain anything. She almost seemed embarrassed for me."

"I have no idea where she would have come up with something like that. I just don't understand."

"Son, there's a lot of things I haven't understood for a long time either." Rob's dad winked at Charlotte. "I have to confess that I bought into everything I read in all those magazines as well." Aunt Charlotte knew there was a double meaning to his confession and gave him a pat on his hand.

Aunt Charlotte promised that she would try once again to talk to Abby but Rob asked that she wait until he talked to her first. He needed some answers for himself.

Abby could not believe she had slept all the way through. She knew it was morning but had no idea what time it was. Her heart thumped when she saw Rob sleeping in the chair next to her bed. *He certainly is a handsome man.* He looked adorable with his hair all mussed and desperately needing a shave. He wasn't gay after all and Abby could not believe the pleasure she found in that. He had won her heart but she had no idea how he felt about her. Calling a woman "babe" was probably second nature to him so she did not want to draw any conclusions. She tried stretching but realized she could not straighten her arm…it was in a sling. Rob woke immediately after her slight movements. "Good morning sweetheart, how are you feeling?"

"Much better thanks; I think I've slept enough for the entire week." *Sweetheart, now that's a new one.*

To Abby's surprise Rob leaned over and kissed her on the forehead. "You have to be hungry. I'll bring us some breakfast."

"That sounds good but I think I can get up now and get my own. You certainly do not have to keep waiting on me." But when she put one leg out from under the covers she realized she only had her underpants on. "Oh my, I guess I won't get my own breakfast just yet."

Rob winked at her knowing she was probably wondering who undressed her. "Hmm, it was Aunt Charlotte who got you into bed yesterday. She didn't want to disturb your arm so she left your top on but took your jeans off."

"That was sweet of her to help. I will be sure and thank her."

Rob left immediately to fetch them something for breakfast. It wasn't long before he returned with bagels and cream cheese, pastries, and plenty of coffee. He insisted she stay in bed and for the most part she knew there was no argument there considering how she was dressed.

He knew it was now or never that he approached the subject of how on earth she thought him to be gay. "Abby, there is something I need to talk to you about. Yesterday when I laid you in the bed you woke for just a moment but not before looking up at me and saying, 'you're not gay'. Where would you get the idea that I'm gay?"

Abby looked utterly embarrassed. "Oh my, I actually said that to you?"

"Yes you did, and Aunt Charlotte heard it too. Why would you ever think I'm gay?"

Abby began to tell him about the conversation she overheard between him and Josh. "I heard Josh tell you how much he loved you and you telling him how much you loved him too and then you told him to spend the night."

"Yeah he did spend the night…on the couch."

As confidential as it was, Rob knew he had to explain the whole situation to Abby. He told her the difficult time Josh was having and the new partnership that was formed. Yes, he loved Josh; even more than his own stepbrothers. "We've been close ever since college. We were roommates all four years; I was best man at his wedding seven years ago." Rob saw the smile on Abby's face but was unsure what it meant. He knew she had a difficult time with his reputation as a playboy and he was counting on Aunt Charlotte to set things straight on that issue.

After breakfast Abby said she really needed to take a shower, and thought she would be okay on her own, although washing her own hair was going to be difficult. Rob left her alone but said for her to holler if she needed him. Abby definitely saw the twinkle in his eye when he offered. "I should be fine, but thanks anyway." It was difficult, but she managed to shower and wash her hair as best she could. Dressing was difficult and it took some time before she felt presentable. Instead of dressing all the way, which was impossible, she put on the plush resort robe leaving the right side to drape over her shoulder. Keeping a towel around her head, she emerged from her bedroom. Rob noticed her huge pleading green eyes and immediately jumped to his feet. "Abby are you okay?" The tears forming in her eyes made his heart ache.

"Rob, I don't think I can blow-dry my hair. It really hurts my shoulder too badly."

"Not a problem. I can try and blow-dry it for you."

Together they walked into Abby's en suite bathroom and Rob pulled out the vanity chair for her to sit on. As he removed the towel, her hair cascaded down way past her shoulders. It was beautiful. Rob began to blow-dry it but felt like he was all thumbs. "I'm sorry Abby but this is something I have never done before."

She handed Rob her brush and told him to brush it along with drying it. The natural waves began to come to life and Rob thought he was brushing the hair of an angel. The more he brushed, the more he wanted to bury his face in her hair. The vanilla scent was almost more than he could handle and he had to reign in his thoughts and desires that were beginning to take hold of him. "Abby I think I'll set up appointments for you at the salon. I'm sure they will do a much better job than what I'm doing." Rob knew if he brushed her hair like this too often he would go crazy. She drove him crazy as it was.

That afternoon they sat watching TV in the living room. Aunt Charlotte and his dad stopped by to see how Abby was doing… at least that was their excuse for Abby. After a few minutes, Aunt Charlotte gave Rob a wink and he got the message that it was time for him to find an excuse to leave. "If you folks will excuse me, I told Josh I would meet him in my office in fifteen minutes."

After some small talk it wasn't long before Aunt Charlotte began directing the conversation to Rob and even mentioned the talk that he had asked her to have when they were in California. "Yeah, I guess I kind of blew that one Aunt Charlotte. I really thought I knew what you were going to talk about. Rob told me how that, um, misunderstanding took place. I guess I really jumped to my own conclusions."

Aunt Charlotte told Abby how different Rob was from what was written about him. "Abby, you have to believe me when I tell you that Rob never had an intimate relationship with any of the women you read about; in fact, not any woman."

"It is hard for me to believe but you certainly know him better than anyone and I trust you, Aunt Charlotte."

"Abby dear, I'm his dad and I believed everything I read. I have to admit that I have been wrong in judging my own son."

"Well, I did what I promised Robby I would do and that's the talk I said I would have with you. What you do with it is up to you."

"I have to love Rob for Rob. Not for what he has or hasn't done. I know that the commitment he made last week was real and it doesn't matter what his past has been like. He's forgiven and he is a new person. I realized I loved him a long time ago but knew if he did not believe in God as I do, it would never work…thinking he was gay was the icing on the cake; and even after believing that I still struggled with strong feelings for him. I just don't know how he feels about me. Oh, please don't tell him how I feel about him.

I would be totally embarrassed and I don't want to put him in a position to have to fall in love with me."

Charlotte and Mr. Stevenson simply smiled at each other but promised her secret was safe with them. "How about we all go out for dinner tonight? We can go to the grill."

"That's sounds lovely but I don't know if I can get myself dressed."

"Nonsense my dear, I'm more than willing to help you. Why I think I can even manage to help with your hair," said Aunt Charlotte while taking a good look at Abby's new hair style.

"It was Rob that brushed it out for me after my shower. He did his best."

As Abby prepared for Aunt Charlotte to come in and help her dress, she took one look at her wedding ring. Yes, it was time to take them off. As she wiped a few tears from her cheek, she slipped them into a drawer. She would find a better place for them later. Aunt Charlotte helped Abby pick out a blouse that buttoned in the front and then helped with a loose fitting pair of dress pants. "This should be easy for you to get out of before going to bed tonight." Charlotte told Robert to give Robby a call and that they would meet him at the grill at six o'clock, giving Charlotte time to do Abby's hair.

When they were ready to leave, Abby looked absolutely stunning. She was so impressed with the way Aunt Charlotte did her hair. Her floral green and fuchsia silk blouse really showed off her eyes and her three inch fuchsia mules matched perfectly. She would have preferred wearing her skinny jeans but her white slacks would be much easier for her to remove on her own later. Aunt Charlotte was certainly fussing over her wanting to get everything just so. Abby was pleased with how she looked but thought Aunt Charlotte was a little over the top with all the primping.

They arrived at the grill five minutes after six, not too bad considering all the fuss Aunt Charlotte had made over her. She was pleased to see Josh and Mary Beth along with Rob waiting for them at a large round table. Both men stood as the women came to the table and Rob gave Abby a squeeze and an unexpected kiss on her cheek. They all ordered steak and Abby was reluctant to order a filet; however, Rob insisted that he would cut her meat for her. She acquiesced to his reasoning and looked forward to an amazing meal. Conversation was easy among everyone but Abby noticed a slight nervousness in Rob and how difficult it was for him to fully enjoy his meal. Dessert arrived with everyone getting an individual chocolate volcano. This happened to be Abby's favorite dessert at the grill. She looked at Rob and thanked him for remembering that this was her favorite. Everyone seemed to wait with baited breath as they watched Abby cut into her cake. The hot fudge wasn't the only thing that flowed out of the volcano but something very large and sparkly. Abby's eyes grew larger by the minute as she realized what was happening. Rob took the ring, quickly washed it off in his water glass, and got down on one knee. Abby's heart was racing and she could not believe what was happening. *Is this all a dream?*

Not knowing what her answer would be, Rob took the chance anyway. "Abby, I fell in love with you when I was Bob York and I have loved you more each day. I promise to cherish and protect you… and Abby, I really have no idea how you feel about me but I hope you love me, although I don't think you could ever love me as much as I love you."

Abby could not keep the tears at bay and for the moment it was only Rob and her in the entire room. "Rob I love you so much. Forgive me for ever doubting anything about you. I love you with all my heart." She wrapped her one good arm around him and he kissed her with such passion she was sure her toes curled. When their eyes finally opened they realized the whole restaurant, patrons and staff, was on their feet clapping and cheering. Rob looked at Abby. "Babe, you have made me the happiest man alive."

Epilogue

Abby's emotions were running the gamut. For six months they planned the wedding and her love only grew deeper. She wanted him so badly she thought her heart would burst.

For Rob, the wait was unbearable; he had no idea how he would keep from taking Abby to bed with him before their wedding night. Abby would not hear of such a thing and Rob knew she was right. Abby's promise that it would be worth the wait kept the anticipation building. To keep from being tempted, Abby moved back into her house. She loved her job and wanted to keep her CFO position with Stevenson Enterprises for as long as possible and it was good to keep busy.

Rob was ready to elope right after his proposal and it certainly didn't take much to convince Abby to go along with it. She already had her "big wedding day" and thought once would be enough. It was, however, for Aunt Charlotte they were doing this. She wanted Rob and Abby to have a very memorable wedding and it was something she had looked forward to for all of Rob's life. Aunt Charlotte had asked if she could have free reign in planning their wedding and they acquiesced to her pleading. Abby knew it would be a fairytale wedding and one she could never talk Aunt Charlotte out of.

Aunt Charlotte asked Abby if she would be okay having the wedding in her backyard. That sounded lovely to Abby but it became much more than she ever imagined. The yard was converted into an unbelievable wonderland with white lights twinkling everywhere. Tents were erected but not without beautifully hung chandeliers throughout, white roses were everywhere. The round tables were elegantly set with beautiful linens, fine bone china with pink roses in the pattern, crystal stemware, and sterling silver place settings. The centerpieces were more white roses with a few pink roses added for color. All the chairs had white back covers with beautiful white bows, white and pink roses were added to the center of the bow. It was overwhelming and Aunt Charlotte knew it would be way beyond Abby's expectations.

The tent that was erected for the ceremony was equally extravagant with chandeliers and stands of white roses. The white chairs were covered and the end chairs decorated with all white roses and green ivy cascading down. Aunt Charlotte was so pleased how everything had turned out and she knew Abby would be pleased as well. She also knew Rob was anxious to get the wedding over with and get on with their honeymoon.

Abby's mom, Lois, helped Abby into her gown. It was a simple gown, very tapered and accentuated every curve she had and yet tastefully elegant. Swarovski crystals and seed pearls covered the entire dress. The train was just enough to kiss the ground. Her Jimmy Choo satin shoes were accented in diamonds and made her look and feel like Cinderella. What Abby did not know was that many of what she thought were Swarovski crystals, were actually diamonds sewn into the dress bodice. Rob would not allow her to know the cost of anything. He knew she would protest to such extravagance. But absolutely nothing could be too much for his Abby.

It was their wedding day and Rob would not see his bride until she walked down the aisle. Pastor Mike officiated and stood at the front with Rob. Josh was Rob's best man and his brothers also stood in front with them. Abby's best friend, Jenny, was her matron of honor, and Rae and Mary Beth also stood waiting for Abby to appear.

A small orchestra played as guests arrived. Aunt Charlotte came in on Mr. Stevenson's arm and Abby's mom, Lois, on her dad, William's arm. The orchestra began with "The King's March" and when Abby appeared they began playing "Jesu, Joy of Man's Desiring". Rob took one look at his bride and his chest immediately expanded with such pride he thought it would burst. Abby's heart pounded like it never had before and she knew without a doubt that this was the most amazing day of her life; and Rob the most amazing man she ever knew. She loved the man standing before her so much and she knew without a doubt; Rob shared the same love for her.

Rob could not wait until the reception ended, and once they had visited guests at each table, thanking them for attending, he grabbed Abby and whisked her out of the tent.

"Abby, Doug and Len will be ready to take off in forty-five minutes. Let's change and get to the airport." Abby giggled at how anxious Rob was to leave. She had no idea where they would be heading for their honeymoon and Rob insisted he could not tell her; only that the flight would be several hours. She knew immediately after the plane was in the air why Jenny did not have to work this flight as Rob whisked her back to the master bedroom. They experienced the most amazing night of a lifetime soaring twenty thousand feet in the air. The remainder of their honeymoon was spent in Rob's tropical home in the Fiji Islands.

They both agreed…it was so worth the wait.

CPSIA information can be obtained at www.ICGtesting.com
Printed in the USA
BVOW08*1838210416

444801BV00016B/26/P